JESSICA DREAMS OF PUTTING OUT FIRES BUT CAN SHE COPE WITH FANNING THE FLAMES OF KEVIN S SMOLDERING HEART?

When she turns thirty, Jessica realizes time is running out if she wants to pursue her dream of being a firefighter and paramedic. Kevin offers her the opportunity to make her dream a reality, but both are unprepared for the flames of desire their meeting ignites.

But what's with Kevin? He flirts with her, then pushes her away. Not that she needs the complication of starting a new job with a reputation anyway. Jessica decides she'll just concentrate on her training instead of the dreamy guy who can't make up his mind.

Friends complicate the matter even further, wreaking havoc on Jessica's plans to stay focused solely on her goal. As Jessica's tests approach, she and Kevin must come to terms with their burgeoning love for each other. Will circumstances snuff their chances for happiness?

SPARK OF DESIRE

By

CHARLOTTE MCCLAIN

Lyrical Press, Inc.
New York

LYRICAL PRESS, INCORPORATED

Spark of Desire

13 Digit ISBN: 978-1-61650-164-8

Copyright © 2010, Charlotte McClain

Edited by Pam Skochinski

Book design by Renee Rocco

Cover Art by Renee Rocco

Lyrical Press, Incorporated

337 Katan Avenue

Staten Island, New York 10308

http://www.lyricalpress.com

PUBLISHER'S NOTE:

This book is a work of fiction. The names, characters, places, and incidents are products of the writer's imagination or have been used fictitiously and are not to be construed as real. Any resemblance to persons, living or dead, actual events, locale or organizations is entirely coincidental.

The publisher does not have any control over and does not assume any responsibility for author or third-party Web sites or their content.

Published in the United States of America by Lyrical Press, Incorporated

First Lyrical Press, Inc. digital publication: January 2010

First Lyrical Press, Inc print publication: May 2010

DEDICATION

To Rox, who believed in me even when I didn't.

CHAPTER 1

Jessica Decker had just started alphabetizing Weddings for the second time this month when she sensed a crowd gathering outside of the Reference section. It sounded like they'd rounded up the entire staff. Pulling out her ponytail, she tidied up her shoulder-length chestnut hair, knowing one of them would have a camera and not wanting to look like a slob in yet another picture in the bookstore photo album. Who'd leaked today was her birthday? Short list. She'd hoped to forget it herself, but she'd had a lot of fun at others' expense on their birthdays so she had to be civil about this, no matter how unpleasant and painful it promised to be.

About the time she'd worked her way to the D's, they started.

"Happy birthday to you, happy birthday to you, happy birthday, dear Jessica, happy birthday to you!" The entire staff clustered around the end of the shelf, all grinning and laughing. Jessica noted Bess and Diana were absent. Probably stuck at the register and information. Tony started the *how old are you now* verse but Mindi started clapping to drown him out. As the probable source of the leak, she'd better keep control of it. Mindi might throw her under a bus for cake, but she'd better be prepared to call the paramedics.

"Happy birthday, Jessica." Mindi leaped forward and hugged her as Karen snapped a picture for the album. "We got you a cake. It's in the break room."

Jessica forced a smile. Yup, cake. Chocolate cake with huge sugary roses. "Thanks. You can start without me."

Mindi mocked a frown. "But it's chocolate."

Jessica sighed. Definitely Mindi. "Let me finish this, and I'll come back. If I leave Weddings half alphabetized, I'll have to start all over when I come back."

Mindi bobbed her blond head. "Well, okay. I'll save you the piece with the big rose."

Jessica watched the rest of the staff filter away. Mindi would end up with the rose anyway. She sat down on her stool and pulled out the book about wedding flowers. If she stayed out here long enough, the first round of revelers would eat their cake and get back to work before she had to deal with questions about her age. The wedding flowers book should burn a good chunk of time. Normally, she liked looking at the beautiful pictures of other people's weddings and imagining her own. Today, she shoved the book back on the shelf where it belonged before she'd even gotten past the second chapter. A thirty-year-old virgin with no romantic prospects on the horizon, trapped in her job. Sighing, she worked her way through Weddings knowing she'd be doing this again in about two weeks.

She'd never meant to still be working at the bookstore six years after she took the job, she'd just never left. When she took the job, she'd innocently hoped she'd meet some nice, good-looking, intelligent guy who would inspire her to get herself together and do something constructive with her life.

So far Mr. Right had not appeared to get her life together for her. It wasn't much of a plan anyway.

At the end of Weddings, she turned the corner and started work on the Careers section. Maybe she needed to move. California would be nice. She took down the San Francisco job almanac and started leafing through it. There had to be lots of things she could do with a degree in biology. Somebody had just been telling her California had a huge teacher shortage. What if she ran away and became a teacher. How hard could it be to be a teacher? Jessica shuddered remembering the torture she'd put her own teachers through in school. Maybe that wasn't a good idea.

She put the almanac away and scooted her stool over a shelf so she could work on the test study guides. Looking at those books, she decided going back to school wouldn't be bad either. The problem wasn't lack of options, it was too many options.

"Excuse me. Do you work here?" A deep masculine voice spoke behind her.

Jessica turned around, smiling. "Can I help you?" Ah yes, *him*. He hung around the store all the time. Dark hair threaded with gray. Deep, dark brown eyes that matched his voice. Powerfully built without being cumbersome. Five years ago, he would have been interesting, even attractive enough to make her tongue-tied. Of course, five years ago, he still would have been much older than her. Too bad. He seemed nice and wasn't bad to look at, but she guessed him to be about forty-five. Too old.

"Do you have any books on Gaelic?"

"Gaelic." She turned to the foreign language shelf behind her.

"You thinking about learning the language?"

"I'm toying with the idea of going to Ireland."

"You know you don't need to speak Gaelic to get around in Ireland. They speak really good English. It's amazing. You'd think it was their native tongue." She glanced at him, but he didn't laugh or even smile to make her feel better about such a bad joke. Did that mean he was stupid, or that he had good taste? "You might be better off with a travel guide if you really want a book."

"No, I like the music too, and some of the old songs are in Gaelic." He shrugged. "Besides, I'm not going for a long time."

"Let's see." Jessica ran her fingers along the edge of the oak bookshelf. "The languages are in alphabetical order, so Gaelic should be..." She slid the book out and handed it to him. "Here it is. And Irish is right over here, on this second shelf from the bottom. It looks like there's only four books there."

"What's the difference between Gaelic and Irish?" He opened the Gaelic book and scanned the table of contents.

"Beats me. I always wanted to shelve them together, but I used to work with a guy who terrorized me into keeping them apart. He swore they were different languages. I can't tell them apart. Was there anything else you needed?"

"Do you know if any of these is better than the others?" He looked over the dozen or so books on the shelf with the glazed expression of the overwhelmed. It made him look sort of helpless and cute.

Jessica sneered to herself. Her birthday was going to her head if she was feeling sorry for the customers. Most days she wanted to hold them off with a whip and a chair. She smoothed her hair off her face. "It depends on you. I think each one is written to a different learning style. You'll just have to look through them and see which one suits you best."

He put the first book back and took down another one. "Okay. Thank you."

Shoving the stool over to another case, she started shelving the SAT books. He'd picked a good time to come over. A few minutes earlier and she'd have had to retreat to the warehouse to wait for him to go away. Now she could keep working without crowding him out of the section.

"So when are you planning on going over?" she asked. At least he didn't know it was her birthday and she was trapped and single. She wouldn't have to bear his ribbing or his pity.

"I don't know yet," he said. "Sometime before this day next year."

Jessica laughed. "Sudden decision?"

"I guess so. A friend of mine just proposed to his girlfriend, and I realized I was spinning my wheels."

Jessica decided she could listen to his voice all day. It sounded like velvet, and not the modern synthetic stuff, either. Antique velvet. Soft and smooth and warm. Probably single, too. Not that it mattered, as old as he was. "I can understand that. Are you planning on going in high season or low season?"

"What's that?"

"High season runs from about April to September or October, I forget. Everything's open and the weather's nicer, but the prices are twenty or thirty percent higher." Jessica finished test study guides and started on vocational study guides. "Low season you get better prices and fewer crowds, but you risk bad weather. Wet, cold, really unpleasant. After a while you start to feel like a mushroom."

"You went to Ireland?"

"About three years ago. It was incredible." She sighed, remembering the trip, taken at one of those points in life when everything seemed possible. Slouching down on the stool, she reached for the lower shelves. "I'd love to go back."

"Why don't you?"

She shrugged, not turning around to look at him. "Lack of money, lack of get-up-and-go, don't really want to go alone again. You know?"

"You went alone?" He sounded shocked. Most people were.

"Yes."

"But you went with a tour group."

"No." She tucked her hair behind her ear again and put the LSAT books back into alphabetical order.

"How?"

Jessica turned around to look at him. With his expression more animated, he seemed younger. Maybe thirty-five. She smiled. In younger days, he must have been a lady killer. Ten years ago she would have been a week getting her tongue untied if she'd tried to talk to him. "I bought a ticket, got a train pass, and stayed at hostels every night." Every time someone reacted this way it reminded her of what an accomplishment it seemed to most people.

"Wow. Weren't you worried? A woman traveling alone."

Jessica stood up. "I'm not exactly a little girl." Standing beside him, she decided he must be about six foot, which made him two or three inches taller than her. She was nobody's idea of a delicate female.

"I guess not."

She sat down again. "I'm the store bouncer," she added. Men always got that expression on their faces when they took a good look at her. That *She could beat me up!* look. Not that she thought she could beat this guy up. He was in good shape, on closer inspection. His shoulders were nice and broad. Not like an over-muscled gym diva, but he could certainly pin her in a wrestling match.

A sudden, unexpected heat raced up her throat at that thought. She focused on the CPA test guides, hoping it would go away before he noticed.

"Jessica?"

She looked up. The general manager, a thin nervous man, fidgeted in the aisle beside her.

He crouched. "I'm sorry about this."

"What is it, Eric?"

"It's Julie."

Jessica rolled her eyes. At least this topic distracted her from the thoughts of wrestling that had been flashing through her mind. "Now what?"

"It's just the usual. Could you talk to her?"

"I've talked to her. She isn't doing anything wrong," Jessica grumbled.

"I know, but if you could just tell her to back off. You know how

Darla is." Eric twisted his hands together between his knees.

"Yeah, and I know how Julie is too." Jessica shook her head. "I'll talk to her."

"Thank you." Eric sighed, relieved at having handed off that confrontation.

Jessica watched him walk away. She had to get out of this job before the death match between Darla and Julie burned a hole in her stomach.

"Who's Julie?"

Jessica jumped. She hadn't forgotten about the customer with the deep dark chocolate voice, but the sound of it right behind her brushed across her cheek like a touch. "Julie? She's the magazine clerk who won't let sleeping dogs lie if she doesn't like them."

He nodded. "I think I know the type."

"I like her. It's just not fun to ride herd on her sometimes."

"So why do you get to ride herd anyway?"

"I have the great fortune to be her manager. They warned me she was unmanageable when I got the job." Jessica pulled out her other favorite book to look at while shelving this section. The professional training section had three different firefighter exam books and two emergency medical service exam books. That's what she really wanted to do. She'd watched every hospital-based show on television since she was old enough to sit still for an hour. In college, she'd started out pre-med and become disenchanted. Besides, she didn't want to be a doctor or a nurse or even a tech. She wanted sirens.

"You planning on taking the test?"

Jessica didn't jump this time, even though he'd leaned over her shoulder, presumably to get a better look at the book. "Maybe. I've always wanted to be a paramedic, and to be a paramedic, I have to be a firefighter first."

"Move to Cambridge and you won't have to join fire service."

Jessica snorted. Julie had been clipping all the articles about the Cambridge EMS fight from the papers for her. One side said it was better service to have two separate departments giving the same service, plus it was cheaper because the EMS service was contracted. The other side said the fire department ended up responding to many of the calls anyway, negating the savings, so it would be better to just send the department in the first place. So far, they'd managed to decide to wait and study the problem more. "They're going to have to bring it into fire service eventually. The fire department is faster and better. If I get in there, I'll have to join up in a year."

"The fire department is more expensive."

Jessica closed the book on her lap. "People don't tend to care about that when they're in the middle of a cardiac arrest."

"They care at the polls when they're voting new taxes." He smiled as if he was enjoying the debate.

"They also remember which politicians wanted to cut costs on public safety."

"So you think it's inevitable?"

Jessica nodded. "Sure of it. It costs more on the surface, but the EMS system doesn't work now. The fire department gets called out in one in four cases. Besides, you can't be a paramedic with a private ambulance company anyway. The best you can do is Advanced Life

Saving. Sometimes ALS isn't enough."

He knelt on the floor next to her. "So why haven't you taken the test?"

"I don't know." Jessica opened the book and started leafing through it. "It all looks so complicated. Three sets of exams, tons of math, tools. I guess I need to find a firefighter to guide me."

"You went overseas by yourself, and you think the fire exam is complicated?"

"Going to Ireland was no big deal. It's easier than it looks. I didn't have to learn another language, I just had to remember to look at the bottom of the street signs for the English name. This is in a different language."

"How?"

Jessica looked down at the book in her hands. She'd stopped at the section of tools. "I don't know the difference between a bench grinder and an offset box wrench."

"You've got plenty of time. Arden's age cut off is thirty-one. You can learn that stuff on a few trips through Sears. The hardest part is the physical training."

"Thirty-one?" she blurted out, vaguely aware he'd been saying something. Jessica's throat constricted. Thirty-one? She had one year left. If she couldn't get it together in the past six years, what made her think she could manage in one?

He reared back. "Arden hires between twenty-one and thirty-one. You've got a couple of years at least."

"I turned thirty today," she wailed, remembering the singing and the cake and her absolute dread when she woke up this morning because it was her birthday. That hole in the pit of her stomach started to gnaw itself a little larger. "I've only got a year left."

He seemed stunned for a moment, but she couldn't tell if it was her age or her outburst, and she was too busy trying not to cry to worry about it. Suddenly the minor annoyance of re-alphabetizing Weddings every other week and dealing with Julie and Darla's ongoing conflict seemed endless. She'd be trapped here forever. She would die a virgin with a laundry list of unfulfilled dreams because she couldn't just jump in with both feet.

He held out his hand. "Kevin Marshall."

Jessica shook his hand, wondering what he was getting at. Then she realized she'd confessed something only a few people knew about to a total stranger because he had a reassuring voice. "Jessica Decker."

"I'll help you."

"Help me what?" Jessica drew back, stopping just before she fell off the stool. She wanted to run into the warehouse and hide in the magazine back stock until she pulled herself together. This was awful. Only a year before she became too old.

"Help you pass the test."

She tapped the book in her lap with her finger. "This test?" He must be crazy. Naturally, the day she could least handle the crazy guy she got him. "How are you planning to do that?"

"I'm a firefighter. I took it and passed it."

"You're a firefighter?"

"That's how I know the cutoff age." He put his hand on her

shoulder. "Are you okay?"

The weight of his hand distracted her by reminding her of wrestling matches, but she needed to be sure he was saying what she thought he was saying before she turned skittish and silly. "You're really willing to mentor me?"

"Sure. I'm not busy right now. They just did exams about a week ago, so you've got ten or eleven weeks to study and get in shape before the next round. From the look of you, it won't take that long." He looked her over again.

Jessica started at him with her mouth open. Ten or eleven weeks. With his help, she could have a new job, her dream job, by the time the weather turned. "You really want to do this? Even though I'm a woman?"

"Doesn't matter to me. We all look about the same in turnouts."

Jessica threw her arms around his neck, nearly knocking him to the floor. "Oh, thank you, thank you, thank you."

"No problem." He reached up and took her arms from around his neck. "Happy birthday."

"It is now." She bit back a sob. "You're going to need my phone number."

"Yes, and I'll give you mine," he said, holding her wrists with just his fingers.

She backed away, pulling her hands away from him, feeling the bright blush on her cheeks. What had she been thinking, hugging him? Still, the overwhelming glee at his offer bubbled around in her veins, and she wouldn't have been able to control herself if she'd tried. If she'd thought she could get away with it, she'd hug him again. Right about now, she'd have hugged Darla if she'd been handy, although hugging Kevin Marshall was a more exciting prospect. "There's scrap paper over here." She led him to the History desk and found paper and a pen.

"I'll find out when the next exams start, and we'll plan a schedule for you," he told her. "You might want to pick up one of those exam books for the questions. And you'll want to get to your doctor for a physical before we start training."

Jessica nodded as she wrote down her full name, phone number and address. "I can call the doctor's office today and set up an appointment. He can usually get me in within a day or so." She handed Kevin the pen and another piece of paper.

"Call me when you get your appointment so we can meet right away. We're on a pretty tight schedule."

"What if I'm not ready by then?" Jessica finger-combed her hair. Her hands trembled, tangling in the ends.

"You'll be ready." He handed back the pen and paper and looked at her face. "Don't worry, if something goes wrong, they'll have the exams again in December. So I'll hear from you soon?"

"Today or tomorrow."

"Okay. We'll get you into the department, and then we'll work on paramedic certification." He held out his hand again.

She shook it. "I don't know how to thank you."

"Finish training and pass the test." He folded the paper and shoved it in his pocket. "See ya soon."

"Yes. Very soon." He had a purposeful, rolling gait and a nice tight rear, which, if he turned around and caught her looking at, would be embarrassing. Blinking at the paper he'd given her, she tried to focus on the thick block letters he printed his name and address with. The address wasn't far from her house. About ten blocks.

That cute, commanding, deep-voiced guy was going to help her become a paramedic. She had to tell somebody, and Mindi would freak out. No, she needed somebody who would be happy for her.

Jessica scurried across the sales floor, dodging a stroller and a floor stack of books to get to the magazine section. "Guess what?"

Julie turned around with a pile of magazines on her arm. "Aliens just landed, and they think you're our leader."

Jessica groaned. Someday Julie would take something seriously. Something other than her battle with Darla. "No. I just met a guy who's going to help me get into the fire department. He's a fireman."

"Really? Is he cute?"

"What do you care? You're married."

Julie shrugged. "Doesn't mean I can't window shop. So what's this guy going to do?"

"He's going to help me work out and study for the test. What's a good weight-lifting magazine?"

Julie led her to another shelf and pulled out a magazine with a built woman posing on the purple cover. "This one. It's from the same company that puts out *Muscle and Fitness*, but it's for women. Which is why it's called *Her's Muscle and Fitness* and why it's got a purple cover. Last month it was hot pink."

"What would I ever do without you to point that out for me?"

Jessica flipped open the magazine, looking for the contents page.

"You'd probably be wandering around the interior design section wondering why you couldn't find what you were looking for. People do it all the time." Julie tidied the rack in front of her. "So when do you start?"

"As soon as possible. Kevin said–that's his name, Kevin–he said they're holding exams in about three months, and I have to get into shape." Jessica closed the magazine. "I can't wait to get started."

"Good. Let me know if you need anything. You better get a piece of birthday cake while you still can. It's chocolate."

"Mindi told me."

Julie finished straightening the shelf. "You looked like you wanted to bite somebody before. Thirty's no fun."

Jessica sighed. Julie only had 3 years on her, but she made it sound like decades. "This is about the best birthday present I can imagine."

"You never said if he was cute."

"You know him. He's in here all the time. Black hair going gray. Brown eyes. Pretty well built. About six foot. Good-looking for an older guy."

"I think I know who you mean. The *Fire Apparatus Journal* guy? He's pretty cute. Can't knock an older man. They've learned things. They have experience." Julie wiggled her eyebrows.

Jessica ignored the innuendo through force of will. "I've got to go call my doctor and set up an appointment for a physical. This is the most exciting thing that's ever happened to me." She started out of the magazine section, but stopped and turned back. "Wait, I was supposed to talk to you about something. I can't remember what."

"Probably Darla. I know the lecture. Quit bugging Darla. Leave Darla alone. Do your own job and don't bother Darla even when she's in your way, underfoot, and pushy for no good reason. I'll wait a few days before I put another dead rat in her locker."

"Julie!"

Julie grinned and went back to shelving magazines.

Jessica went back to the office and got her cake out of the refrigerator before sitting down at her desk to call the doctor. While she listened to the phone ring, she wondered if Julie *would* put a dead rat in Darla's locker. It would make things interesting. Of course, Julie didn't have much room to call anyone else pushy, and Jessica didn't relish the idea of being on the wrong side of her.

"Dr. Masciano's office, please hold."

Jessica scraped the garish blue rose off her cake and placed it on the extra plate Mindi had provided. The cake was chocolate, as advertised. This birthday was starting to have some promise.

"Dr. Masciano's office. Can I help you?"

"I'd like to schedule a full physical for as soon as possible."

"Is there a specific complaint?"

"No, I need a full physical." Jessica sliced off a section of cake with her fork. Mindi had gotten the cake with the good frosting at least, even if it did have big blue roses on it.

"There's a block open tomorrow afternoon at one-thirty."

She didn't have to come to work until four, so she had plenty of time. "That's fine."

"Your name?"

"Jessica Decker."

"Jessica Decker? According to the computer, you had a physical last April."

"I did, but I need another one. I'm going to be doing some physical training, and I want to be checked out before I start."

Mindi stopped at the edge of her cubicle, staring at her. Jessica held out the rose, which Mindi took and proceeded to ignore.

"He'll expect you tomorrow at one-thirty, Miss Decker."

"Great. Thank you." She hung up the phone and grinned at Mindi. "One of the regular customers just offered to train me to join the fire department. I'm going to be a paramedic."

Mindi's mouth fell open.

Sonya popped her head around the corner. "Did you just say you were going to be a fireman?"

"Yes."

"Get out. That is so cool. Which customer?"

"The guy with the black hair going gray. Broad shoulders, about six feet tall."

Sonya shook her head.

"He's got a voice that could move mountains."

Sonya pointed at her. "I know who you mean. Large hot cocoa, shot of caramel." She sighed. "He's cute. I could listen to him talk all day. He's a fireman?"

"He sure is." Jessica rocked her chair back and forth, making it squeak. "He said the department is holding exams in September, and he thinks I can be ready in time."

"Wow. You could miss Christmas rush. I'm so jealous."

"You can't," Mindi wailed. "You could get hurt. You could get killed."

"You could get to ride around town with a siren," Sonya added.

Mindi turned on Sonya like she wanted to throttle her. "This is not funny," she shouted. "It's a very dangerous job and you're egging her on. I thought you were Jessica's friend."

Sonya put her hands up. "Don't get all unhinged on me. Sheesh."

"What's all the yelling? I could hear you on the floor."

Mindi whirled on Julie, who stumbled backward a step, holding a section of newspaper in front of her like a shield. "I suppose you think this is just dandy, too," Mindi screeched.

"What?" Julie lowered her newspaper.

"Mindi, will you calm down? I'm not volunteering to go to the Middle East to campaign for women's rights. I'm not even planning on jumping out of any airplanes." Jessica ate another bite of her cake. It was good chocolate, too.

"Unless you become a smoke jumper," Julie offered. "Then you would be jumping out of airplanes to fight forest fires."

"Oh, that would be cool." Sonya sighed.

"I can't believe either of you. Any of you. This is incredible." Mindi threw the sugar rose on Jessica's desk. It slid into a stack of books, smearing blue icing on the pages.

"So this would be a bad time for this?" Julie turned around the newspaper in her hand so they could see the picture on the front page. The masthead was missing, but Julie had kept the headline intact. "Apartment Fire Leaves Three Families Homeless." The large picture showed a burning building. Below that picture a smaller picture showed a firefighter being treated for a minor injury while holding the hand of a dazed-looking woman. "Cop hero's widow finds new love."

"Why is that news?" Mindi shrieked.

"It's news because her husband was killed a couple years ago by another cop," Julie said, her voice dripping sarcasm. "If you remember, it was all over the papers for about three weeks."

"I can't believe you two." Mindi pushed between them and stormed out of the office.

"She seems upset," Sonya said.

Jessica reached for the paper and skimmed the article. The article had a small mention of the couple, which said she agreed to marry him to the delight of the crowd, otherwise it concentrated on the early morning fire which was thought to have started because of an overloaded electrical outlet in a third floor kitchen.

"I pulled it for you about a week ago and kept forgetting to give it to you," Julie said. "I just noticed it on my desk."

"This is great. Thanks. I think I'll hang it up over my desk." She looked at the collection of pictures taped to the wall over her desk. Movie stars and burning buildings. Julie clipped out every article she noticed about fires, but most of them didn't end up on the wall. Jessica cut the picture of the burning building and the happy couple out and taped them to the wall. "This is great. Thanks, you guys. I'm going to be a paramedic."

CHAPTER 2

Kevin sat in his sweltering car looking at the bookstore and wondering what had possessed him to offer to help her. In sixteen years with the department, he'd never offered to help someone get in. The guys he'd helped study for exams had always been guys he already worked with. He didn't know how to train a rookie, let alone tutor a hopeful.

Through the front windows he could see Jessica talking to the moody girl who did the magazines. Now that one was more his type, small and feminine. Or at least shaped like a girl. That one was pretty prickly under the wrong circumstances, though. Besides, she was married. Her left hand had a damning silver wedding band. Too bad. He did prefer the small curvy type.

Not like Jessica. Jessica was too tall, for starters. Nearly as tall as him. She had broad shoulders like a guy too. Plus, she was too young. No matter how old she claimed to be, she looked about twenty-two. How could he be attracted to a too-young tomboy? He liked women who were sophisticated and confident. Women who tended toward perfume, lipstick and dresses. Women who could turn him inside out with a well-timed smile.

But she had a great, infectious laugh. When she hugged him, it hadn't been unwelcome either. He'd forgotten what a nice feeling it was to have a woman throw her arms around him. For a minute, he'd forgotten to let go of her hands. Her body was soft, and yielding, too.

Which it wouldn't be in a few weeks.

Why was he sitting here in the parking lot with the windows rolled up, staring through the store windows at a woman so wrong for him? Too tall, too boyish, too exuberant. She'd just about knocked him over when she hugged him.

It had to be because Jack and Kate were getting married. It had to be. The last couple of months watching Jack pursue Kate had left Kevin a little jealous. Even when Jack had been unhappy, and Kevin had been on the verge of killing him, he'd noticed something different about his friend. Something he wanted. When Kate showed up at the apartment fire, Kevin could still see the joy on her face when Jack proposed. So what had he done? He'd latched onto the first woman to cross his path. Good thing the magazine girl was married or he'd be courting her now. It was probably for the best that she wasn't available. Kevin had a feeling she'd work him over good, given the chance. No, he wasn't attracted to the inappropriate Jessica Decker. He just wanted what Jack had.

As he watched, Jessica left the magazine section. Probably going to call her doctor. He remembered how excited he'd been when he trained for the test. That would be fun, at least. Sharing her enthusiasm. Watching her work for the goal. As long as he kept in mind that she wasn't his type, he'd be fine. He had to learn to think of her as one of the guys. Like Bobbie down at eleven. He never imagined he was attracted to Bobbie, and he'd worked out with her before. Hated jogging with her. She could out-distance him. According to her, it had something to do with female anatomy, but he just didn't run with her anymore. Maybe he could call Bobbie and ask her if she wanted to help him out with Jessica.

That might not be a bad idea. Give her another woman to talk to, and give him another person to distract him from Jessica.

Starting the car, he rolled down the window and put it in gear. The minute he got home, he'd call Bobbie. He needed another person between him and Jessica.

At home, he dropped into his favorite chair and dialed Bobbie's number, priming to get her machine. While he listened to the phone ring, he looked around his house. Bobbie referred to the decorating scheme as *guy chic*. The walls were hunter green, the carpet navy blue. The furniture was all blue- and green-striped except for his favorite chair, which he couldn't part with. That was tan.

"Hello?" Bobbie said.

"Hi, Bobbie?"

"Nobody else answers my phone. Who is this?"

Kevin frowned. He'd forgotten how abrasive Bobbie could be if she wanted to. "Kevin Marshall."

"Hey, Marshall, what do you want?"

Kevin considered lying to her and finding someone else to help him train Jessica. Jack couldn't help him. He was too busy being a newlywed, even though the wedding wasn't for a couple of months. Dan wouldn't be able to stop hitting on her, and that would drive Kevin nuts. Lew? No, he didn't have the patience to deal with Lew and train Jessica at the same time. Besides, she'd be better off with another woman. There had to be stuff she'd need to learn from another woman.

"Marshall, do you usually call up people to daydream?"

"No, I was–never mind. Listen, I met this girl today—"

"And you want dating tips?"

"No." Kevin dug his fingers into the arm of the chair. Arden had one other female firefighter, but he didn't know her very well. Not well enough to call her up today. "She wants to join the department, and I told her I'd help her study and train."

Kevin had to move the phone away from his ear so Bobbie's braying laughter wouldn't give him a headache. He could still contact the other woman. City hall would have her number if no one else did. She couldn't be worse than Bobbie.

"What did you do that for?" Bobbie howled when her laughter had subsided to the point where she could speak again.

"I don't know." He couldn't tell Bobbie that the minute he'd started talking to Jessica, he'd been drawn to her. That he didn't even want to admit to himself yet. "I just did. Look, I thought you might be able to help."

"Help you what? Get her in bed?"

"I'm not trying to get her into bed." Kevin thanked his lucky stars he wasn't having this conversation with her in person. If she could see how hot he was around the collar, she'd start howling again. He wasn't sure if he was telling the truth, either. "I'm trying to get her into the department. She said she's always wanted to be a paramedic and she just turned thirty today, so she's running out of time."

"She sure is. Do you really think she's going to make it on the first try?"

Kevin shifted in his seat. Somehow, with Jessica, he'd forgotten about the competition. Talking to her, he'd felt like nothing could stop her. Nothing but all the other guys and possibly a couple of women who also wanted to work for the fire department.

"It took me five tries to get in, and I was younger and probably in better shape. Training almost killed me. Then it got hard. Or should I say difficult?"

Kevin rubbed his eyes. How had he forgotten about the competition? He didn't know how many slots were going to be open for the September tests. "She's got a year. She might not even make it through our training."

"Our? No way, pal. This is your baby."

Kevin opened his mouth to snap that Jessica wasn't his baby, but caught himself because he realized she meant *baby* as in the training, not the girl. Why did this simple offer keep getting more difficult to fulfill without making a fool of himself?

"I'll talk to her, but you're the schmuck who said you'd help her. When are you meeting her again?"

"I don't know. She was going to see her doctor, and then we were going to figure out a training schedule."

"Okay. When you guys sit down to plan out her training schedule, count me in. We'll see how quick she scares."

"What are you going to do?" Kevin grumbled, feeling very protective.

"Just talk to her, sweet cheeks. There's a thing or two she should know, and you seem to be real forgetful all of a sudden. Besides, it's been a long time since you took that test, old man. I just took it a couple of years ago. Give me a call. I'm on A shift now."

"Thanks, Bobbie. I appreciate the help."

She laughed again. "We'll see. Bye, Kevin."

"Bye, Bobbie." Kevin hung up the phone. If she worked A shift, she'd have one day off, the same as him. Her twenty-four-hour shift started tomorrow at eight, his didn't start until eight the next day, exactly when she got off. That was very good. If she and Jessica hit it off, he'd still only have to see her once every third day. Unfortunately, it meant he'd be alone with Jessica once every third day too.

* * * *

In her paper gown, Jessica perched on the examination table, looking at the inspirational posters on the wall. The office desperately needed new ones. For six years now, she'd been staring at the same cute picture every Spring during her annual checkup, and occasionally at other times of the year when she had a cold she couldn't shake. It might help if Masciano raised the temperature in here to something above freezing, too.

The door opened, and her short, overweight doctor stepped through it. "So, Jessica, to what do I owe the honor of this visit? Head cold?"

"I'm going to be a paramedic." She grinned and bit her lip to keep from giggling.

Dr. Masciano stopped with the door half open and stared at her. He usually closed the door to keep anyone from peeking into the exam room, but today he looked too stunned to move. "You're going to what?"

"I'm going to train to join the fire department so I can be a paramedic."

He closed the door behind him and consulted the chart in his hand. "There it is. Full physical. I thought it was a mistake. You always have your physical in the spring. Well, well, well." Sitting down on the stool, he studied her. "Did you have any head trauma recently?"

"No. Why?"

"Because you've got to be crazy. Firefighter? Do you know what you're putting yourself up for?" He started ticking things off on his fingers. "Lung disease, heart disease, various and sundry cancers from toxic smoke inhalation, broken bones, pulled muscles, and trauma. As a paramedic, you're fair game for every communicable disease going. Add the fact that you're twenty-nine years old—"

"Thirty, yesterday."

"You're thirty. So you won't heal as fast as a younger person when you do get hurt. And I have a feeling the physical tests aren't going to be a piece of cake, even though you are in very good physical condition."

"I've got someone helping me train." Jessica started swinging her feet back and forth under the exam table, banging her heels on it. "There's three parts to the test, and it doesn't start until September."

"I'm not going to change your mind, am I?"

Jessica shook her head. She'd been too excited to sleep last night.

"I guess I'll be able to afford that boat, now that you're going to be visiting me more regularly." He watched her face for any change in expression. "Have you talked to your parents about this?"

Jessica stopped grinning. She'd meant to call her parents in Florida last night, but never gotten around to it. They were not going to be pleased. Mindi's fit would be nothing compared to her parents'. Or, rather, her mother's. Leave it to the doctor to find the one part of this adventure she was nervous about.

"I see. I guess I'll leave that up to you." He stood up and took the blood pressure cuff off the wall. "Let me take your blood pressure."

"The nurse already did."

"If you're going to be one of the city's bravest, I think I'll want to double-check a few things. I want to have a good baseline to work from when you hurt yourself. Note I didn't say *if*. Give me your arm."

Jessica held out her arm.

He wrapped the cuff around her arm and pumped it up. "So you've found yourself a nice fireman to train you." Glancing at her face, he positioned the stethoscope on her arm. "I see you have good color. He must be attractive."

"He's okay. He's too old for me."

"Hmm." The doctor counted her pulse before speaking again. "If *too old* can turn you pink like that, I'd hate to see what would happen if you found *just right*, Goldilocks."

"Goldilocks?"

He reached through the back of her hospital gown and pressed the stethoscope against her back. "Yes, Goldilocks. Deep breath. This porridge is too hot. This bed is too soft. This fireman is too old. Again."

Jessica took another deep breath. Was she being picky? He did seem pretty old, but older men looked distinguished sometimes. Sonya was right. That voice—she could listen to it all day long. The doctor shifted to the other side and requested two more deep breaths. She'd never envisioned herself with an older man, though. In all those weddings she'd envisioned while leafing through the wedding flower book, she'd pictured a younger groom. Younger, black hair, tall, more wiry than bulky, deep soft brown eyes. The doctor tested her lungs from the front and then he listened to her heart. He was being overly thorough, in her opinion.

He picked up her chart. "Yup, excellent color. Are you still taking birth control, or do you just collect the little round boxes?"

"I'm taking them."

"Even though you aren't using them for their intended purpose?" He looked at her through his eyebrows. "I'm your doctor. There's no need to be embarrassed. Medically, you're safer waiting."

"The boxes are rectangular," Jessica grumbled. She stared at the wall, willing her blush away. It had to be a record. Thirty years old and a virgin. "And I want to be prepared."

"Nothing wrong with that," Dr. Masciano murmured, bending her knees. "You know, if you want a job where people throw up on you, you could become a nurse." He took out his rubber mallet and tested her reflexes. "It's going to take a couple of years of college, but there's no age limit to start."

"I was pre-med tending toward Emergency Medicine in college."

"You could do that too. It's much like the fire department in many respects, except the job is always in the same place and there's less smoke." He probed her glands. "I could even help you out."

"Maybe if I wash out of the fire department." Jessica didn't want to admit to that possibility, but knew she had to. She hated the idea of failing in front of Kevin. What if she couldn't make the grade? What if the training was too hard, or if she hurt herself, or she couldn't master the material? For the rest of her life she'd be stuck working at the bookstore and hightailing it to the warehouse every time he walked in.

Dr. Marciano shrugged and made a few notes on her chart. "It's your choice. You're in excellent condition. I want you to come back in six weeks for a follow-up. People have been known to develop heart murmurs and other defects when doing strenuous exercise. Listen to your body. Don't push yourself past your better judgment to impress your fireman friend. He's not going to be impressed if you pull something or pass out because you stressed your system. You still run, don't you?"

"Three or four times a week."

"At least you're not starting from total inactivity. Don't hesitate to call me if you have any questions or concerns." He stood up and held out his hand. "Good luck. Make an appointment for six weeks from now. And don't forget to call your parents."

* * * *

Jessica checked her answering machine when she got home after midnight. It had one message. Mindi had the day off, which Jessica appreciated more than she wanted to admit. She considered Mindi a good friend, but after the stern lecture from her doctor, she didn't think she was ready for another hysterical episode from her best friend. As it was, the rumor had already gone around the store and become distorted. She'd had to explain to one of the coffee bar girls that she wasn't dating a firefighter, she was training to be one. Then she'd had to explain to Tony that she hadn't been in a fire, she wanted to pull people out of them. And just about every woman on staff had told her to bring around some cute firefighters. For some reason, every time someone mentioned cute firefighters, she thought of Kevin.

Kevin was not her idea of a cute firefighter. If he were thirty, she'd have been overjoyed to have him speak to her, let alone have him offer to train her. But he wasn't thirty. He was too old. *Goldilocks.*

"Hello, Jessica."

Jessica sank into the couch at the sound of his voice.

"I spoke to a friend of mine about helping me work with you. She works down at Eleven, and she should have some insight on what you'll need to work on as a woman." He coughed. "Give me a call and let me know when we can meet. Bobbie and I will both be off duty day after tomorrow. It looks like you're right around the corner from here, so maybe we can meet at Meechan's Kitchen."

He pronounced it Meechan's Keetchen so it rhymed. You could always tell somebody was from the neighborhood by how they pronounced the name of the local diner.

"If that's okay with you. Unless you've chickened out already." He laughed.

His dark little chuckle sent a thrill down her spine. No, she hadn't chickened out. If she did, she'd never be able to face him again. She couldn't stand the idea of him being disappointed in her.

"Give me a call. You can leave a message on my machine when you get in. I'm looking forward to hearing from you. Good-bye, Jessica."

Jessica's chest tightened. He was looking forward to hearing from her. If only he wasn't so old. She'd never get to sleep now. Until the moment she heard his voice on her machine she'd been tired. Now she wanted to run a marathon, but she wasn't sure if she was excited because he called or because she was training to join the fire department. Pulling on some sweats, she left her apartment for a quick run around the neighborhood.

* * * *

"So who's your new girlfriend?" Dan asked before Kevin had even gotten out of his car.

"I don't have a new girlfriend." Kevin slammed his car door, cursing himself for ever involving Bobbie in this.

"Bobbie said you were helping some woman train to take the exam. Since one and one usually equal two, she must be cute."

"She is not cute." Kevin almost bit his tongue. It was sort of a lie. She was good-looking, but if he admitted that to them, they'd never leave him alone.

"Kevin the celibate has a girlfriend?" Doug Reynolds asked, walking out the back door of the station. Once more he'd managed to shave his entire head except for the spot directly under his nose.

Kevin kept his eyes on the ground. Doug was too perceptive and too mean. Jack would have known when to back off, but Jack was still out with his sprained wrist, playing house with Kate, and that's why Kevin was doing stupid things like offering to train strange women for the department test. This was all Jack's fault. "I do not have a girlfriend." Kevin walked past them to the station. "I'm just helping her out."

"Why? You've never done that before." Dan and Doug trailed

him into the locker room.

"She works at the bookstore, and I know her pretty well." That was an outright lie. He'd talked to her on a couple of occasions, but he didn't know her at all. "She mentioned that she wanted to be a paramedic."

"And why wouldn't she? It's the coolest job in the station," Dan said.

"Unless you get to be captain."

The three men turned around to face the captain in the doorway.

"Come on, you clowns." The captain jabbed his thumb over his shoulder. "Time for PT. Marshall, hold up."

Dan and Doug ducked out of the locker room, leaving Kevin alone with the captain. Kevin pulled on his sweat pants, racking his brain for why the captain wanted to talk to him alone. He couldn't remember doing anything unusual last shift.

"Kevin." The captain sat down on the bench bolted to the floor in front of the lockers.

That was a bad sign. The captain never wanted to have heart-to-hearts like this. Either he'd screwed up bad, or somebody else had and he had to clean it up.

"I understand you're going to help a woman train for the department exam."

Kevin's mouth went dry. It wasn't against regulations to help outsiders train. A couple of guys he knew almost made a hobby of it. The department encouraged women to join too. Was that why the captain wanted to talk to him privately? Did he want him to discourage

Jessica? Kevin knew he couldn't do that to her. Not after the look in her eyes when she realized he had offered to help her.

"I don't quite know how to say this." The captain steepled his fingers under his nose. "There isn't really a regulation against couples being in the department, but if the two of you are an item, it's going to be harder for her to get in."

Kevin blinked. A couple? His heart started beating again. They weren't going to ask him to break her. They assumed he had an ulterior motive. Which he didn't. He hoped. "We're not a couple."

"There's nothing between you?"

"No." Kevin wondered if he was lying again.

"Then why the heck are you training her?" The captain stared at him, baffled. "You've never shown any interest in recruiting for the department before."

Kevin shrugged. "It seemed like a good idea at the time. And I figured I could use a refresher." He needed to think of a good answer for that question. Too many people were asking it.

"Ha." The captain slapped Kevin's shoulder. "Well, now that we've got that cleared up, get a move on. They're waiting." He stood up and walked out the door.

Kevin followed the captain out to the back courtyard for calisthenics. He couldn't be attracted to Jessica. She wasn't his type.

But if she wasn't his type, why couldn't he get the sound of her laughter out of his mind?

CHAPTER 3

Jessica stood in front of Meechan's Kitchen watching the road for Kevin. She was at least ten minutes early, and she wouldn't recognize his car if it ran her over, but she couldn't stop herself from looking. Her head felt as if it would never stop spinning. Three days ago she'd been shelving reference, bemoaning her fate, and now she was about to start training to join the fire department. Diana and Sonya waved from the other side of the street before strolling into the grocery store. This morning she'd borrowed all three of the study guides from the store, but they were sitting in her car at her apartment. She'd got home from work and not bothered to even go inside before hurrying down here to be too early. Since he offered to help her, she hadn't been able to sleep from the excitement, and she almost had herself convinced it was the fire department and not the firefighter that was keeping her awake. She saw him walking down the street and stepped into the middle of the sidewalk.

There was a woman with him, tall and thickly built with short curly blond hair, and she was laughing. Jessica suffered an unwelcome stab of jealousy. When Kevin said he'd asked a female friend to help, she'd envisioned a hatchet-faced, grizzled woman with a gray crew cut, not a pretty blonde. Jessica envied how the other woman carried herself with such grace and confidence. Jessica had always felt a little uncomfortable with her size. This woman seemed to have no such problem. She also seemed to have no problem chatting with Kevin, who grinned and shook his head at something the woman had just said.

"Jessica, you're here." Kevin smiled. "This is Bobbie Kelly. I told you she might help us out."

"Hi, Jessica." Bobbie shook her hand. "Why do you want to be a firefighter?"

Jessica blinked. She'd been considering the question in quiet moments, expecting someone to ask, but hadn't expected to be asked so soon. "I want to help people?"

Bobbie raised one eyebrow. "What, don't you like sirens?"

"That's a perk."

Bobbie laughed.

"Ladies, can we go inside?" Kevin asked.

"Ladies? Marshall, do you have a fever? I don't get that out of you unless I'm wearing a dress."

Kevin rubbed his forehead and reached for the door handle. "Come on. All the good tables are going to be gone."

Meechan's was a neighborhood fixture. Most of the residents ate at least one meal a month there, if not more, despite the cramped dining room and lack of air-conditioning. The three of them jostled around a too-small table. Jessica hung her purse from the back of her chair and noticed Bobbie hadn't carried one. She wasn't sure if it mattered or not, but it made her uneasy.

Bobbie picked up a menu from the rack on the center of the table and studied it. "Nice place here, Marshall. You always take me to the best greasy spoons."

"Kelly, quit complaining." Kevin put his elbows on the table, looked at their position relative to her, and dropped his hands into his lap.

Jessica noticed Kevin didn't look at a menu. Regulars knew it by heart. She wondered why she hadn't noticed him in here before. Glancing around the packed dining room, she saw all the usuals. The woman who tried to bum a cigarette off every person she saw every time she saw them, even when they'd repeatedly told her they didn't smoke. The old man with the fedora he wore rain or shine all year long and doffed to every woman he met. The weird artist girl with the piercing blue eyes.

"So." Bobbie snapped her menu closed. "You want to be a firefighter. Let me tell you the single most important thing about being a woman firefighter. Never wait to take a leak."

"What!" Kevin protested.

"It never fails, you gotta wiz and you get a call. There is no place at a fire for a chick to take a p—"

"Bobbie!" Kevin slapped his hand on the table, rattling the condiments in the center. "Oh my God. You are so crude." His face was bright red.

"It's a hazard of the job. Crudeness." Bobbie shrugged. "You'll get used to it." She patted Jessica's hand.

A waitress sidled up to their table and took their orders.

"Have you ever started a chain saw?" Bobbie blurted out as soon as the waitress turned to leave. The waitress hesitated, decided the question wasn't directed at her, and left.

Jessica blinked at Bobbie. "A c-chainsaw?" She shook her head. "With a rip cord? No."

Kevin dropped his head into his hands, groaning. Jessica eased back in her chair so he wouldn't elbow her in the chest.

"You better learn. The guys can just rip that sucker." Bobbie jerked her hands apart above the table demonstrating and nearly smacking Kevin's head. "But most women can't. I was in training with a woman who couldn't do it. She just couldn't get it. She quit. I have to put it on the ground and brace it with my foot. For some reason women can't jerk it like the guys do."

Kevin groaned again.

"It's a lack of upper body strength," Jessica said. She thought she'd been dizzy before, but Bobbie was the human equivalent of the Tilt-A-Whirl. "Most of a female's strength is centered in her hips. Men's strength is in their shoulders."

"Really? That's neat. Did you know that, Marshall?"

Kevin shook his head without lifting it up. Jessica noticed the tips of his ears were red. Was he embarrassed or angry? Was she failing some kind of initiation?

"There's a way you can do it. I'll show you." Bobbie started spinning her butter knife on the table.

Kevin looked at Bobbie. "Are you finished?"

Bobbie shrugged.

He sighed, staring at Bobbie for a minute before he spoke. "Okay, this is what I found out. I got you an application when I was down at the office the other day—"

"Wasn't that sweet?" Bobbie batted her eyelashes at him. "Did you go all the way down there just for that?"

"No," Kevin said. "Jack needed to go in, and I drove him. While I was there I checked a few things. I thought you were finished." He turned back to Jessica, pulling the application out of his pocket along with a second piece of paper. "You need to fill this out and return it to the office. The address is at the top. The next round of tests starts on September first. That's the written. The physical is on September third and the oral is on September seventh. There are fifteen openings." He double checked the notes he'd written before folding the paper into his pocket.

Bobbie whistled. "That's bad."

"Why?" Jessica asked, looking from one to the other. She folded her hands into her lap, trying to keep from jostling one or the other of them. Glancing over her shoulder, she discovered if she moved her chair back more than two inches she'd be sitting at another table. She was surrounded.

"You're gonna have a hundred fifty, two hundred guys going for those fifteen spots. Some of those guys are going to be vets so they'll get extra points added to their score. Pretty slim odds."

"There won't be that many vets. Maybe fifteen," Kevin grumbled.

"Fifteen is enough to soak up the openings," Bobbie said.

"There's no way all of them are going to pass the test. Half are going to fail outright and half the guys that pass aren't going to score high enough."

"There's one other minor thing you seem to be overlooking, Marshall. She's a girl." Bobbie pointed at Jessica without looking at her.

"So?" Kevin grumbled.

"Do you know how many women have tried to get into the department? Sixty-four. How many made it?" Bobbie held up two fingers. "Me and Peggy Spinelli."

"But what's the percentage of men who've succeeded?" Kevin shot back. He leaned across the table, caught up in the argument.

"Probably better than eight percent," Jessica murmured.

Kevin dropped back in his chair.

Bobbie folded her arms. "It's not going to be a piece of cake, and you've only got a couple of months to train."

"Six percent chance of success at best. Five, really," Jessica mumbled looking at the table.

"It is?" Bobbie asked.

Jessica looked up, catching the last flickerings of surprise on their faces before they hid the expressions. She didn't know what had surprised them, but didn't think this was a good time to start asking questions. The odds weren't inspiring, but it was better than nothing, and she didn't want to give up before she started, not with Kevin defending her so ferociously. "That's not zero percent, so I might as well try. What do I have to do?"

"Do you run?" Bobbie asked.

"Bobbie, why are you so wound up today?" Kevin growled. "You're like a caffeine transfusion."

Bobbie grinned at him and turned back to Jessica. "So, do you run?"

"I jog."

"How much?"

"Three or four times a week for about a half hour. Two and three miles each time." Jessica glanced at Kevin. She'd rested her elbow on the table and now his arm was brushing hers, interfering with her ability to pay attention to this woman. There was a test happening here. She couldn't start failing this early, but with Kevin this close she could barely manage to keep her eyes on Bobbie. Forget where her mind was.

But she wasn't attracted to Kevin. He was too old.

Bobbie nodded. "You need to up that to about six miles in that half hour. You need to do weight training, too."

"I can't believe you're doing this," a familiar voice hissed behind her.

Jessica squeezed her eyes closed before turning around to face Mindi. They were watching her. Kevin was watching her. He would want to know how she reacted in a crisis. Mindi freaking out in a restaurant was a crisis of magnificent proportions. Of course he didn't know Mindi, so he didn't know what she could get like. Jessica hoped he would never know. "Mindi, calm down."

"Calm down? Calm down?" Mindi's voice rose to an unpleasant screech that rang off the narrow restaurant walls, causing half the patrons to stop eating so they could devote full attention to the floor show. "I can't believe you're even thinking about doing this."

Jessica stood up. "Excuse me." She seized Mindi's arm and pulled her out of the restaurant before she could start in on a serious temper tantrum.

* * * *

Kevin watched Jessica tow the cute but distressed blonde outside.

"Maybe she's an idiot savant with numbers," Bobbie suggested.

"What?" Kevin couldn't stop staring out the window. For a few minutes there he'd managed to stop thinking of Jessica as a female, but watching her outside the window with her friend, he remembered again. For a too-young, too-big, unfeminine female, she filled out her short-sleeved blue cotton blouse enticingly. While he watched, she put one hand on her generous hip. Her little friend's voice carried through the window like the whine of a dentist's drill. She seemed like a fragile toy next to Jessica. Kevin tore his eyes away from the scene outside the window.

"An idiot savant. You know, one of those people who can do calculus in their heads without notes or anything. What are you looking at?"

Kevin's eyes had turned back to Jessica and her little friend outside. Jessica brushed her silken brown hair off her face with one hand, remaining calm while her friend did everything but jump up and down screaming.

"Uh oh. Looks like a lovers' spat."

Seemingly without his permission, Kevin's head snapped around to look at Bobbie. "Lovers' spat?" Ugly coldness developed in his chest and start flowing through his body.

"That's what it looks like to me. It looks like Jessica has a girlfriend." Bobbie sneered at him. "So maybe you won't be getting her into bed after all."

"A girlfriend?" Kevin stammered.

"Yeah. You know, she's a woman who wears comfortable shoes. She prefers her women short and sweet. Her middle name is Butch." Bobbie drew a deep breath, preparing to pelt him with more euphemisms.

"I get it," Kevin cut in before she could. He looked out the window again. Jessica was still listening to her hysterical friend with an almost perfect calm. Her sweet face focused on the other woman, her hair falling across her cheek and her hands folded in front of her. Two other women walked up to them. Kevin thought he remembered one of them from the coffee bar at the bookstore.

"But then you weren't interested in her anyway, were you?"

"No, I wasn't. It's just... I never thought... She just doesn't look like the type."

Bobbie raised one eyebrow. "Oh really. What does the type look like?"

"I don't know. Not like her." He stood up. Suddenly the heat of the restaurant was too much to bear. "I have to use the restroom before I eat." Jessica couldn't be like that. He stalked toward the back of the restaurant, grinding his teeth. If she was, it made his job easier. If she didn't like men, she wouldn't be hitting on him, and he wouldn't be thinking about it, either. But he wasn't, was he? If he wasn't, why was he noticing how her clothes fit? If he did hit on her by accident, would she deck him? Pushing open the door to the men's room, he noticed his hands were shaking.

In the mirror over the sink, he studied his face. It still looked like the same face he'd shaved this morning, but it didn't feel like it was attached right anymore. He splashed cold water on it, and discovered the bathroom had run out of towels.

If she was a lesbian, that should make everything easier. There wouldn't be any messy attraction to get in the way. It would be like working with one of the guys. Cap said she'd have a harder time getting in if they were a couple. This ruled that out. In addition to being too young and too unfeminine, she wasn't attracted to men in the first place. It also gave him the perfect answer for the guys when they started harassing him . Of course, it would just give them another tack to work from.

Bobbie would have it all over the department in under twenty-four hours.

* * * *

Jessica sat down at the table, looking around. "Where's Kevin?"

"The john. What's up with your friend?" Bobbie leaned her cheek on her fist. The waitress stopped next to her and put plates in front of them.

"Mindi? She hates not being the center of attention. We've been friends since college, but I get the sneaking suspicion she never heard a word I said." Jessica surveyed her plate. All three of them had ordered burgers and fries. At least she wouldn't have to change her diet much. She didn't feel much like eating right now, though. Her stomach still churned from her chat with Mindi. If Diana and Sonya hadn't dragged her away, they'd still be out there.

"Oh? How do you mean?" Bobbie ignored the food in front of her.

Jessica looked toward the restroom. Where was Kevin? She liked

Bobbie, but felt leery of her at the same time. "I guess she's happy working at the bookstore and husband hunting, and I'm not."

"Not happy husband hunting?" Bobbie pressed.

"Working at the bookstore." Jessica poured ketchup on her plate.

"All the guys are going to assume you're a lesbian."

Jessica almost dropped the ketchup bottle. "What?"

Bobbie picked up her burger. "The guys. They're going to assume you're a lesbian. No regular woman wants to be a firefighter. It's not a great place to find a husband."

"I'm not looking." Jessica's mouth went dry. Did Kevin think she was husband hunting? What a stupid way to do it. Right about now, that was a secondary concern. Sort of. She hoped to marry someday, but looking at the wedding flowers book was getting more and more depressing. Tall, dark, and good-looking in a tuxedo wasn't showing up. Locating a husband required finding an acceptable male who was looking for a wife. Joining the fire department she could do on her own, mostly.

"Oh." Bobbie bit into her burger and then spoke with her mouth full. "So are you?"

"Am I what?" Jessica glanced at the bathroom doors again. What was Kevin doing in there? She needed him to protect her from Bobbie's insistent and strange questions. Wiping sweat off her cheek with her palm, she had the horrified thought that Bobbie might be flirting with her. Hopefully, Bobbie would supply her with an easy out if she was.

"A lesbian."

Jessica sighed. As easy an out as possible. "No. If it matters."

"Doesn't." Bobbie shrugged. "Don't worry. I'm not looking for a girlfriend either."

"I didn't assume you were." Jessica studied Bobbie across the table. Something about this whole line of questioning did and didn't fit into the rest of her conversation. "You're doing this on purpose."

"Doing what?" Bobbie salted her fries.

"You're trying to throw me off." Jessica narrowed her eyes. "You keep pitching curve balls."

Bobbie grinned. "Smart girl. I'm just trying to prep you for the guys. Kevin's a really nice guy. Too nice. He'd keep encouraging you and pumping you up until you fell on your face. I think it's better to be prepared before you get kicked in the teeth." Bobbie leaned her elbows on the table. "They don't just do this to women. In training, they will put you through hell. They need you to break down early if you're going to so you don't kill somebody because you freeze up."

"Strength of character as well as strength of body," Jessica murmured.

"Exactly." Bobbie shoved a french fry into her mouth. "Speaking of strength, what do you bench?"

"I'm not sure. I know some of the boxes we receive are about seventy pounds, and I don't have any trouble with those."

"You're going to need to be able to carry one hundred and sixty-five pounds over your shoulder for about a hundred feet."

Jessica nodded.

"Don't worry, Kevin has weights in his basement. Don't you, Kevin?"

"What?" Kevin slid into his seat. He glanced at Jessica, swallowing hard.

Jessica noticed the collar of his t-shirt was wet. He didn't seem to want to meet her eyes and when he sat down, he'd moved his chair away from her, crowding against Bobbie.

"Weights. You've got a set, don't you?"

"Sure." Kevin coughed, busying himself with salt and ketchup.

"She said she can lift sixty-five pounds comfortably." Bobbie's eyes shifted from Kevin to Jessica and back again.

Kevin nodded. He started going through a list of physical requirements she'd have to meet, but Jessica couldn't seem to concentrate. Each of the three books she'd borrowed had a slightly different list of requirements, and she felt pretty confident the department would tell her their set.

What she didn't feel confident about right now was Kevin. He'd almost turned away from her in his chair and wouldn't meet her eyes. She felt herself sinking into a pool of self-loathing. The last time she'd felt this way was her eighth grade dance when she walked into the middle school auditorium in her first pair of high heels only to discover that they made her taller than all the boys in her class. A lot taller.

"So you lift three days a week, jog every day," Kevin instructed, bringing her back from her adolescent insecurity and plunging her right into her adult insecurity.

"You should do some running, too. Get your speed up." Bobbie polished off her fries. "You know where that gym up the road from your store is?"

"Yes." Jessica's throat dried up.

Bobbie leaned on her fist, squishing her cheek into her eye. "You should join. You can't be at Kevin's house every day, and I don't have good weights anymore."

"What about the tests I need to pass on the written exam?"

"Don't worry about that," Kevin grumbled.

"Why not?"

He met her eyes for the first time since he came back from the restroom. "Because I said so."

"That isn't a good enough reason." Jessica heard herself baiting him and couldn't believe it. She was provoking him into an argument just to make him look at her. This wasn't the best way to establish a relationship, even a friendship.

"Trust me. I know what I'm doing," Kevin snarled.

Jessica drew a breath to snap right back, but Bobbie cut her off.

"Whoa." Bobbie put her hands up. "Cut it out. It's not even cute. Jessica, get your strength and stamina up and then we can work on drills."

"We?" Kevin turned on her.

"Yes, we. You asked me to help, remember. I work a different shift than you, so I can help her when you're on duty, and I belong to the gym I told her to join." One side of Bobbie's mouth curled up. "Jealous?"

"No." He turned to look at Jessica again, and she saw something flicker in his eyes. When he spoke again his voice was gentler. "We'll work on drills starting in August. Plan to work out for at least an hour every day and study. The first test is the written."

"On September first." Jessica felt his eyes searching hers. A strange surge of emotion welled up that she didn't want to deal with right now, and she shoved it aside. Mindi showing up had really thrown her off her stride. It had nothing to do with Kevin. It couldn't have anything to do with him.

He clapped her on the shoulder. "You've got better than a five percent chance."

"Except for the tools," Jessica said. She had to work to keep her voice even. The spot where his hand had touched her warmed. The waitress came around to pick up their plates and refill their drinks.

"Tools?" Bobbie asked.

"I'm not very good with tools. I can learn to use them, I just can't tell them apart," Jessica wasn't embarrassed by her lack, but it did irritate her. Was Kevin embarrassed by it? Men grew up breathing tools, girls got dolls. When Jessica had been resuscitating her dolls, it hadn't occurred to her that she might need a crowbar to get the doll out of her overturned Barbie Corvette.

"Take her to the station," Bobbie suggested to Kevin without looking up.

"No!"

Bobbie and Jessica turned to Kevin. Jessica had started to convince herself that he wasn't acting odd around her and judging by the look on Bobbie's face, this was very odd. "Why not?"

"I can't take her to the station." Kevin shoved his chair away from the table and it rocked back on two legs. He grabbed for the table, but missed. Jessica caught the back of his chair and tipped it forward.

"Slick move." Bobbie clapped. "Going for the Olympic Chair

Ballet team?"

"No." He slouched and his face turned pink as he studied his section of table like he wanted to lean on it. Bobbie was leaning on her elbows, and Jessica had her arms folded on her edge. There was still plenty of room if he didn't mind being close enough to feel her body heat. Apparently he did. He folded his arms across his chest. Jessica found herself annoyed that he didn't even want to touch her by accident, but pleased he didn't want to touch Bobbie either. Neither emotion sounded like something a woman who wasn't interested in a man would feel.

"Well?" Bobbie snapped.

"Well what?" Kevin snapped back.

"Why can't you take her to the station?"

Jessica held her breath, waiting for the answer. She'd been so caught up watching him not lean on the table she'd forgotten there was a discussion going on. By the look on Kevin's face, he'd forgotten too. Why wouldn't he take her to the station? Was he embarrassed by her already?

"They'll eat her alive."

"So? They're gonna do that anyway."

"No," Kevin said. He focused on the ketchup bottle. "We'll go to hardware store in the plaza by the bookstore and look at what they've got."

"That's stupid. Sears won't have an SCBA tank."

"SCBA tanks aren't on the exam."

"How do you know? You haven't taken the exam in sixteen

years."

Kevin turned to Jessica, ignoring Bobbie. "Why aren't you asking what an SCBA tank is?" His blush had become a deep red and there was a vein throbbing on his temple.

"Because I know." Jessica pressed back into her chair. He seemed to dislike her again. She wished he'd make up his mind. If he would make up his mind, she'd at least have an idea where to start making up hers.

"I'll take her to my station if you're embarrassed," Bobbie snorted.

"What makes you think I'm embarrassed?"

Bobbie rolled her eyes. "Don't worry, Jess. We'll go over everything until you're comfortable. Mr. Shy will have to get over it."

"I'm not shy." Kevin turned to Jessica. "Really, I'm not shy. I just don't think it's going to be useful to drag you into the station prematurely."

Bobbie put her hand beside her mouth as if she didn't want Kevin to hear what she was saying and then stage-whispered so he couldn't help overhearing. "He doesn't want the guys to see you until he's ready."

Kevin groaned. His face glowed red by now. "I'll meet you at the bookstore tomorrow, and we'll walk down to Sears. What time do you have lunch?"

"Ten."

"In the morning?"

Jessica nodded. She had to go at ten or wait until two, but she didn't feel like explaining that to him.

"Fine." He stood up and pulled out his wallet. "I'll meet you tomorrow at ten."

"It's not going to help," Bobbie sang.

Kevin dropped some bills on the table. "I'll talk to you later." He walked out.

Jessica stared at the door long after he left, wondering who he was going to talk to later. Her or Bobbie? "He was really mad," she said.

"No, that wasn't mad. Mad is much quieter. He was flustered, and it was funny. Kevin doesn't get flustered. He's pretty level. This is going to be a blast." Bobbie grinned. "You can come to my station to play with the toys."

"Thanks." Jessica stared out the door, wondering if Bobbie had read him right. He'd looked more angry than agitated. Or had she been too flustered to know what he felt?

Bobbie sipped the last of her drink. She put down the empty glass and started turning it on its ring of condensation. "He's never done this before."

"Done what?"

"Helped anybody train to get into the department." Bobbie didn't look up from her careful glass spinning.

"Is that unusual?"

The waitress stopped by with the check and picked up Kevin's empty glass.

"It is for Kevin. He's quiet. He keeps to himself. Doesn't date. I tried." Bobbie grinned, but Jessica thought she saw something odd in it.

"For a while I thought there was something wrong with me, but it's him. I've known him for four years and never heard of him seeing anyone. I have to wonder why he picked you out of the crowd."

Jessica shrugged. "I went to Ireland." How could a smart, attractive guy like Kevin manage to stay home on a Saturday night? He should be beating women off with a stick, or a crowbar.

"Really? He'd probably be into that. He's into all the traditional music. He's a classic firefighter. Irish Catholic, tough, stubborn. You know the type."

Irish Catholic, tough, stubborn. Why then did he keep changing his mind about her? Why did it matter? "How old is he?" she asked before she could stop herself.

"Not sure. Sometimes he looks older than God and sometimes he's a big kid. I know he's been in the department for about sixteen years and the earliest you can join up is twenty-one."

"So the youngest he could be is thirty-seven."

"Something like that." Bobbie stood up and flipped over the check. "That rat."

Jessica looked at the check and the bills Kevin had left on the table. "What?"

"He paid for lunch. What a guy, huh?" Bobbie dropped a single on the table. "He's cheap, too. You always have to watch his tips. Hey, are you free Monday?"

"I'm off all day." Jessica stood up and collected her purse.

"Good. Meet me at the gym at nine. I can show you the machines and get you started. Time's short, you know?"

Jessica nodded and followed Bobbie out. As she walked home, she considered Kevin. Irish Catholic, tough and stubborn. Never trained anyone for the department exam before, but offered to help her out of the blue. "Pretty level", but he'd been half crazed throughout the encounter, and he'd vanished to the men's room forever, apparently to wash his face. She still wasn't sure why she'd tried to provoke him. Had she just wanted him to look at her? Acknowledge her? Anything? Was she turning into a child, acting out to get attention?

At her car, she stopped to collect the books she'd borrowed and walked up the rickety stairs to her apartment. She'd been trying to get the landlord to fix them since she moved in two years ago. As she unlocked the door, she heard the phone ring. Throwing open the door she dived for the phone before the machine picked it up.

"Hello?"

"Hi, honey. We got your message. What's the big news?"

Jessica sank onto the couch. Last night, in a split second of courage, she'd called her parents intending to tell them she planned to take the fire department exam. Unfortunately, her courage deserted her now when her mother decided to return the call. "News?" She stalled.

"You left us a message saying you had news. What's going on?"

Last night she had hoped her father would answer the phone. He'd be much easier to deal with about this than her mother. Of course, the way Mindi was acting, she should be glad both her parents were in Florida. "Well..." Jessica opened her mouth to say she had started training to take the fire department exam, but that's not what came out. "I met someone."

"Really?"

"Yes. Really," Jessica said through her teeth. So far, she told herself, it wasn't a lie. She had met someone. Two someones so far. She couldn't help how her mother took the news. Right?

"Tell me about him. What's his name? How old is he? What does he do?"

"His name is Kevin Marshall. He's a firefighter."

"Oh honey, you always did like firemen."

"I want to be a firefighter, Mom." Jessica started picking her fingernails. Her mother had never gotten over the idea that her little girl wasn't very little or very girlie.

"But honey, it's so dangerous, and it's very hard work."

Jessica remembered now why she'd dropped out of pre-med. Her mother repeating over and over again "it's such hard work." She pictured her mother the way she always had, a tiny woman wearing a pastel blouse with a lacy collar, matching slacks, and a permanently perplexed expression on her face. "But Mom, I want to be a paramedic, and you can't do that without being a firefighter."

"Honey, I thought you called to tell me about your new boyfriend."

Jessica gritted her teeth. This is where it curved into lie territory. "Is Dad there?"

"No, he stepped out. I'll tell him you said hello."

Jessica kept her groan away from the phone. Her father would have at least listened. He'd been more than willing to put her through med school. He'd encouraged her to go to Ireland. He didn't think anything was too difficult.

"Did you get your birthday card?"

"Yes, Mom. Thank you."

"When are you going to come visit? You're probably going to be busy with your new boyfriend this summer."

"Probably." By not correcting her mother she'd managed to lie without opening her mouth.

"You must really like him. How old did you say he was?"

"He's kind of old. He's thirty-seven."

"Baby, that isn't old. Your father is twelve years older than I am."

Jessica looked at the family picture hanging on the wall over the television. It had been taken three years ago before her parents moved to Florida when Dad retired. Mom in a pastel pink lace-collared blouse. Herself wearing a burgundy blouse. Dad standing behind them in a black suit with a blue- and red-striped tie. Her dad had been thirty-five when she was born, but her mother had been twenty-three. Twelve years difference.

Kevin wasn't that much older than her.

"Hello? Jessica?"

"What?"

"You were daydreaming."

"Just distracted for a minute. How's Aunt Rose?" Jessica launched her mother on a topic that should keep her occupied for the rest of the conversation. She didn't want to have to make up more lies about Kevin. At this point, she could dig herself out with very little suffering, but the longer her mother went on, the worse it got.

Eventually she'd have to tell her parents what she was doing. She couldn't just pop up one day with a badge, but she might as well find out if she could do it first. No reason to panic her mother before she knew if she could handle the training. She was going to be spending most of her summer with Kevin. Flipping open one of the study guides, she listening to her mother babble about her friends at the retirement village. Her mother could believe the white lie about Kevin for a few more weeks. It would make her happy. Give her something to brag about with the other women. If, by her next doctor's appointment, she was still training, then she would tell them.

Handling her parents was going to be the easiest part.

Figuring out Kevin was going to be a bit trickier.

CHAPTER 4

When Jessica stopped next to her cart of reshelves, Julie looked up from the magazine rack she was kneeling in front of. "I didn't do it," she said.

"Do what?"

"Whatever you're about to yell at me for."

"I'm not here to yell at you." Jessica checked her watch. "You haven't seen Kevin, have you?"

"Kevin? *Fire Apparatus Journal* guy? No. Is he coming to take you to lunch?"

"He's meeting me here, and we're going to Sears."

"Oh. Hardware stores are so romantic."

Jessica leaned on the cart. "It's study. I need to look at tools for the exam."

"You started studying?" Julie stood and scooped up a pile of magazines.

"Last night. Except for the tools, I don't think I'm going to have much trouble with the written exam. I took one last night and got an eighty-six."

Julie started putting away the magazines in her arms. "Let me know if you need any help. I can quiz you. Mindi's still freaking out, isn't she? Sonya said she and Diana had to drag her away yesterday."

"They did."

"It's not like she didn't know you wanted to do this." Julie walked into another aisle with her pile of reshelves. "I knew, and I haven't known you since college."

Jessica stared out the window. The sun scorched the parking lot. The summer was shaping up to be a lousy time to do any physical training. She'd gone running this morning before work and at five-thirty it had already been hot. What if her mother and Mindi were right? What if it was too hard?

"Hey, are you going to look like this?" Julie held out a weightlifting magazine. The woman on the cover wore a bathing suit made of two three-inch strips of silver material, and she arched her back so the suit ran in a taut line from between her legs to where it tied at her neck.

"Yuck." Jessica opened the magazine to the photo spread of the cover model. She always had her back arched as much as possible. Her long blond hair showed about an inch of dark roots and her breasts were as perfect and pert as Tupperware bowls. Her shoulders, arms and legs showed hours of hard work. She looked like she could lift a Clydesdale. "I hope not. You could shoot arrows off her spine."

"Do you think that bathing suit would slice her in half if she stood up straight?" Julie snickered.

"No, but she'd probably need to go to the emergency room to have it removed." Jessica felt her lip curl with disgust. Never in her life had she thought of working out for the sole purpose of working out. "I don't think I'll end up like that. Bobbie Kelly isn't this bulky. This chick is built."

Julie looked over Jessica's arm at the magazine. "You could look just like her, though. Think of all the hotties you could pick up. All those great big guys who talk about creatine and protein shakes."

"Is this really attractive?" Jessica asked.

"Not to me."

Jessica jumped at the sound of that velvet voice over her shoulder. She tried to close the magazine too quickly, and it flipped out of her hands. Julie leaped backward. The armload of magazines she'd been carrying slipped out of her grasp onto the floor. Julie cursed and knelt down to pick up the magazines.

"Uh, hi. I didn't see you come in," Jessica stammered.

"I noticed." He glanced down at Julie, who was working around his feet, and looked back at Jessica. His face was blank. Like he had woman crawling on the floor in front of him all the time. Maybe he did. Maybe Bobbie didn't know him as well as she thought she did.

Jessica crouched down to help Julie clean up the mess and pull herself together, but Julie waved her away.

"No, go on. It's your lunch hour, and if I don't pick up mass quantities of magazines at least once a day I go home unfulfilled." She glanced up at Kevin. "*Fire Apparatus Journal* should be here in about two weeks. I'll tell Jessica."

"Thanks. You ready?"

Jessica nodded.

Kevin held the door for her as they left the store. The switch from the cool air-conditioned store to the baking sidewalk was almost suffocating, but Jessica hadn't been breathing right since he'd snuck up behind her. He didn't say anything and walked with his hands in his pockets.

"Hot out," Jessica offered.

Kevin nodded. "It looks like it'll be a toasty one."

Jessica folded her arms, and they stuck together. She wished she hadn't left her purse behind so she'd have something to fiddle with. He seemed angry or something. Jessica couldn't put her finger on it. What if he had changed his mind about helping her and now felt obligated? She didn't want him to feel trapped. She wanted him to do this because he wanted to. If she let herself get down to brass tacks, she wanted him to help her because he wanted to spend time with her. "I filled out the application. I'm going to take it downtown Monday after I meet Bobbie."

"Good. They'll send you some information after you turn in your application and you'll have to sign a record search. They will want to make sure you're clean." He stared straight ahead, once again not meeting her eyes.

"I am," she murmured. She looked in the windows of the furniture store. All those beautifully arranged rooms tumbled together and not a soul in any of them. "Are you upset about something?"

"No."

"You just seem awfully quiet."

"Did you eat lunch yet?"

Jessica wasn't prepared for the subject switch. People didn't like to answer those kinds of blunt questions, but they didn't flip into another subject, either. "No."

"Let's stop at the bagel place, then. It's not a good idea for you to start skipping meals."

"Okay, Dad."

He turned and glared at her.

"What?"

He shook his head, his mouth twitching into a frown. "Nothing."

Jessica stopped in the middle of the sidewalk. Kevin took a couple more steps before he realized she wasn't beside him anymore. Tears burned behind her eyelids, but she wasn't going to give him the satisfaction.

"What?"

"What is wrong with you today?" Jessica demanded.

"Nothing."

"You know, a couple of days ago when you were bothering me in Reference, I couldn't get you to shut up, and now you can barely string two words together. I'm supposed to think nothing's wrong based on that?" Jessica felt her jaw tightening against the tears. If he'd changed his mind, she might be able to do it on her own. Or Bobbie might help her.

"I've just got stuff on my mind."

Jessica didn't want to ask in case it involved a woman. Or she'd been right and he didn't want to train her. She could find other help, but she didn't want other help. She wanted Kevin. "Are you sorry you offered to train me?"

"No." He shifted back a step, tucking his hands behind his back. "I just don't have anything to say."

She watched the movement. He had something to say, but he wasn't saying it. Why not? What was he hiding? "Don't you think I can do it?"

"Of course I do. If I didn't, I wouldn't be giving up my free time like this."

"So why are you so crabby?"

"I'm not crabby." He put his hands up in front of him.

"Then what's on your mind?"

He opened his mouth and closed it. For a minute he grumbled under his breath before announcing, "My best friend is getting married in two months, and I don't have a date to the wedding."

He didn't put his hands behind his back again, so she guessed it was at least partially true. Partially true and absolutely not an invitation. "Oh. Well, I do work in a store full of single females if you want me to ask around." Jessica wanted to bite off her tongue. Find him a date? Was she insane? Had the heat cooked her brain? Had all the running bounced her senses right out of her head?

He didn't look enthused by the offer. "Thanks, but I think I can handle it."

"I wasn't trying to be insulting."

"I know." He started walking toward the bagel shop.

Jessica caught up with him. "So why don't you ask Bobbie?" She kept the sour expression her face wanted to form to herself. Why did she keep asking questions she didn't want to know the answers to?

Kevin laughed bitterly. "No, I don't think I'll do that. Besides, she'll be invited anyway." He pulled open the door for her.

Jessica stepped inside the cool restaurant. He wasn't worried about not having a date to a wedding. Not for a wedding two months away. In her experience, men started worrying about those things when the wedding loomed within a week. Something else was going on, but she didn't know the magic words to make him talk. She doubted saying "open sesame" would work. At the counter she ordered lox on a plain bagel and watched the kid make it.

"What is lox?" Kevin asked. He'd stopped right next to her, where he could watch her lunch being made too.

"Smoked salmon."

"Is it good?"

"Sure. I like it. It's really fatty, though. Mindi says it tastes like waxed paper to her."

"What do you think it tastes like?" He watched the kid behind the counter slice the package of salmon in half.

"Really fatty smoked fish? You've never tried it? I thought you were into all things Irish."

He seemed calmer now. Maybe he had needed to get out of the heat. That didn't click either. What kind of firefighter couldn't take a little heat? Maybe it was the neutral topic of conversation.

"I am." He watched the counter kid layering the pink-orange slices of fish on her bagel.

"Don't be a coward. Try it. You're Irish. You're genetically predisposed to like salmon." She accepted her bagel from the counter girl and went to the register to pay. When he arrived at the table, she realized he'd ordered the salmon.

He peeled a small section away and tasted it. For a moment he looked uneasy, then less so.

"How does it taste?" she asked when he didn't offer a verdict.

"It's not terrible."

"Just wait. It gets better with each taste. I wasn't so sure the first time I had it either. But I was in a restaurant overlooking Galway Bay at the time, and that'll improve the flavor of anything."

"Really?" He leaned forward with his sandwich lost in his big hands. "When were you there?"

Jessica tore her gaze from his hands to meet his shining eyes. She smiled in response to his eagerness. "Three years ago in March. I was on Galway Bay about halfway through the trip. I had just walked down from the Burren, which is this huge area of exposed limestone with a famous standing stone on it. It's not a cairn. This one is three stones standing upright supporting a fourth stone. They call them wizard's tables sometimes."

"Poulnabrone Dolmen," Kevin supplied.

"Yes. It's funny because there's this megalithic stone structure and over the years people have built little ones from the loose limestone. As far as the eye can see, there're little dolmens." She held her hands about a foot apart to demonstrate the size of the miniature dolmens. "And it's really windy. It took me half an hour to comb out my hair that night, and I'd had it pulled back all day."

"You were on foot?"

Jessica leaned toward him to bask in his excitement. He seemed more enthusiastic about her trip than she remembered being herself. "Yes. I took the train where I could, but the only way to get to the dolmen was on foot. It took me about half a day to get down into this little town right on the bay. I walked right into town and booked myself a bed and breakfast, and then I went out to find dinner. The sky was gray, the stones on the shore were gray, the water was gray. It all looked like it might disappear. Like I had imagined it. I found a little stone building with beautiful golden hardwood floors and the obligatory upright piano. It had a bar across the entire back wall with a mirror behind it and a couple of old salts drinking their pints. That's where I first had smoked salmon." She took a bite of her sandwich.

"That sounds incredible." Kevin ate the last of his sandwich. "What was the weather like? It was gray?"

"I had freakishly good weather. The locals were commenting on it. I went in March and they told me the weather was better that March than it had been all the previous summer. The day I spent in Galway was the only rain I saw."

"Did you get to many of the megalithic structures?"

"Not as many as I would have liked. You need a car for that, and all I had was a train pass and my feet. I got to several of the usual tourist spots, but anything off the beaten path was difficult."

"Are you going to go back?"

Jessica shrugged. "I want to. I don't know if I can afford it."

"Why did you go alone in the first place?" Kevin shoved his tray aside and leaned his elbows on the table.

"My mother told me it would be too hard." Jessica rolled her eyes.

"My mother thinks everything is too difficult. To hear her, you'd have thought it was the 1850's and I was going to America on a steamer from the old country to settle the Wild West."

Kevin laughed. "Is your mother always overprotective?"

"No, she's not overprotective. I think it has more to do with learned helplessness. She's never challenged herself, so she thinks everything is too hard to even try."

"What does she think about you training to join the fire department?"

Jessica shoved the last bite of her sandwich in her mouth to buy some time. The second to last thing she wanted to do was lie to him. The very last was explain why she couldn't tell her tiny mother what she was doing. Chewing, she considered her options. Lie and tell him what her mother would do when she found out, as if she already had. Tell the truth and explain how her mother would react when she found out. Blow off the question by telling him a half lie like the ones that had led her mother to think she was dating him. Every option sucked. He sat across the table from her, looking at her attentively. Right now he liked her. She wanted to keep it that way.

"She doesn't know." Jessica waited for his response.

"Chickened out, huh? Couldn't tell her? I didn't tell my parents until I had already passed the test and was about to start training. My mother didn't know whether to be proud or spank me."

Jessica smiled. She'd picked the right choice. They now had one more thing in common than they did five minutes ago. Later she could jump for joy when no one was watching. "Why?"

"She had uncles in the department. It sort of runs in my family on her side, but skipped a generation. I think she would have joined if she could have, but back then women didn't join the department. Her family was surprised when she didn't marry a firefighter."

"What does your dad do?"

"Dad is an accountant. He was really mad. He told me I was wasting my education." Kevin shrugged. "But that was all a long time ago. They got over it. What about your dad? How do you think he'll react?"

"I think my dad would be happy if I were a circus clown if that's what I wanted to do." She pushed aside her tray and picked up her empty milk carton. "He was prepared to fund medical school."

"Medical school?"

"I started college as pre-med, but I switched. No sirens."

"Oh. I can understand that." He nodded, smiling.

Jessica set aside her milk carton and leaned on her hand. Sonya was right. She could listen to his voice all day long.

* * * *

She walked through the doors a little late getting back from lunch and heard her name paged before she got through the inside foyer doors. Grabbing the phone at the register, she answered the page, which started her on an afternoon of running. For the next half hour she bounced around the store on one errand after another.

"Good lunch?" Mindi asked when she met up with Jessica in the cash office getting change for the registers.

"Great lunch." Jessica sorted through bundles of ones and fives, putting bigger bills away in the safe. "I think he's starting to like me."

"The fireman?" Mindi let the door close behind her. She hopped onto the stool in the corner of the cramped office.

Jessica nodded and kicked the safe closed. "We sat over lunch and had a great conversation. Then we went to the hardware store and he showed me some of the tools I need to learn. He opened doors. He listened to me. He's so wonderful."

"Lunch is a start." Mindi nodded.

Jessica stood, leaning her hip against the desk. "It was great, Mindi. I have never known a guy like this."

"You think he's the one?" Mindi's eyes brightened and she leaned forward.

"I don't know. I've never been right before. I don't want to jinx myself." Jessica scooped up the money on the desk. "It's funny, I've seen him around the store a hundred times and never looked at him twice, but now... Everything's different." Jessica hugged herself, remembering the way he looked at her over lunch. Attentive and kind. Almost hanging on her every word. Never had she felt that comfortable on a date, with the guy or with herself. It had been strange and normal at the same time. Like some part of her that had been out of joint had slipped back into place. For that hour it had been okay for her to be five-ten and broad-shouldered.

"That was a pretty smart idea, telling him you wanted to train for the fire department."

"What?" Jessica's mind ground as it tried to change gears.

"You got him to spend lots of time with you. That was smart. You had me really freaked out." Mindi rolled her eyes. "I thought you were serious. I honestly believed you wanted to join the fire department."

Jessica's hands dropped to her sides. "I am serious. I do want to join the fire department."

"You just said you were trying to catch this fireman."

"I never said that. I said I thought he was starting to like me." Jessica's mouth went dry. Why did Mindi think this was a trick? Would Kevin think it was a trick? "This isn't a joke or a gimmick to get a date. I want to join the fire department. I always have. Don't you remember when we were in college I worked security?"

"Yeah, but that was just walking around campus with a flashlight." Mindi bobbed her head side to side. "How cool, I have a big flashlight. You got to meet all the cute security guys."

"I didn't do it to meet security guys. You ended up dating all the security guys," Jessica shouted.

"That's because you didn't seem to mind. You kept bringing them home and introducing them to me," Mindi shouted back.

"They were my friends. That's why they came to the dorm."

"They were also cute. You're just mad because you didn't have as many dates in college as I did."

Jessica felt herself starting to shake. The office was too small and too cramped for her to be this angry. "That is totally unrelated. You always do that. It's time to play Bait Jessica Until She Goes Ballistic."

"You're the crazy woman whose greatest goal in life is to run into a burning building."

Pounding rattled the door. "Hey! Hey! Open the door," Eric shouted.

Jessica could hear him fumbling to fit his key into the lock and she jerked the door open. Eric fell into the room, catching himself on the safe. Behind him, a crowd of coworkers stared.

"Will you two keep it down?" Eric whined. He stood up and realized he was trapped between them, nearly brushing into Jessica. "We could hear you on the floor."

"The discussion is over." Jessica pushed past him and walked out of the office. The crowd parted for her. She carried the change to the register without speaking to anyone. The morning had been nice. A good run, an easy opening, nice conversation with Julie. Fantastic lunch hour.

Now she could only feel the steady boil of her own temper.

It had always bothered her that every time she brought home one of the security guys, Mindi hit on him. More often than not she ended up dating them while Jessica went to the campus movies by herself. Jessica had made very certain to never invite over a guy she had any interest in. She'd felt like a third wheel in her own room when one of the guys stopped over to study or socialize and cute little Mindi started flirting. Once she turned on the charm, Jessica might as well have been furniture.

Mindi did it every time. Even after Jessica asked her not to. What kind of a moron was she to keep hanging around with her? She had to have some redeeming qualities, Jessica just couldn't place them right now.

Mindi had never listened to a word she'd said. Every time she'd asked her friend to do something that she didn't want to, Mindi would forget. Every dream or hope she'd confided in Mindi that didn't fit Mindi's world view had been forgotten, too. At this point, Kevin knew her better than Mindi did. Jessica left the register and started toward the coffee bar to see if they needed anything, just to be doing something. If she stopped too long she'd start screaming. Or crying.

"Jessica?"

A hand fell on her shoulder. She jerked around and found herself face to face with Kevin. "What are you doing here?" Taking a step backward she stumbled into the greeting card fixture. Why did he have to turn up now? She didn't want him to see her like this.

He frowned. "Are you okay?"

Jessica clenched her teeth. Her fury dissolved into a rush of tears that threatened to spill down her cheeks, mortifying her. The day had now bypassed bad and barreled straight for hellish.

"What's wrong?" He looked so concerned her heart ached.

"Why are you here?" she countered.

"I wanted to look for a gift for my niece." He shrugged.

"How old is your niece?" Jessica groped for the familiar role of bookseller to hide in. She should have told Eric she needed a break and gone outside, but she hadn't and now she was trapped. Either it was a good thing Kevin had stopped her instead of a customer because he knew her, or terrible because she had been trying so hard to be strong in front of him. At this moment, she couldn't tell which. Bursting into tears would be definite weakness.

"Ten. You never told me what was wrong," he persisted, stepping closer.

"Ten. Let's head back to the kid's section and see what appeals to you." She turned away from him, and he grabbed her arm.

"Jessica."

Jessica focused on a frail, white-haired old woman standing at the end of the register. Something about her didn't look right. Her eyes were wide and she was breathing through her open mouth. While Jessica watched, the old woman grabbed the counter. Jessica pulled away from Kevin. She reached the woman in seven strides and reached for her arm. "Ma'am? Ma'am, are you all right?"

The old woman shook her head.

Jessica could hear her labored breathing and see her blue-tinged lips. Jessica looked up to survey the scene. Tony was scheduled at register, but he was headed toward her and someone else had walked up behind her. "Tony, call 911."

CHAPTER 5

Tony spun toward the nearest phone. Jessica looked over her shoulder. Julie stood behind her with a stack of magazines in her arms. "Julie, get me a chair from the coffee bar."

Julie stood there like a deer in headlights.

"Julie. Get me a chair now," Jessica ordered.

Julie jumped and whirled around, sprinting toward the coffee bar with the magazines still clutched in her arms.

"Can you tell me your name?" Jessica asked. She glanced toward the far end of the register. Tony had the phone to his ear and was speaking calmly.

The old woman shook her head. She still struggled to draw shallow breaths through her mouth.

"That's all right. My name is Jessica. I'm one of the managers here. We have help on the way. Everything's going to be just fine." Jessica kept her voice level and calm. Eric hadn't turned up yet, which was a good thing. She was panicked enough without his handwringing. Jessica adjusted her hold on the old woman, who had begun to slump against her. Where was Julie with that chair? "Are you here with anyone?"

The old woman shook her head again.

The chair appeared next to her.

"Here we are. This should help." Jessica eased the old woman into the chair. She didn't seem to weigh more than a bundle of newspapers. Jessica glanced up and realized Kevin had brought the chair. Julie stood helplessly to one side, still carrying magazines in her arms like a security blanket. "I don't think we need a crowd here, Julie," Jessica said. "Why don't you get back to work?"

Julie blinked. Jessica almost expected her to say something snide, but then she turned and walked away.

Jessica knelt beside the chair. "Is this better?"

The woman nodded. She still had her mouth open, gulping shallow breaths, but her lips were returning to a more normal color. Her eyes didn't seem as wild as they had a few minutes ago. She clutched her hands around her black patent leather purse.

"Okay. We'll just wait here until the professionals arrive." Jessica patted the old woman's hands. Her skin felt like tissue paper. The old woman smiled faintly at Jessica.

"What's going on?" Eric arrived with the peak of tension Jessica had anticipated. The old woman looked up at him, startled.

"It's under control." Jessica noticed Mindi standing behind Eric. "She's having a little trouble breathing. We've called 911."

"Is there anything else we can do? I mean, can we make you more comfortable, ma'am? Is there anything you need?" Eric jabbered.

"Why don't you go outside and look for the ambulance?" Jessica suggested.

"Okay." Eric sprinted for the door.

"Mindi, can you make sure everybody's where they belong? We don't need an audience."

"Audience?" Mindi turned around and saw the three booksellers Jessica had noticed, wandering over to see what the excitement was all about. She set off to redirect them.

A paramedic truck pulled up out front and the siren cut off. Jessica let herself be hustled to one side and ended up standing next to Kevin, watching the paramedics work. They only seemed to be there for a few minutes, collecting what information they could before they loaded her onto a gurney and into the rig.

Eric stood staring after the rescue truck as it sped down the plaza to the exit, siren wailing. Jessica thought he might be shivering. He wasn't good in a crisis. Kevin, however, had reacted better than her staff. Jamming her hands in her back pockets, she wondered what Kevin thought of how she'd handled the situation. Had she done a good job in his eyes, or did he think he had a lot of work ahead of him?

After a moment, Eric turned around to Jessica and Kevin standing side by side behind him. He coughed. "Um, Jessica, can you write up the incident report?"

Jessica looked at his face. Eric was pale and sweaty. She considered telling him to go lie down before he had a heart attack. The nearest paramedics were busy right now and wouldn't be able to respond. "Sure," she said instead. "I'll have it to you by the end of the day."

"Thank you. You did a good job." Eric hurried into the building.

Jessica watched him go. He looked like he'd been saved from the guillotine. One of these days they were going to have a crisis at the store and he'd have to handle it himself. Imagine the paramedics' surprise when they showed up to find not one but two patients.

"He's right. You did a good job," Kevin said.

Jessica felt her heart swell in her chest. He thought she'd done a good job. Was it a good job for a civilian, or for a paramedic hopeful, or should she just take the praise he'd offered? "Thank you." Turning her face to the side, she let a silly grin creep across her face. A compliment was a compliment, and this one was from Kevin. Her toes curled inside her tennis shoes.

"But you still haven't told me what happened before."

Jessica's ballooning pride crumbled. Before. Mindi. Kevin apparently never forgot anything. "It was nothing." Then she remembered how hot the parking lot was and how cool and comfortable the store would be.

"It upset you." Kevin didn't seem to be willing to let her retreat into the cool and comfortable store.

She shook her head. "It was stupid. I shouldn't be surprised, but I am. I'm just mad at myself."

Kevin grabbed her shoulders.

Jessica froze. His hands gripped her and her knees turn to jelly. She wondered if he knew how much of her weight he was supporting.

"Listen to me," he rumbled. "Whatever happened to put you in that mood, much, much worse things will happen on the job, and you're going to have to get used to talking to people about it. You can't keep this stuff down. It can kill you. Why don't you practice spilling your guts now and tell me what happened?"

Jessica's mouth felt too dry to speak. She could feel his hands on her in every nerve. Most of the blood in her body must have rushed to her face, but she couldn't tear her eyes from his. This could be it. He was the perfect distance to lean down and kiss her. Would that make working out with him more difficult, or less?

"I had an argument with a friend," she stammered.

"That little blonde from Meechan's?"

Jessica nodded. For an instant she didn't think she'd be able to stop her head from nodding and it would roll off her shoulders and bounce on the pavement. How would he feel if she lost her head for him right now?

He flushed too. "A friend? That's it?"

"She's been a friend for a long time. We went to college together. I guess she never realized I had a reckless streak." Jessica forced a grin. Her face felt rubbery and numb. "She's one of the reasons I'm afraid to tell my mom. My mom will be much worse."

"Oh." His expression froze in that startled, open-mouthed manner for a moment. Then he coughed. "Well, you did a great job with your patient. I've got to go." He let go of her and stepped back a pace.

Jessica kept herself upright with strength she didn't know she had. Why was he leaving? Why was he being so strange? "I thought you needed a gift for your niece."

He stepped off the sidewalk, stumbling when one of his shoes caught on the curb. "I'll pick it up another time. I'm late for something." He turned around and strode across the parking lot.

Jessica retreated to the foyer to watch him get into his car and drive away. Nice morning. Great lunch. Fight with Mindi. Startled by Kevin. Old woman in respiratory distress. Weird conversation with Kevin, and now he was fleeing the scene. She'd been up and down so many times in the last hour she felt like she'd ridden the world's wildest roller coaster and now she felt sick.

Why did he take off? He'd nearly fallen off the sidewalk getting away from her. She must have read him wrong. He hadn't been anywhere near kissing her. He'd been trying to teach her a lesson. This was part of the job for him. He'd committed himself to helping her whether he liked it or not. Any attraction she thought she felt was one-sided. Spinning around, she hurried to the office before anyone could stop her. She threw herself into her chair and put her hands over her face. Ten weeks until the exam.

* * * *

Kevin gripped the steering wheel like it might get away from him. Which it might because his hands were so sweaty they felt like they would slide off the slick leather. Bobbie had to be wrong. He'd stood there holding her and watching her react. At least as much as he could. His own body had been racing ahead of his mind. If it hadn't been, he wouldn't have blundered so horribly.

What had he been thinking, demanding to know what had happened to upset her? He wanted to believe he was preparing her for the job, but he knew full well it had nothing to do with the fire department. He'd wanted to protect her. Someone had hurt her, and he wanted to protect her.

Which was why the brass didn't want couples in the department. He remembered watching Kate panic at the apartment fire on Jefferson and not understanding why she was throwing such a fit.

Until now.

Would he be able to watch Jessica run into a building or would he try to protect her then, too? What about when the guys started razzing her? Did he have any right to protect her? She was an adult, she'd made her choice to do the job he did and had done for years.

Wasn't that the other sticky part of this problem? What right did he have to say *I care about you too much to let you do what I do*? He'd convinced Kate that Jack would survive the job, why couldn't he convince himself? Because he knew too much, that's why. He knew all too well surviving was the easy part. Staying sane was a little more tricky. If he acknowledged that he loved Jessica, he wouldn't be able to send her to training and on to the job knowing what she would face.

Plus he'd nearly kissed her. That was the worst of it. He'd stood there like a schmuck, clutching her shoulders, watching her dark eyes dilate and her breath quicken, on the verge of pulling her close and kissing her.

The first mistake had been touching her at all. When he'd grabbed her shoulder to stop her because she'd stormed past him without even seeing him, his entire body had reacted. The more distressed she became, the more he wanted to pull her against him right there between the cards and the magazines and hold her. Later, after watching her deal with that old woman so well, he almost hadn't been able to let her go outside. He'd been so proud of her. Obviously upset and yet handling a patient like a pro. Assessing the situation and issuing orders without hesitation. Keeping her perimeter under control. Getting rid of disruptive influences so she could keep her patient calm. Getting out of the way when the professionals arrived. She would make a heck of a good paramedic.

Which was another reason he couldn't have her. If they were a couple, it would affect her ranking. If he were dating her, she might not get into the department, which meant he could protect her from the rigors of the job. But if he did care about her, he would want her to fulfill her dream of becoming a paramedic.

He detoured past Jack's house, but Jack's truck was missing from the garage. He needed to talk to somebody, but his first choice apparently wasn't at home. Driving to his own house, he parked his car in the garage. When he unlocked the door, the house echoed.

He liked his house. Liked the privacy. Liked to be alone.

Why did he find himself wishing Jessica were here to greet him when he came home?

* * * *

"Okay, the curiosity is killing me. What the heck has got you in such a mood?" Bobbie kicked her left foot up on an extra chair in the gym's little café area. A frighteningly fit, vacuous blond wandered around the room straightening displays of t-shirts and supplements.

Jessica slouched. The gym felt cold now that she'd stopped exercising, and she was tired. Really, really tired. She'd gone for a run again last night after she got home, trying to burn off some stress, and she'd overdone it. Afterward, she'd spent a couple of hours soaking in the tub, turning herself into a prune, to think about the whole stupid argument with Mindi followed by the odd encounter with Kevin. This morning she hadn't even been able to run because of soreness, and Bobbie had cut her off a couple of times when she went overboard with the machines. Yet, tired and sore as she was, she still felt agitated past a comfortable threshold. "Just a bunch of stupid stuff happened yesterday."

"Oh?" Bobbie started spinning the cap of her juice bottle in the table. "You were going to look at tools with Kevin, weren't you?"

"That went okay. Everything just went a little nuts afterward."

"What happened?"

Jessica stared at the table. "All hell broke loose. Mindi thought I was doing this to catch Kevin, and we ended up having a screaming match in the cash office."

"Really?" Bobbie leaned forward, still playing with her bottle cap. It seemed to require all of her attention.

"It wouldn't be so bad if the cash office wasn't the size of a small walk-in closet. Shouting in a tiny room is a really bad idea." Jessica had spent part of her soaking time last night looking at old photo albums from college. Lots of pictures of her and Mindi, a few of her working security, more of Mindi headed out on dates with security guys.

"But you're not."

Jessica looked up. Bobbie hadn't stopped watching herself spin her bottle cap. "Not what?"

"Not trying to catch Kevin."

Jessica groaned, clenching her fists. "That was the other part of the waking nightmare that was yesterday." She craved his approval like she'd craved her father's as a little girl and like she'd craved the attention of her high school's star linebacker who had been her first serious crush. The linebacker had never given her more than a puzzled glance when she happened to stumble across his path. Kevin gave her more than puzzled looks, but she didn't understand what the looks he gave her meant half the time. She'd spent some soaking time considering that, too. Without knowing Kevin's intentions, she couldn't *catch* him, but she wouldn't mind if he seemed interested in hooking her. Which, at the moment, he didn't. "I don't think he likes me."

"Why?"

"He just, well, he acts weird around me sometimes. We had a good conversation over lunch and then after the argument with Mindi, he forced me to tell him what happened. Then he jumped into his car and drove away."

"Oh yeah?" Bobbie took a swig from her juice.

Jessica nodded.

"Did he say anything?" Bobbie bit her lip.

"He said I did a great job with my patient, and he had to go. He didn't even get the gift he said he needed for his niece." Jessica stared at the table top.

"What patient?"

"Oh, a little old lady had trouble breathing. We had to call 911. She's okay. They didn't even keep her overnight." Jessica sighed. "Anyway I ended up handling the incident, and he said I did a good job, but he still took off like a shot."

"He wouldn't have said you did good if you hadn't. He's not that nice." Bobbie slid back in her chair and finished off her juice. "I'm sure he likes you fine. He likes women like you."

Jessica looked up. "Women like me?"

"You know. Women who act like women."

Jessica plucked at her sweaty t-shirt. "I sure am winning awards in that area. Liz Hurley. watch out."

"No, never mind. I'm sure he likes you. He wouldn't have offered to help you if he didn't like you."

"Are you sure he didn't just feel sorry for me? It was my birthday. I was a little hysterical when he told me I only had a year before the cut off age."

"You're thirty? You don't look that old."

"Thanks," Jessica muttered. She'd been hearing that all her life. About now she should start taking it as a sincere compliment. "I guess I should mean that. I've always looked young."

"Don't worry. Working for the fire department adds years pretty fast." Bobbie sat up. "Hey, I found out something you might be interested in. Kevin's birthday is coming up. He's turning thirty-seven on the sixteenth."

"So he's just thirty-seven this summer." Jessica nodded. Seven years difference. Not that much. Not when she considered her parents were twelve years apart. Of course, it didn't matter. Despite what Bobbie said, she felt pretty sure, deep down, Kevin didn't like her.

"You could—" Bobbie hesitated. "You could throw him a surprise birthday party."

"A birthday party? Would he like that?" Jessica frowned. She loved hosting parties, but she hated being the focus of them. Kevin didn't strike her as the type who liked it either.

"Who doesn't love having a party thrown for them? Look, we'll order some pizzas, get a keg, call up the guys, and we're all set."

"Pizza and a keg? Is that all you think we need? I mean, I can make some food and we should have a birthday cake." Jessica paused. If Kevin 'liked women who acted like women' would he like a woman who planned a party for him? "Are you sure he'd like that?"

Bobbie grinned, but something about it seemed strange. "Sure. He'll love it. Listen, you plan the menu, I'll get the guys, and I'll choke a couple of bucks out of them for food and stuff."

Jessica stood up. "You know him better. Why don't we shower, and you can come back to my place so we can plan a menu and pick a date."

Bobbie stared at her. "Plan a menu? You take this party stuff pretty seriously, don't you?"

Jessica nodded. If Kevin did enjoy being the center of attention, she might be able to do something he'd like. "I love throwing parties. Come on."

* * * *

Jessica walked up to the front door of Kevin's two-story gray wooden house. The sticky hot weather made her miss the air-conditioning at the gym. She hadn't seen him since the outing to the hardware store six days ago. Bobbie had started making phone calls to round up his friends for the birthday party less than two weeks away. Jessica had gotten the day off and started gathering supplies. She'd talked Bobbie out of beer and pizza. Instead, she was cooking up some barbecue fare, but in honor of Kevin's interest in all things Irish, she'd cleaned her grocery store out of canned Guinness, as she understood it was better than the bottled. After consulting with the store's music aficionados on the best Gaelic folk music, she'd purchased a couple of

CDs. Normally, it took about two hours to set everything up, and she planned to ask Kevin to pick her up at home to go running that day. The way the backyard lay hidden behind the house ensured she could hide thirty or forty people out of sight. If only she was sure Kevin wanted a surprise party. Bobbie seemed positive he would.

She'd walked here, which she thought she might pay for on the way home, but it gave her plenty of opportunity to check out Kevin's house. Minimal landscaping, he seemed to take the mow-it-and-forget-about-it approach. His porch had a swing hanging from the ceiling, and what she'd thought was an enclosed porch was in fact a solarium that opened from inside the house. She judged the house to be from the 1920's. Old and romantic.

Kevin opened the door and looked her over. "You're early."

"Am I? Sorry." She smoothed her hand along her hair. Suddenly the exercise outfit of bike shorts and tank top she'd been wearing to the gym seemed all wrong, even though Bobbie had never commented on it. Kevin's gaze made it less comfortable and silly.

He shrugged. "Come on in." He stepped through the small entry way into the living room.

She glanced down at the blue and white honeycomb tiles on the entry floor before looking up and realizing the living room spanned the entire front of the house. "Wow." One side appeared to be his dedicated living area with a couch, two chairs and television set grouped together. The other side held the fireplace.

"It's nice, isn't it?" Kevin said, grinning. "I just bought it a year ago. I don't really have everything set up yet."

"You really need a chair in front of this fireplace. A rocking chair would be good. Or you could move that tan easy chair over here. It doesn't seem to fit with the rest of the furniture over there." Jessica admired the large mantle and the built in cases on either side before she glanced at Kevin.

Kevin studied the space and she wondered if she should have made the suggestion. "Maybe. Come on. My weights are in the garage."

He led her down a short hall and out the back door. She kept to herself her observation that the kitchen remodel, which looked like it predated Kevin, had been ill-conceived. His garage had old-fashioned doors that opened on side hinges instead of rolling up on rails. Because of the equipment, he'd had to squeeze his car against the far wall. "How has your studying been going?" he asked, leading her inside.

"Good. The only part I'm worried about is the tools. I consistently get those wrong on the practice tests."

"You're taking practice tests?"

Was that admiration or irritation? "Yes. I tried one the day I talked to you first, just to see what my shortcomings were, and then I tried another one yesterday to see if I'd learned anything."

"Did you?"

"It's hard to tell. The practice tests are only fifty questions."

He nodded and turned his back to her, setting up the bench. "How did you score?"

"Eighty-six the first time, ninety-two yesterday."

He started sliding disks on the bar.

She wished he'd turn around or say something. Had she been

wrong to take the practice tests so soon? Between the three books, she had about fifteen of them. She could take one every week from now until the testing started and not run out. Did he think she was being too gung-ho? Was it possible to be? Had he gotten to the same idea Mindi had? That she was using training as an excuse? Her parents could give him written affidavits that she'd played fireman as a little kid. Provided she managed to tell her parents. Maybe the scores weren't good enough, and he didn't want to tell her?

"I'm going to start you out at seventy pounds. You need to do fifteen reps," he said.

Nodding, she stretched out on the bench. He stood over her with his hands under the bar like he thought she might drop it on herself. The flash of irritation surprised her. He wasn't doubting her, he was spotting. Normal procedure.

She did the repetitions without even changing the expression on her face. Bobbie had warned her it would take a while to build up strength, but they had already worked up to one hundred pounds of resistance on the upper body machines at the gym.

"Good job," he said. He leaned down and started loading more weight disks on the bar. "Now let's go up to eighty."

Eighty pounds was not much more difficult than seventy had been. While he stood over her, ready to catch her if she slipped, she had the opportunity to watch him. He seemed anxious, with his hands forward and his feet set in a wide stance so he would be more stable if he did have to reach over her and lift the bar off her chest. The more prepared he seemed, the more irritated she felt. He was fully prepared for her to fail.

"Very good." His tone still rang hollow. Part of her rose up to meet the compliment while another part of her scorned it for being an empty courtesy. She wanted him to be impressed, but she wanted it to be for a good reason. "We'll just increase to one hundred then. You seem to be in better shape than you thought."

This time it took a little more concentration to not change her expression. The free weights were more difficult than the machines. She had a hard time keeping the bar balanced. Her shoulders and upper arms burned. When she finished this set of repetitions, he helped her rest the bar in the cradle and turned toward a table against the side wall. Why wouldn't he look at her?

"You can sit up. We'll do some biceps curls next." He sounded like her doctor telling her she could get dressed now before he left the room. That cool, professional tone. Detached. It fanned her fury higher.

"Why don't you want me to do any more bench presses?" She slicked sweat off her forehead with her hand.

"Because you're going to exhaust the muscles. To get a really good work out you need to shift around. We'll go back to that later." He didn't turn around. "The hand bells are against the back wall. Pick a weight that's comfortable, but not beyond your capacity. You aren't here to impress me."

Scowling, she walked to the back of the garage and located the hand bells. Sorting through the disks on the floor she chose ones that were about the weight she'd been using at the gym. She started a repetition of fifteen because she anticipated him telling her to do one any minute. Most of this kind of exercise came in repetitions of fifteen. She was starting to like Bobbie more than Kevin.

Unfortunately, Bobbie didn't look like that in a t-shirt. He wasn't the type to wear tight shirts to show off his muscles, something she appreciated more and more every trip to the gym, but he had something to show off. His trapezius muscles flowed across his shoulders and up to his neck instead of mounding up to his jaw. Her eyes wandered down to his waist. For nearly thirty-seven, he hadn't thickened there like many men around middle age had. Those guys hung around the gym, too. The ones who looked in a mirror one day and realized they'd become their fathers. Bobbie referred to them as *mid-lifers*. The mid-lifers were always ready to buy a girl a drink at the juice bar, or compliment her on her prowess with a machine, but Bobbie pointed out most of them had dents on their left hand ring finger where they'd taken off their wedding rings.

Jessica couldn't see much of Kevin's glutes in his baggy sweat pants. She decided that was for the best as she felt herself getting warm from something other than the exercise. Absently, she wondered if her bike shorts had any effect on him. They did wonders for the mid-lifers. Kevin, however, wouldn't even look at her. Shaving her legs last night had been a waste of time. If he wasn't going to even look at her face, he'd never notice stubble on her legs.

CHAPTER 6

Kevin turned around from the notes he was making, having braced himself to look at her, and noticed the way her eyes darted up to meet his. "What are you staring at?"

"Nothing," she said. "Just staring into space waiting for the next order." She smiled.

"How many of those have you done?" he asked, hoping she didn't hear the tenseness in his voice.

She looked down at the dumbbell she'd been lifting and lowering automatically. "I don't know. I lost count." Her face turned a deeper shade of scarlet.

"Well, switch sides."

She moved the dumbbell from her left hand to her right and started lifting it up and down. He'd thought he was ready to look at her again, but he'd been wrong. From the moment he'd laid eyes on her in that outfit, he hadn't been able to think straight. He didn't want to be juvenile, but all he could think about was how hot she looked in those tight shorts. Standing over her while she worked on her bench pressing nearly gave him a heart attack. He'd dragged all this stuff out here to the garage hoping that being out in the open would help him hold onto a little perspective, but it hadn't. The only way he managed to not stare was to turn his back on her, and then he had to listen to her behind him. Listening was almost worse because then his imagination took over, and her heavy breathing made too good a soundtrack. But if he had his back to her, she couldn't see the dumbstruck look on his face. A draw at best.

"Okay, now what?" She looked up at him with her bright, eager eyes.

"Triceps. Kneel on the bench with one knee and pull up from the floor to about your waist." He hoped his instructions were clear enough that he wouldn't have to correct her position by touching her.

She put one knee on the bench and started her repetitions. "There's a machine at the gym we use for this."

"Oh?" Kevin closed his eyes because she wasn't looking up. He could imagine her at the gym dressed like that, with a horde of young hunks surrounding her.

"The free weights are different, though. They shift around in your hands a little more," she said.

"So do the victims." Kevin opened his eyes. Bodybuilder women always turned him off. They were hard in all the wrong places. Too much like men. So why was watching this woman lift weights turning him on?

"Exactly." Jessica stood up and switched sides. "I was reading last night about what to expect in the exam."

"Oh?" Did she notice how stupid he was all of a sudden? He felt stupid. He couldn't seem to string together a coherent thought. How much worse could he have been inside the house?

"It said the hose drag could be simulated with a duffel bag across a gym floor. Is that likely?"

She sounded so calm. So conversational. No way was she as attracted to him as he was to her. "Pretty likely. When I took the test we had a duffel bag loaded with about a hundred fifty pounds that we had to drag across the parking lot and back. It's supposed to be like dragging a charged hose, but it isn't."

"How is it different?"

Kevin tried to gather his thoughts so he could make an answer that made sense. He missed being able to make sense. "A charged hose is full of water, so it's stiff and sometimes it feels more like maneuvering a two-by-four that's fifty feet long."

She nodded and stood up. "Is that something we'll be able to practice?"

"I can find a duffel. You might have to run up and down the street." He wondered if she would be embarrassed, running up and down the brick street in front of his house dragging a weighted duffel bag.

She looked down his driveway. "All right. What about victim drag?"

Kevin flushed. "Victim drag?"

"The book said part of the test would involve dragging a hundred and sixty-five pound dummy a hundred feet through an obstacle course." She watched him with a serious set to her mouth.

"Maybe you better do that with Bobbie." A squeak leaked into his voice this time. He couldn't imagine Jessica having her arms around his chest and dragging him anywhere. Actually, he could imagine it all too well. Just now he could imagine her arms wrapped around his chest quite clearly. Of course in his imagination he was facing her.

She scowled. "Why?"

"I'm too heavy," he said. "I weigh one ninety."

"So? Isn't it better to over-train?"

He could see a furrow developing between her eyes. Once he'd heard that furrow described as the "I want" line. What did she want and how could he give it to her without having to touch her and risk embarrassing himself? "I guess. But we could just use the duffel. We can load it with however much weight you want."

"But that won't simulate a dummy or a human. I've only got a five percent chance of success. I'm going to need all the help I can get." She reached her arms over her head to stretch out.

Kevin turned around because the sight was too much for him. He looked at the notes he'd made on her abilities. "I need to look at this book you're using."

"Which one? I've got three."

He turned back around. Her hands were on her hips now. The pose was alluring, but not as much as watching her stretch. "Three?"

"I believe in over-training when the odds are stacked against me." She pursed her lips.

The challenge in her eyes bumped his libido up a notch. He wasn't going to live through eight and a half more weeks of this without serious embarrassment. At some point he was going to make some advance that she would be horrified by. Even if she wasn't a lesbian, her dating pool had to include better specimens than him. Younger, smarter, wealthier, better looking, something. If he did make an unwanted advance, the moment she joined the department, everyone would know. He'd be a laughing stock. "Fine. Just don't hurt yourself over-training. I still would like to take a look at the books."

"Come over to my apartment a week from Tuesday."

"Why?" Kevin stepped backward, bumping into the table. Her apartment? He couldn't imagine a worse place to be alone with her.

"It's a mess. I need time to clean up," she said.

"Why can't you just bring the books with you next time we meet?" Kevin tried to keep his rising panic out of his voice. He could do substantially more damage alone with her in her apartment than he could alone with her in his basement.

"I can't," she stammered. "I...borrowed them from work, and I can't risk having anything happen to them." She wiped her hands on her hips and slid them behind her back.

"Can't I just look at them at your store?"

"No. They were the only ones in stock. I can't take them back until I'm finished with them." She bit her lip.

Kevin found himself staring at the point where her teeth sunk into her lush lower lip. "I guess I can come by your place."

"Good." She smiled, pleased. "Now what?"

"Legs. Then we'll start at the top again." He clenched his teeth, wondering how he was going to get out of this. Her apartment was the very last place he wanted to be. Behind that closed door he could really do something foolish. Or he'd find out something that would turn him off to her. Maybe he would meet her girlfriend. Maybe he would find out she was a slob. Maybe he'd discover she liked modern Swedish design, and she had an apartment full of uncomfortable white furniture.

Of course, the fact that she was a tall, weight-lifting, too-young girl should have turned him off already.

Kevin watched her go through a complete repetition, struggling to keep his hands to himself. He wanted to sweep the loose strands of hair off her face and run his fingers down the curve of her back. It helped that she seemed a little defensive. If she thought he was getting too close, she would draw away. That only made him want to follow though.

"So did you find a date to your friend's wedding yet?" she asked, doing the biceps curls.

"Wedding?" His mouth went dry. She remembered. Why did she remember?

"You were worried about finding a date to your friend's wedding in a couple of months." She kept her eyes on her hand, watching herself lift with more concentration than she needed.

"No, I haven't." Kevin frowned. Jack's wedding now loomed seven weeks away and the only available females he knew were Jessica and Bobbie. He couldn't show up dateless. Even Lew would manage to scrape up a date. The only person likely to turn out alone was Jack's sister, and Kevin didn't want to be equated with her or, worse, stuck with her all day because he'd be alone too, which is what Jack's mother would say given half a chance. No, he'd been tricked into one evening with Jack's viper of a sister two years ago, and if he had to spend more than half an hour with her, there might be fatalities. He had to find a date some place.

Bobbie, he ruled out as a matter of course. He needed a girl, and Bobbie didn't count. The thought of asking Jessica to a wedding made him break out into a cold sweat. He could barely contain himself around her now. Seeing her dressed like a bodybuilder was driving him crazy, seeing her dressed like a girl might push him over the edge. Plus, if he was getting all misty because Jack was settling down, being with her at the wedding might be more than he could stand. In an emotional moment, he might pop the question and spend the rest of his life regretting it.

Or would he?

Under cover of making more notes, he watched her put away the equipment. She had a certain grace to her. A purpose and calm he admired. In her own way, she was attractive. Maybe not what he would have chosen out of all the women in the world, but not undesirable. Besides, all the women in the world didn't seem to beating a path to his door. In fact, Jessica was very desirable and intelligent, and she was interested in some of the same things he was. Would it be so bad to spend the rest of his life with that?

Kevin shook himself. What was he thinking? Here he was just *thinking* about the wedding and getting all mushy over Jessica. There had to be another female in Arden who wasn't Jack's sister and who didn't expect one date to end with her own wedding.

"Are we finished for the day, or do you want to start something else?" she asked.

"Finished?" He checked his watch. It was poker night and the guys should start showing up any time. The more time between her leaving and Dan arriving, the better. "We're done for today."

"And you're coming by my place a week from Tuesday."

She wasn't going to forget this. He was going to have to spend some time with her in her apartment, alone. "Yes."

"All right. I'm going to the gym tomorrow after work."

What was she going to wear to the gym? That outfit? One just like it? Something skimpier? Kevin bit back that question. If he was there, he could keep the young bucks from getting in the way of her training. "Okay. Do you want me to meet you there?"

She lifted her chin. "Don't feel obligated."

"I'm not obligated. I thought you might like the company." He'd been so busy thinking about not touching her and how much he wanted to that he hadn't considered why she had been acting so defensive.

She hesitated. "You can meet me if you like. I get off about three and walk up there."

"How far is that?"

"Two miles."

"Then when you're finished, you walk back to your car?"

"Yes." She set her jaw, turning defensive again.

Kevin raised one eye brow. "I'm on your side, remember? I think you should stop doing that because you're going to exhaust yourself. You need to build up slowly."

"I don't have time to build up slowly."

With her eyes flashing, she looked more beautiful. He made a mental note to not make her angry. It made her too appealing. "You have plenty of time. Relax and take it easy. If you don't pass the first time, you have three more chances. You'll pass, and you'll rank high enough to get in. You have nine weeks to train and that's plenty of time unless you hurt yourself overdoing it. That's going to knock you out more certainly than not being trained enough."

"What about the dummy drag?"

Kevin looked down the driveway because he heard a car. Lew was parking across the street. At least he hadn't brought Dan with him. If Dan saw Jessica in that outfit, he'd scoop her out from under him in less than five minutes. "We'll work something out for the dummy drag. We won't practice that until August anyway. Anything could happen by then." Like he could convince somebody to loan him a dummy.

"Hi, guys," Lew called walking toward the garage. "You must be Jessica."

"Nice to meet you…" She trailed off waiting for Lew to supply his name. He didn't because he was too busy peering into the garage.

"Lew Draper," Kevin said.

"Hey, how come you moved all your stuff out to the garage?" Lew asked.

"Because I did," Kevin growled through clenched teeth. Dan or Jack would have picked up the hint and let it drop, but not Lew. No, Jack would have picked up the hint, Dan would have been too busy picking up Jessica to notice the weights or the hint.

"You had it set up real nice in the basement. I thought you said you were going to keep it there."

Kevin glanced at Jessica. She had one eyebrow raised. "I decided since it had been so warm, I would work out here."

"But you said it was cooler in the basement last year. It's too hot to work out outside."

Kevin glared at Lew, wondering how anyone could be so slow on the uptake. "I changed my mind."

Jessica stepped back a pace with a tight, closed look on her face. "I guess I'll go. See you tomorrow at the gym, Kevin. Nice meeting you, Lew." She started down the driveway.

Kevin watched her until she'd turned on the sidewalk. He rubbed his hands over his face. Now he had to get a membership to her gym so he could fend off muscle men despite the fact that he was determined not to date her himself.

"What's the matter?" Lew asked. "She not doing okay?"

"*She's* doing fine." Kevin headed into the house before he ended up explaining that he wasn't doing as well.

* * * *

Jessica walked home, grumbling under her breath. He had to hate her. Had to. He didn't even want her in his house. He'd carried all his equipment outside to keep her out, he'd done his best to avoid looking at her, and he'd evaded the whole dummy drag issue. And when his buddy showed up, he'd hustled her away.

In fact, he'd tried to avoid her meeting his buddies all along. First, he'd objected to taking her to the station to go over the tools, now he was trying to get her away from his house. They obviously knew who she was. Lew had known her name without being told.

He was in for a real surprise in about a week and a half. He wasn't going to be able to keep her away from his buddies when they were all gathered in her backyard.

* * * *

Kevin walked up the stairs to Jessica's apartment feeling like he was walking into a trap. Something about this seemed very odd.

Or it might be him.

Yesterday at the station, the captain had called him into his office to quiz Kevin about Jessica. How was she doing so far? How likely was it that she would be able to pass the test? What about her personality? Would she make a good addition to a crew? Could she think for herself and follow orders? The department anticipated a shortage of paramedics in about a year, and when Jessica's application had turned up in human resources, their ears had perked up.

After her first two weeks of training she was doing very well. She could produce the answers to complicated math problems instantaneously. All three practice tests she'd taken, she'd aced. The crisis at the bookstore had been handled with a great deal of natural skill. The only problem he could see was that she attacked her training more aggressively than he liked. He worried she might hurt herself.

He hadn't been able to convince himself he wasn't trying to protect her by telling her to slow down. If he slowed her down too much, she wouldn't rank high enough on the test. How long would it take her to figure out it was his fault she hadn't passed?

Kevin had no idea how he'd managed to be observant enough to give the captain a clear report. He'd been having a hard time tearing his eyes off her body to see what she was doing. When she showed up at his house wearing bike shorts and a tank top, he'd almost lost his composure. The membership at Bobbie's gym let him work out with her in public. He didn't trust himself alone with her. Unfortunately, the gym was not much better, and there was competition there. In her bike shorts and tank top, she was never without a spotter. That had been driving him to distraction yesterday. The knowledge that she was at the gym, in that outfit, without him to chase off potential Romeos.

Not that he cared. She was too young, too tomboyish, too tall, not feminine enough, and she wanted to be a firefighter. He didn't want to have an intimate relationship with another firefighter. Think of the rumor mill if they broke up. Think of the rumor mill if they stayed together. If they were a couple, it might wreck her ranking, and now not only did she want to join the department, but the department wanted her to join.

He knocked.

Jessica opened the door, looking a little flushed and overdressed for running in jeans and a white cotton blouse. "Hi. I'm not ready yet. Come on in." She stepped out of the doorway, allowing him a full view of her apartment.

He stopped in the doorway. "This is your place? I mean, you live here alone?"

"Yes."

"You don't live with a boyfriend, or a girlfriend?"

"No. One bedroom. No boyfriend, no roommate. I don't even have a hamster." She smiled uneasily. "Why?"

He shook his head. The apartment, while not frilly, definitely belonged to a girl. Scratch that, a woman. The front door led into the dining room. The room felt warm and welcoming with nice, but not saccharine, art prints on the wall. Against one wall stood a drop leaf table with one of the leaves up and a small stack of mail, three fire exam study guides, and a matched pair of brass candlesticks on it. The other two walls were covered with bookshelves. She could have stocked her own library with titles ranging from *Gross Anatomy* to *The Poetry of John Keats.*

She must have been following his gaze, for as if she'd read his mind, she supplied the answer to his unspoken question.

"The shelves? One of the hazards of working in a bookstore. You acquire a lot of books. I just read something really interesting." She bent down and pulled a book off one of the shelves. Kevin had to redirect his gaze before she caught him staring at her derriere. "It says in here that in ancient Rome there were private fire-fighting companies who would show up at the scene of a fire and offer to buy the building. They wouldn't try to put out the fire until the owner sold the place at a huge loss." She held out the book which had a picture of a hand-cranked pump on the facing page.

"I don't think that'll be on the test," he said, amazed his voice sounded so normal. His throat felt too tight to produce the correct tone. He'd almost refused to come here today. This morning, he'd had his hand on the phone to tell her he couldn't make it. Under no circumstances did he want to be alone with her in her apartment, and he was feeling those reasons very clearly through his sweat pants just looking at her and she wasn't wearing the bike shorts. What the hell was going to happen when she went in the other room to change? He'd have to stand out here and imagine her naked. He was already standing here imagining her naked.

She closed the book, looking a little uneasy. "No, I didn't think it would be. I just thought it was interesting." She slid the book back into its shelf.

Turning toward the archway to the living room, he tried to get his mind back to where it should be. He'd spent too much time worrying about Jessica, her bike shorts, and the gym yesterday. Looking at the living room didn't help. In addition to a TV and a couple more prints and burgundy wing-backed chair, she had a big comfortable burgundy couch that made him want to stretch out on it, with her.

Again, she seemed to read his mind. "It's huge, isn't it? Every Thanksgiving we have to drag it into the bedroom so we can open the table all the way for the Cast-Off Thanksgiving dinner." She started toward a doorway that revealed a framed print of another Victorian painting.

"Cast-Off Thanksgiving dinner?" Kevin heard a squeak slip into his voice again, but he doubted Jessica noticed it. Her apartment already felt more like home than his house did.

"Every year I cook dinner for anybody who can't get home to family."

Kevin swallowed hard. She was getting more feminine by the second. Maybe they could skip the run today. If the department needed her that badly, they would bump up her ranking enough to cancel out the drop of having her involved with one of their firefighters.

"Have a seat while I change." She gestured toward the couch, and he decided in that instant there was no way he could sit down on it. If he did, before too long she would end up sitting beside him, and from there things only went downhill. Instead he perched on the edge of the chair. She walked through the door and took a right rather than go through the closed door straight ahead. That struck him as odd because based on the size of the dwelling, if that was a bathroom, it had to be a darn big one and there wasn't room for a bedroom off the back of the place.

"Hey Kevin, can you give me a hand with something?" she called down the hall.

Kevin stood up, feeling like his knees were going to disjoint by themselves. His calculations about the size of the dwelling disappeared under the haze of her calling him to another room deeper in the apartment that might or might not be the bedroom.

"What do you need?" he asked, stalling for time and hoping she'd change her mind while he tried to come up with innocent reasons for her to need him in the back of the apartment. Nothing came to him.

"I need a hand."

Kevin walked to the hall and peered down. She stood in another door that appeared to lead outside. "What do you need?" he asked again.

"Will you just come here? Boy, you're suspicious today." She stepped through the door onto a narrow porch.

He followed, praying that whatever she needed would be over quickly so they could get back out in public where he was less likely to try to kiss her.

"Surprise!"

CHAPTER 7

Kevin stumbled back a step, looking for a place to hide. This had all the earmarks of a very bad dream. He looked down to make sure he was dressed. If he was naked, it would be a dream; if he was clothed, it would be worse. Thirty or so of his nearest and dearest friends crowded into Jessica's small backyard. He saw Jack with Kate and Bobbie and Lew and Dan. They all started singing *Happy Birthday to You*. Jessica watched him with uncertain hope all over her sweet face.

A birthday party. Somehow she'd found out his birthday was Thursday and arranged a party for him. Jessica couldn't have any idea how much he hated parties, especially parties in his honor. Scanning the crowd, he found Bobbie in the back corner. She was wearing a pleased smirk until his eyes met hers. At least he knew now how Jessica knew when his birthday was. He forced a smile.

"Thanks, everybody," he said when the singing stopped.

"Come on down before the beer gets cold," someone shouted. Kevin had been too busy staring daggers at Bobbie to register who.

"There is plenty of cold beer, too," Jessica shouted back. "You just get the keg open." She pressed a button to start the music and walked past Kevin into the house. "I left some beer warm for you. Irish style."

He followed her. "Bobbie put you up to this," he announced, standing in her kitchen door.

Jessica stopped unwrapping cling wrap from a bowl. "You hate it, don't you? I'm sorry. It won't last long. Bobbie thought you'd like it."

"I'll bet she did." Kevin turned to storm outside, but Jessica caught his arm. He froze. Her touch was light, but it went straight to his core.

"Take this with you." She held out a bowl.

He looked at the bowl for a minute before lifting it out of her hands.

"There's a table against the fence. Most of the food is already there. You'll see it. I'll be down in a minute." She smiled at him. "Be nice to Bobbie, she meant well." Jessica turned back to her refrigerator.

Kevin carried the salad bowl to the backyard feeling as if he couldn't effectively hunt down and kill Bobbie while carrying it. Bobbie seemed to be determined to make capturing her as difficult as possible. When he came around the corner of the house, she was standing across the yard by the fence, but by the time he'd reached the food table, she'd slipped past him to the other side of the yard. He set down the salad and looked at the table. The salad he brought out had black beans, chopped tomatoes, and avocado in it. Also on the table was a carved ham, a plate of sliced cheese, a heap of rolls, potato salad, baked beans, and another exotic looking salad composed of lentils, tomatoes and corn. No one had any hesitation about digging in.

He scanned the yard. Bobbie must have done all the inviting. Every off-duty firefighter stationed in this area of the city had shown up, from guys he worked with every shift to guys he saw once a year. The guys he worked with every shift also seemed to be determined to avoid him, so he was constantly congratulated by guys he didn't know well as he worked his way through the crowd.

A brick patio spanned the back of the house where a couple of wooden deck chairs sat, along with an aluminum tub full of ice and drinks. The yard sloped up steeply at the back, and Jessica had planted a row of ferns there. Just over the property line, towering elm trees blocked out most of the light but provided a welcome shade. It reminded him that he hadn't done any landscaping at his house in the year since he'd moved in. He worked his way to where Jack and Kate stood near the ferns.

Jack held up his hand before Kevin could speak. "I tried to stop her. You know how Bobbie is when she gets going."

"It's not that bad," Kate added. "It's a very nice party."

"I hate parties," Kevin growled.

"I already talked to your trainee yesterday. She's going to start running out of alcohol in about two hours and out of food in three. The music will last about as long as the food. Once there's no food and no music, everybody will go away. She has party planning down to a science." Jack shrugged. "If you have to have a party, Jessica is probably the one to host it."

"The food is very good," Kate said.

Kevin glanced at the plate in her hand. It wasn't pizza, he realized. When Bobbie had a party, it always involved pizza. Bobbie may have done the calling, but Jessica catered.

"She seems pretty nice," Jack ventured. "What made you decide to train her?"

Kevin shook his head. "Good question. I need to talk to you, but not here."

"Okay." Jack frowned. "Give me a call. You were going to help me take down that wall anyway."

"When are you coming back to work?"

"The twenty-fifth."

"Good." Kevin looked around the yard. Everyone seemed to be having a good time. If he weren't so worried about Jessica, he'd be having a good time.

"What's this playing?" Kate asked.

"Altan," Kevin answered. The music. Good Irish music, no cheesy *Danny Boy* in sight and no rock. He didn't have anything against rock, but it was one of the things he hated most about these parties. Everybody played the same six CDs. Every party seemed like a rerun of the last one.

This wasn't your everyday Irish folk music either. This was some of the better, more obscure stuff. He recalled having heard Capercaillie, too. Not only had the food been carefully chosen, but so had the music. He decided he would be having a pretty good time if this weren't Jessica's backyard and if he didn't have to watch every guy in the department leer at her.

Jessica walked down the stairs with a bowl in her hands. Joe from A shift stopped her. When Joe gestured to the corner of the yard, Kevin decided he was telling her one of his war stories, not hitting on her, and realized with a start that *this* was the location of the infamous Magnolia Boulevard Unfire. Jessica smiled and nodded. His breath caught in his throat watching her. Brushing her loose hair back with her free hand, she laughed when Joe gestured as though he was overturning a bucket. He imagined she would listen to Joe's stories for hours just to be nice. Glancing in his direction, she caught him staring at her and paled before looking away.

Dan strolled over with a can in his hand. "I didn't know this was the address of the Magnolia Boulevard Unfire," he announced.

"That's because you never really listened to Joe tell the story," Jack said.

"Unfire?" Kate asked.

"There was a call to this address, and when the engine got here the fire was a couple of embers in a half-rotted stump. The tenant put it out with a bucket while they were standing there. She didn't even let the captain do it," Kevin explained.

Jessica broke away from Joe and crossed the yard, stopping to talk to a few other guys on the way. Kevin couldn't take his eyes off her.

"There's Guinness," Dan said.

"Guinness?" Kevin turned his attention back to Dan in time to see him and Jack exchange an amused look. This was what he had been afraid would happen. They were catching on, and the rumors were going to fly.

"Beer. Jessica said she left some warm for you if you wanted to drink it in the true Irish way, or there's some on ice." Dan examined his can. "She said the canned stuff is better than the bottled. More like it is over there. This stuff is bitter."

"It's supposed to be." Kevin found himself searching for Jessica again and forced himself to stop. She got Guinness for him? He was a complete heel. Sure he hated parties, especially parties in his honor, but she must have put hours of work into this, tailoring it for him. Good food, his music, special beer, and he hadn't managed to say thank you.

"She's hot, too." Dan grinned. "I wouldn't mind pulling a twenty-four hour tour with her. Showers would be fun."

A growl developed in Kevin's throat, but he caught it before anyone heard it. He'd predicted the moment Dan laid eyes on her, he'd be after her. Didn't that prove she was attractive? Dan didn't have bad taste in looks, just in brains. Kevin already knew she was smart. "Hands off," he said, trying to keep as much hostility out of his voice as possible.

"Why, is she yours?" Dan asked.

Kevin turned to Dan, his jaw tightening. He still wanted to believe he didn't even have designs on her, but it became less and less possible with each passing moment. "The brass doesn't like the idea of couples in the department. I don't want you costing her ranking."

"That's nuts," Jack said. "Why would it matter?"

Kevin glared at him. He had plenty of reasons. Protectiveness for one. Sexual harassment for another. But he didn't want to start listing those off now. It would look too much like he'd spent a lot of time thinking about it. Which he had. "Ask the captain. That's what he told me. I need to talk to Bobbie." He set off across the yard after Bobbie again. No matter where he went, she'd managed to stay on the opposite side of the yard from him. In the back corner of the yard he got trapped listening to another one of Joe's war stories and before he could get away, Bobbie had vanished again. He sidled up behind Jessica with a can of Guinness in his hand while she was talking to a couple of guys from twelve because they were looking at her the way dogs stare at steak. The trick was reminding them she wasn't fair game while not saying anything.

"Do they actually let you have as much as you can drink?" Roger asked.

"They sure do. If you go through the entire tour of the plant, at the very end you can drink as much as you can hold. Fortunately, the Gardai are very nice to drunken American women who think they can walk on water." Jessica's laughter worked through him like hot coffee on a cold day, warm and welcome.

"Is that what they call the cops over there? Gardai?" Pat Tobin asked.

"Garda is singular, Gardai is plural." Jessica glanced over her shoulder at Kevin, and he saw her tense.

"Hey man, great party," Pat said. "Happy birthday."

"Thanks," Kevin said. He felt awkward standing this close to Jessica and not putting his arm over her shoulders, but then he would feel more awkward standing next to her and putting his arm over her shoulder. "Jessica did all the work."

"Don't I know it? I was really surprised when I showed up. When Bobbie throws a party it's beer, pizza and Bob Seger." Roger grinned. "I'm gonna talk my captain into requesting you once rankings come out. It'd be great to have somebody around who could cook again." He winked.

Kevin felt himself glowering at Roger. A coil of jealousy heated in his chest. They were fawning over her. This was worse than a singles bar.

"You seem to think I'll make it first try. You must have a lot of confidence in me." Jessica tilted her head, and it was adorable. How a tall weight-lifting woman was adorable, Kevin didn't know, but he did want Roger and Pat to stop looking at her.

Roger shoveled black bean salad into his mouth. "Kevin won't let you down. He'll do you right."

"I hope so. If you'll excuse me." She stepped out of the group leaving Kevin with Roger and Pat. All three of them watched her go to the table and start moving things around, removing empty containers and making space.

"Where did you find her, anyway?" Pat asked.

"She works at the bookstore. I met her there." Kevin watched Jessica walk across the yard toward the steps and stop to talk to a couple he didn't recognize. A curly-haired man and a short woman. None of the old marrieds were around. Other than Kate with Jack and two other younger wives, it was all men. Even Dan hadn't brought a date. Bobbie definitely did the invitation list. She'd made sure to include every eligible bachelor within reach to parade Jessica in front of. Another good reason to strangle her.

"If she doesn't make the cut, I might have to marry her," Roger commented.

Kevin turned around to look at him. Why was everybody talking about marriage all of a sudden? "What?" Roger, he remembered, was thirty-three. Much closer to her age and no gray hair.

"Hey, I'd do a lot for this cooking. If you need any help training her, let me know." He peered around Kevin. "I see Cap. I'm gonna go talk to him." Roger ducked past Kevin, headed for his captain.

Pat shrugged. "He's been sore ever since Carl Mendes retired. He swears nobody can cook like that."

"That's not exactly the greatest reason to join the department," Kevin snapped.

"There's worse reasons." Pat, divorced thirty-five-year-old Pat, winked. "Worse reasons to get married, too."

Jessica was walking down the stairs from her apartment again. Even though he hadn't wanted a party, he had to thank her for it. She'd done a lot of work, but he didn't want anyone to see him talking to her, and he didn't want to be alone with her either.

Kevin looked toward the entrance to the back yard and noticed another pair walking around the house. He recognized them from the bookstore. The woman from the coffee bar and the woman who shelved History. The female half of the couple he'd seen earlier was the magazine clerk too. Hopefully Mindi wouldn't show up. Bobbie had wandered close enough that he could catch her.

He stopped behind her and waited until she turned around. When she did, she paled.

"I didn't know you hated parties that much. Who hates parties?" she said. She'd been talking to three guys from Eleven, but they cleared out as soon as Kevin arrived.

"Bobbie, you know I hate parties. Why did you talk her into this?"

"It was her idea."

Kevin scowled. "It was not."

"Okay, so it wasn't. Don't be a baby. It's just a party. Lighten up." Bobbie folded her arms across her chest. "Or didn't you want everybody else to meet your girlfriend?"

"She's not my girlfriend," Kevin hissed.

Bobbie smiled slyly. "That's what you think. I think she has a different idea."

"What's that supposed to mean?" Kevin's head spun. Jessica, his girlfriend? Did she have designs on him? Was that the point of the party? To make him fall in love with her? He couldn't. Not even if he wanted to.

"Nothing, clueless." Bobbie licked her lips and grinned.

"You said she didn't like men." Kevin's voice dropped to a low growl.

Bobbie shrugged. "I'm entitled to a mistake."

"How do you know?"

"Girl talk. Are you jealous?" Bobbie batted her eyelashes at him.

"No, and we are not a couple."

"Anything you say, big guy, but you should be having this talk with her, not me. I know who you're not dating, even if no one else does."

Kevin turned, looking over the yard. He didn't see Jessica. Walking around the house, he saw her as she stepped through the door into her apartment. He might not be able to convince the rest of the department he wasn't dating Jessica, but he could convince her. Running up the stairs, he leaned through the door. "Jessica!"

"Back here," she called.

He stalked to the hall and walked through the door that had been closed when he first arrived before realizing it was her bedroom. In the far corner sat her bed, shoved against the wall. With its high head- and footboards, it seemed to have walls of its own. Covered with an Indian-patterned purple satin spread, it made a passionate cocoon he wouldn't be able to forget soon. She stood in front of a dresser with a cake on it. It didn't say anything, but it must be his birthday cake.

"Did you want something or did you just want to admire your naked cake?" she asked. Her voice didn't sound sarcastic, rather it was pleasantly teasing.

His hands started to sweat when she said *naked*. "We are not a couple," he said.

"I noticed." She picked up the cake. "Anything else?"

He stared at her. *I noticed?* What kind of a response was that? He hadn't considered what kind of response he was hoping for, but bland acceptance wasn't it. She could be a little more heartbroken. A little upset. Some kind of emotion. Unless she really didn't care. Damn, was he the only one who felt some kind of connection here?

She shifted the cake in her arms. "Can you move so I can take this to the kitchen and write on it? For a guy who wants a short party, you don't seem to be interested in expediting the process."

He stepped back, and she walked past him, carrying the cake to the kitchen. He followed. Bobbie needed to explain herself. She'd made it sound like Jessica had been telling everyone they were involved, but Jessica didn't act like she'd ever considered the notion. So what did Bobbie mean? And why did he feel so let down? "What do you mean, you noticed?" he asked.

"Kevin, you have made it abundantly clear that you wish you'd never offered to help me." She put the cake on the tiny counter and turned to take a bag of frosting out of the refrigerator. "Is *Happy Birthday Kevin* all right with you, or do you have a special request that isn't more than seven words long?"

"What makes you think I don't want to train you?"

"That is ten words and won't look good on the cake, so *Happy Birthday Kevin* it is." She leaned over the cake, squeezing frosting through the plastic tip. Her hair fell across her cheek, hiding her expression from him.

"You didn't answer the question."

"I didn't want to."

Her voice sounded tight, like she might be fighting tears. The thought of her in tears alarmed him. He'd seen her push herself past where a lot of guys gave up and didn't like to think what it took to make her cry. However, this was more the response he'd hoped for. Tears meant she wasn't completely ignorant of him, so she must feel some kind of attraction too. "Then why did you put so much work into this party if you think I don't want to train you?"

"Because I like to give parties and because you are training me. Even though you don't want to." She paused halfway through writing *Birthday* because she'd made an *h* that looked more like a *b*. "You want this?" She scraped the frosting off the knife and held out the crumpled *h* on the tip of her finger.

For an instant he considered licking it off and shook his head before thought managed to translate to action.

"Your loss." She licked the frosting off her finger, leaving a smear of green on her lips. Kevin forced himself to look away. This whole conversation was taking too long, and there was a yard full of guys who would ride him mercilessly if they noticed. Still, he didn't want to leave her right now. She still sounded upset and it had to be his fault. Plus, he hadn't thanked her for the party yet. Getting a look at where she lived hadn't cooled his desire at all. She had an apartment so welcoming and comfortable he'd gladly move in tomorrow. Everyone said she was a great cook and none of those guys would lie to be nice. She planned a party tailored for him and she used that cake decorator like a professional.

"You're really good with that," he commented.

She barked a laugh. "It's all in the hands. You should see me dissect a frog. I'm a wonder."

"It's a really nice party. Thanks," he said, trying again. "I guess it's not all parties I hate, just the ones I get invited to."

"I host a mean brunch, too." She spelled out his name with sure, even strokes. "I even have my own melon baller."

"I want you to know I appreciate it."

She nodded and straightened. Reaching around, she put the frosting back in the refrigerator. As she licked frosting off her fingers she didn't look teary or upset, but she had another green smudge on her cheek. "Just think, in six and a half weeks I'll be out of your hair." Her mouth quirked into a sarcastic smirk.

He stepped forward so quickly she jumped back a step, flattening herself against the wall. Her dark eyes went round, looking up at him in alarm. Grabbing her shoulders, he murmured, "You have no idea." The frosting still on her lips sweetened the kiss. Her body curved against his as his hands slid down to her waist. Even after the workouts she wasn't hard in all the wrong places. He wrapped his arms around her waist, lifting her off the floor in his eagerness. Her hands grasped his shoulders, pulling him against her as her lips parted to his probing tongue. A soft moan escaped her, shivering through him. He tangled his fingers through her hair, luxuriating in its satin texture. His need for her was growing beyond his control. If he hadn't wanted to be seen talking to her, he certainly couldn't be caught having sex with her.

He stepped back as abruptly as he'd moved forward, leaving her leaning against the wall dazed and breathing through her open lips. Her cheeks were stained with a faint blush.

"You can't tell any of them about this," he said trying to catch his own breath.

"Okay." She nodded. Her eyes were round and uncomprehending. Cap would be happy to know she knew how to follow directions. Too bad he couldn't explain to Cap how he knew that.

"You better go out first. Tell them I went to the bathroom if they ask." He looked behind himself at the hall. "Where is it?"

"Through the bedroom." She brushed her hair off her cheek.

"Okay. I'll be out in a few minutes. You're not going to put candles on that, are you?" He frowned at the cake, wondering if anyone had noticed they'd been gone a long time.

She looked at the cake too, as if she'd forgotten it was there. "I don't have to if you don't want me to."

"I'd rather you didn't."

She nodded. "All right. I'll just take it out then."

Kevin paused. He wanted to kiss her again. To drop a courtly kiss on her cheek, but if he did, it wouldn't remain courtly. "I'll be out in a minute." Hurrying through her bedroom, he tried not to look at her bed. It looked too inviting, and he had enough damage control to do. He closed the door of the narrow bathroom behind him and pressing his forehead against it.

Now what was he going to do? She was a kid. They'd call him a cradle robber. There were at least two captains out there. His little stunt could screw up her ranking. Getting through the exams in the first place wasn't going to be easy, without having to deal with some kind of other problem. How was she supposed to concentrate on training when he was concentrating on her? He had no right to put his own desires above hers. No matter how raging his need seemed to be. She wanted to be in the department and the department needed her. In comparison, his wishes were infinitesimal.

He stood up and looked around the room. This room too, for all its functionality and the design forced on her by the landlord, felt comfortable without being frilly or girly. Just like the rest of the apartment.

Just like Jessica.

CHAPTER 8

Jessica remembered watching movies of foals trying to get to their feet after birth. Still wet and wild-eyed, they flailed around trying to get their long, ungainly legs underneath their bodies and maintain some balance. She now understood how they felt.

Gathering her legs under her, she pushed away from the wall. For a second she thought her knees might give, but she got them under control and stood in the middle of the room, swaying.

No one had ever slammed her against a wall and kissed like that before. Most of her previous kissing experience involved either linebackers who were more force than finesse or guys too overwhelmed by the fact that she had to lean down to be very much fun. That alone explained why she was thirty and a virgin. What was there to look forward to, and why spend time chasing it when you could repaint the bathroom?

Kevin had balanced force and finesse pretty nicely. Her lips felt swollen, but a quick fingertip inspection revealed them to be about the same size as normal. She took a deep breath. What in heaven's name possessed him to kiss her? When he leaped forward the way he had, she hadn't known what to expect. If she'd had a split-second to think, she doubted kissing her would have made the top ten.

"Well," she murmured, picking up the cake with nerveless fingers. "I guess this means he likes me." Liked her? Definite understatement. Based on his reaction, he would have been more than willing to carry on in the other room if she didn't have twenty-seven firefighters in her backyard.

Carrying the cake through the living room to the door, she wondered why, if he liked her, did he tell her not to say anything to anyone? What was the big secret? They were adults and this could make lifting weights at his house much more interesting. He must have a good reason.

She hoped he had a good reason.

The door latch wasn't closed. Occasionally the door didn't close all the way, but she thought she'd heard it click after Kevin when he came in. That had been a while ago. She could be misremembering. If she got to the bottom of the stairs and everyone was looking at her funny, that would end the charade Kevin seemed to want to play.

Everyone was too busy staring at the cake to look at her. The older man with all the stories followed her across the yard to the table, telling her about the country club fire where they'd had to pull down every wall in the office area to put it out, but managed to save the wedding calendar.

"Can you believe a ritzy place like that still had tube and knob wiring? And there they were, running computers and fax machines and all this equipment off this lousy wiring," Joe finished with a flourish.

"Pretty silly. You'd think they'd have been able to afford to replace the wiring."

"At least it sparked at night. Nobody in the building at the time." Joe nodded.

Jessica set the cake on the table and wiped off the bread knife and waited. She wanted everybody out as soon as possible. Any other time she'd have gladly trundled the last guest off around midnight, but today had just taken a sharp left. Joe launched into another story about tube and knob wiring.

"Oooo, that looks good. When are you going to cut it?" Roger asked, leering at the cake and cutting off Joe midsentence.

"As soon as the birthday boy comes down." Jessica fidgeted with the knife in her hands. She felt like she was standing on the deck of a ship during a storm. This was the kind of thing she would discuss with Mindi if Mindi weren't being nuts. Did Bobbie fall under Kevin's admonishment not to tell *any of them*? Jessica frowned, glancing around. She couldn't see over the crowd. For probably the first time in her life, she couldn't see over most of the heads around her.

Sonya ducked through the crowd. "What's wrong with you?" she asked.

"Nothing."

Sonya raised an eyebrow, but didn't ask again.

Kevin came down the stairs.

"Hey, Marshall, get over here. Jessica won't cut the cake without you," Roger yelled. "Are we going to sing again?"

"No." Kevin stopped a few feet away from Jessica, but didn't look at her.

Jessica held out the knife. Her hands were shaking too hard to cut straight.

"You do it. You're better at it," Kevin said. He put his hands behind his back like she might force the knife into them.

Jessica held the knife out to Sonya. "You've got plenty of experience at this. You do it."

"Why? You can do it. It's not surgery." Sonya's face wrinkled with total confusion. She wouldn't leave now until she had answers. At least she didn't fall under Kevin's category of *any of them*.

"Julie can do it then. Where's Julie?" Jessica started to hold up the knife and realized as she did that the long blade exaggerated how badly her hands were shaking.

"No way," Julie yelled from the other side of the crowd. "We're not at work. You're not the boss of me."

"Give that to me." Roger snatched the knife out of her hand and stepped between them. "I'll cut it if you're all afraid."

Jessica stepped back and watched Roger hack into the soft cake, smearing frosting everywhere and cutting the largest pieces Jessica had ever seen.

"It's not a door, it's a cake," someone heckled.

"It'll still be edible." Roger dumped the first pieces on plates and Jessica grabbed the knife out of his hand.

"Why don't you let me finish so we'll have enough to go around?"

"Sure." He grabbed one of his huge pieces and a fork. "This is great. What kind of frosting is this?"

"Cream cheese." She bit her lip, remembering that she'd decided on the tart frosting because she thought Kevin was being tart with her. She'd read him all wrong too. So far that was Mindi *and* Kevin. Who was next? Would her mother do handsprings at the idea she was training to be a firefighter? Would Eric develop a backbone and offer her a huge raise to stay at the store? Would Julie and Darla become best friends?

"Wow. Hey, Cap!" Roger waded through the crowd, leaving Jessica standing next to Kevin to cut up the rest of the cake. After Roger had done so much damage, no one would be able to tell her hands were shaking. Kevin grabbed the first plate he could get his hands on and put as much distance between them as possible. Half an hour ago that would have incensed her. Now it explained a few things.

Like why he moved all his weights out of the house.

And why he wouldn't come near her when they were working out.

What it didn't explain was why he didn't want her around his friends or why she wasn't allowed to tell anybody. Was there something wrong with her? Was he embarrassed?

She looked over the crowd and her eyes settled on his friend Jack and his friend Jack's soon to be wife, Kate. They had done introductions when they arrived. She hadn't thought much of it at the time. Yet another small woman, ho hum. Now, Jessica's gaze fell on her a little more critically.

Kate was really small. Not much more than five feet tall, she guessed. Long hair, long fingernails. Wearing a blue cotton sundress that showed off her curves. Standing beside Jack, they looked like one of those comical Great Dane/Toy Poodle combinations. Kate smiled up at Jack, looking adorable and small and in need of protection. Like

Mindi and her mother. Men liked women who needed protection. They liked to be needed.

Jessica had never needed protection in her life. She'd beat up her own bullies in elementary school, escorted nervous girls after dark on campus in college, and now had started on a path that, hopefully, would lead to a full time job rescuing people. Men, she'd learned, were turned off by women who stood up for themselves. Kevin probably thought he was attracted to her because he was training her. Sort of like nurses falling for their patients. As long as she needed him, he would believe he was in love with her. Once she passed the test, if she passed the test and joined the department for real, she wouldn't need him anymore. Once she didn't need him anymore, any interest he had would vanish. She met his hooded eyes through the crowd. From that expression she couldn't make anything out, but didn't think it mattered.

As giddy and happy as she'd felt a few minutes ago, she now felt sick. The last few pieces of cake waited on the table but she didn't think she could stomach eating one. Everyone could go home now. Including Kevin. She picked up the knife and carried it inside for an excuse to leave.

"Okay, what's going on?" Sonya demanded, following her into the apartment. "You look—Jess? What happened?"

Jessica put her hands over her face. "Nothing. Just taking stock of my life and realizing what's on the debit side."

"What did Kevin say to you?" Sonya stepped into the kitchen. "You guys were talking for a long time."

"He wanted to thank me for the party."

Sonya looked over her shoulder. "He looked like he was enjoying himself for a half second there."

Jessica snorted. "You could say that." She couldn't tell Sonya now. The thought of talking about the kiss Kevin had given her made her feel sicker. She had adapted to not being every man's dream woman a long time ago, but for a little while there she'd thought she could be one man's dream woman. Until reality dawned on her.

"Do you need anything? Is something going wrong with your training? Jess, you're a mess," Sonya said.

"Thank you." Jessica pulled herself together. The house was still full of people, and she needed to endure it for a little while longer before she could deal with it. Turning on the water in the sink, she washed off the knife. She needed Kevin for six and a half more weeks. If she could stop daydreaming long enough about the things she couldn't have and focus on the things she could get, she could pass the exam and move on.

Someday, she and Bobbie could retire to the old firefighters home and tell each other stories about their exploits like Joe out there. At least Bobbie was on her side. "I'm going back down. You coming?"

"I guess so." Sonya moved so she wasn't blocking the door.

Jessica mingled with her guests, feeling as if her face was made of plastic and had been glued on badly. When the CD player ran out of songs and shut off, she nearly collapsed against the fence. She'd kept herself far away from Kevin. Any time he seemed to be headed toward her, she worked her way in the opposite direction. She chatted with various guys, listening to yet another one of Joe's stories, and smiling when Roger told her he might have to marry her because she was such a great cook. Julie, Diana, and Sonya had started dragging things upstairs. Normally, they would have been picking up stray trash, but the firefighters cleaned up after themselves. Last party, it had taken half an hour to pick up the discarded paper plates and cups in the yard. This time there were none to collect.

Jessica stationed herself at the corner of the house so everyone could say their thanks and good-byes. Kevin joined her. They stood side-by-side, not speaking to one another. It made her ache all over to be this close to him. Just because her head knew he wouldn't be in love with her in two months time didn't mean her body and her heart believed it.

"You survived," she heard Jack say.

She turned. Nearly everyone had gone already. Roger hung around in the kitchen picking through the leftovers as Julie and Diana tried to pack them up, and two other guys were dismantling the food table. Julie's husband walked past them to throw down the rope she used to pull up the table rather than carrying it around the house, up the stairs, and through the apartment.

"I survived. It wasn't the normal party though," Kevin said. His deep, melting voice flowed through her. She felt her face getting warm. It certainly hadn't been a normal party.

"It was great party." Kate smiled and shook Jessica's hand. "And it was so nice meeting you."

"It was nice meeting you, too," Jessica said. She'd have liked Kate if she didn't stand for everything Jessica wasn't.

Roger bounded down the stairs with a plastic bag in his hand. "You don't mind if I take some leftovers, do you?"

Jessica shook her head.

Roger kissed her cheek. "I love you, and I'm working on my captain." He spun around and hurried down the driveway before she could move.

Jessica glanced at Kevin. He was too busy glowering at Roger's back to notice her look or the smiles on Jack and Kate's faces. When he turned to Jack, he scowled.

"You have icing on your back," Jack announced when Roger was well out of earshot.

"What?" Kevin reached over his shoulder.

"Yup. It's been there since you came downstairs after Jessica brought down the cake. The one that had green icing on it." Jack grinned as Kevin turned bright red. "I'd be interested in knowing how a green icing fingerprint got there."

"Why didn't you tell me before?" Kevin demanded. "Do you think anyone else saw?"

Jack shrugged. "Nobody said anything, and you know they would have. Good thing it's a gray shirt. When's poker night?"

"Next Monday." Kevin groaned. He was still groping his shoulders, trying to find the spot of icing.

Jessica watched him, amazed at how embarrassed he was to have been caught. Apparently he thought the worst thing to happen to him was being caught kissing a big awkward cow like herself. She heard banging at the side of the house and used the opportunity to go check on their progress with the table. The rest of the yard was clean. Great, as soon as she got rid of everyone she'd be able to crawl into bed and bawl.

Julie's husband pulled the table onto the porch and untied the rope, letting his end dangle from the pulley she'd attached to the porch for this purpose. "Thank you," she told the two men in the yard.

"Anytime, my lady," one of them said, bowing.

"Dan," Kevin scolded coming around beside her.

Dan grinned. "Wonderful party. Thanks for inviting me."

"Yeah, it was a great party," the other man agreed. Him she recognized from Kevin's house. Lew Draper.

Dan slid his arm through hers and started walking with her to the edge of the yard. "Tell me, do you cater?"

"I don't know. I guess it depends," Jessica said. Where was this going and why was it going there? She had that vertigo feeling again. Could she make it through the rest of the day without getting tipped off the planet?

"How about an intimate dinner for two?" He stopped at the edge of the asphalt beside her car. "You and me."

"Dan!" Kevin snapped.

Dan looked at Kevin without letting go of Jessica's arm and raised one eyebrow. "Yes?"

"What did I tell you?" Kevin's normally soothing voice had a steely, almost frightening, tone.

Dan sighed. "Something about ranking and dating and brass. You never said she was yours."

Jessica's throat threatened to close. Any moment she expected Kevin to grab her other arm so they could play tug of war for real. What was Dan talking about—*ranking and dating and brass*?

Kevin stepped forward and Dan backed off, releasing her arm.

"You are no fun anymore," Dan told Kevin. "I'm afraid we'll have to postpone that dinner until after you pass the test and probably after training. I'll pencil you in for September. If not then, December." He leaned over and kissed her hand.

Kevin bristled beside her, and she would have stumbled backward when Dan let go of her hand, but she sensed Lew right behind her. When she looked up she saw Sonya, Diana, Julie and Julie's husband all crowded onto her tiny door porch, watching. Should she feel flattered or humiliated? She chose humiliated because it seemed closer at hand about now.

"That never works, you know," Kevin said. His voice had gained some calm.

Dan grinned. "That's what you think." He nodded at Jessica. "Jessica."

Lew stepped around her. "I'll see you later." He shook her hand and followed Dan down the driveway.

Kevin watched them go.

Julie scampered down the stairs. "You're all cleaned up," she announced, grinning. "I'll see you at work. Come on, dear. How come you never fight for me like that?"

Her husband snorted. "You fight all your own battles."

Sonya and Diana both passed them, smiling and waving. Once they disappeared at the end of the driveway, she realized she was once again alone with Kevin and now they didn't have a yard full of guests to stop them. Good thing or bad thing, she wondered. He had sort of just fought for her, but if he thought he was in love with her because she needed him, then it was a hollow victory.

Of course, nothing was stopping her from taking advantage of the moment. It wasn't like she'd have to marry him if one thing did lead to the bedroom. She could enjoy it while it lasted and deal with the rest later. Women did it all the time.

But if she was one of those women, she wouldn't be a thirty year old virgin.

Today had been too long to wrestle with this dilemma, better to get rid of him. "So I guess you'll be going now," she said.

He looked at her, a little surprised. "Going?"

"Home. The party's over. No reason to hang around here." She folded her arms, wanting him to object. To inform her that he was staying. To fight another battle for her.

"Did you see Bobbie leave?" he asked.

Jessica blinked. Just when she thought she knew where he was going he changed direction. This was developing into a routine with him. "No."

"I didn't either." Kevin looked around the backyard like she might be hiding behind a tree or something.

"Maybe she left early. Why does it matter? Bobbie is a big girl. She can take care of herself." Jessica's breastbone tried to make contact with her spine. Sure, Bobbie could take care of herself, but could Jessica?

"I know, but she gets funny sometimes. You know how w—" Kevin stopped and looked like he might start choking.

"How women are?" Jessica finished. "No, how are women?"

"I didn't mean that."

"It is what you said." She tilted her head, trying to look as smug as possible.

"Can we go inside?" Kevin asked. She detected a slight whimper in his tone and it was the only thing that kept her from saying no.

Turning, she walked up the stairs and he followed. She didn't want him inside her apartment again. She didn't trust herself with him. Part of her wanted to cut all ties with him even if it meant losing the opportunity to ever be a paramedic. Another part wanted to go to bed with him. Yet another part wanted to travel back in time a month and take her entire birthday week off. Fly to Florida and visit her parents. Max out her credit cards and go back to Europe. Something. Anything to avoid being in this position now.

"Listen, I'm very sorry," he started as soon as he closed the door behind them.

"About what part?" She stood in the middle of the living room, not inviting him to sit and not sitting herself. Hopefully it was clear to him he was barely welcome and at any minute that welcome might be withdrawn.

"About? Okay. About the whole day. Will that make you happy?"

"I don't think this is about making me happy." She watched his face, wondering if he wanted to kiss her again. This conversation held less and less promise in that direction with every word.

"Jessica, let me explain something." Kevin reached toward her, but made no real effort to touch her. She wasn't sure if it bothered her. Once he did leave, she was going to have a whole bunch of things to figure out. "Not long after I started training you, my captain called me into his office to ask me if we were a couple. If we were, he was going to try to talk me out of training you."

"Why?"

"There's no regulation against couples being in the department—"

"Of course there isn't. It would be illegal."

Kevin licked his lips. "Just because there's no regulation doesn't mean they couldn't make it more difficult for you."

"More difficult?" Jessica felt her heart pounding in her chest. This sounded very suspicious, but not impossible. She imagined a bunch of old chiefs who never wanted women in the department in the first place but had Equal Opportunity rammed down their throats, fighting back any way they could.

"You've seen sample questions for the written exam. A lot of the answers are subjective. All you need to do is slip a few points and it could cost you ranking. The physical exam is worse, and the oral exam is worse yet. If you drop in the ranking, it could keep you out. There's only fifteen slots open in the first place, and if you rank sixteenth, you lose."

"I can do the math," Jessica grumbled. "Why would it matter if we were a couple?"

"One wild guess? They might be worried about one of us getting protective about the other if we're working the same scene. Most likely me because I tend to be outside working the pumps on my engine. There's all kinds of other stuff too. You getting harassed by the other guys on your shift and me getting pissed off about it. The calls that go sour. Maybe me blaming somebody on your shift if you got hurt. I think they are worried about one of us getting over-protective." Kevin closed his mouth, as though he realized he was babbling.

Jessica's heart stopped beating. Protective. He already felt protective of her. Once he realized there was nothing to protect, he would be out of her life and she might gain a reputation she didn't want in the gossipy fire department.

"Jessica, when I kissed you before, I did it out of desperation. I've been fighting so hard to keep my hands off you for the past three weeks I can't believe I've only kissed you once."

A chill dripped down her spine. He wanted what he thought she was. A helpless female. Someone to protect. "I'll do my best to stop being so enticing. Are we still going to work together?" she asked.

"I want to if you want to." He stepped forward, but again stopped short of touching her. "I really like you, Jessica. I like you more all the time. I like you so much that I don't want to jeopardize your dream. Especially not since I can wait. In a few months we can start over. For real this time."

How noble of you, she thought. Putting me ahead of yourself. Tears pricked her eyes. If he'd offered the decision to her, she knew she'd have made the same choice, but she had the sinking suspicion the postponement of their relationship would end up being permanent. She nodded. "All right. Should I pencil you in for December?"

"I knew you'd understand." He reached out and clasped her shoulders in a very brotherly way. "Can I take a look at those exam practice books you've been reading?"

Jessica gestured to the table behind him. "They're over there. I have to use the bathroom." That wasn't true. She had to get out of the room before the swirl of emotions engulfed her.

Retreating to her cramped bathroom, she stared at herself in the mirror until she knew she wouldn't cry. He'd answered most of her questions. It was even flattering. He didn't look at her so he wouldn't be tempted. Never had a man had that response to her. The weights were moved to the garage because he couldn't trust himself alone with her behind closed doors. Also flattering. Nobody could know why he kissed her and why he couldn't do it again because he didn't want to wreck her plans. Gallant of him.

That didn't explain why he'd been so reluctant to have her meet his friends.

Washing her face, she went back out to deal with him. More relaxed and calm than he'd looked all day, he sat at her dining table bent over one of the books, studying the table of contents. He had everything in the world to feel relaxed and calm about. Her stomach felt tied in knots because she still had to choose between a career and a man.

"I have one question," she announced, standing at the edge of the living room.

He looked up.

"Why didn't you want me to meet your co-workers?" She clenched her teeth against the emotions that wanted to rise up again. She couldn't let that happen because she didn't have another excuse to run out of the room.

"What?" He blinked at her, confused. Good, for once she'd thrown him off track.

"You won't take me to the station to check out the tools, and you wanted to get rid of me before they showed up to play cards at your house."

Kevin shifted. "Well, two reasons. First of all, you saw how Dan was. He's always like that. He'll hit on any woman in the vicinity. He's a Lothario. I didn't want him to get all smarmy and charming with you."

"Jealous?" She noticed his language changing. He had a better vocabulary than to use a word like 'smarmy.' Over the years she'd noticed people's vocabularies changed when they were stressed. It almost pleased her that she could stress him.

Kevin scowled. "I am not. I just didn't want him to confuse you."

"Confuse me?" she repeated. It sounded like jealousy to her. It had sounded like it outside, too. This one, she decided she should let go. By his face, he was working to come up with an answer, and if he had to work that hard, it wouldn't be the truth. He wasn't about to admit he was jealous of his friend Dan. "What's the other reason?"

"They would take one look at us and know something was going on."

"Like they did today?"

Kevin shrank into himself like a pouty little boy. "I guess. I mean, I'm sure there'll be rumors."

"Since there's nothing going on, the best way to prove it to them is to be very professional. I can meet you at the station on your next shift, and you can show me the tools. Then they can see that there's nothing going on between us." She lifted her chin, challenging him to refuse her.

"I guess." Picking up one of the books, he held it out. "You know this one has a whole section on tools, right?"

She faltered. "It does?" That one she hadn't looked at much. It hadn't looked as interesting as the other two.

"There's a whole chapter here." He flipped it open about midway and she could see rows of illustrations from across the room.

"Oh." Her breath was getting short the way it always did when she got nervous. What she wanted was to make him agree to meet her at the station so he would see her on that turf and she could prove to him she could do it. That was her best chance to prove her professionalism to him and, if the opportunity presented itself, to his captain. She wouldn't be the protective one causing problems at a fire scene. Her father always told her to pick her battles and this one looked like a good one. "But it would be better for me to see the real thing, wouldn't it?"

"I guess," he reluctantly agreed. "If you really want to."

"You're on duty Sunday. I have something I need to do in the morning, but I'll be free about three. I'll come to the station about four. All right?" She dared him to say no.

"Fine. Can we look at this here first?" He pointed at the books in front of him.

Crossing the room she sat down in the other chair at the table. She didn't know how happy she should be to win, but she was. If she wasn't going to get him to love her, she was going to make him respect her.

CHAPTER 9

It took another hour to get Kevin out of her apartment. Sitting next to him at the table had been agonizing. The act of concentrating on the book between them sapped her strength. She still wanted him to kiss her again. Every time his arm or hand had brushed her, it felt like an electrical shock.

She dropped onto the couch and reached for the phone. But who could she call?

Mindi would get hysterical again, and Jessica didn't feel up to that right now.

Julie, Sonya and Diana would listen, but they didn't know the whole story.

Bobbie fell under the tell-no-one restriction Kevin had given her.

She dialed her parents' house and hoped her father would pick up. Sometimes he did, when she was lucky and she needed him.

"Hello?"

No luck today. "Hi, Mom."

"Oh, hi, honey. How are you?"

If she played this right she might get something worthwhile out of her mother without revealing anything that would make her crazy. "I'm really tired. I just had a long talk with Kevin."

"About what, dear?"

"Our relationship."

"Oh. That doesn't sound good." Her mother sounded unusually understanding tonight. Jessica suspected she'd been waiting all her life for her little girl to come to her with man trouble. "What happened?"

Jessica groaned. What hadn't happened? "He's afraid that if people find out about us it's going to cause me problems at work."

"Why would it cause you problems at work to be dating a fireman? You work in a bookstore."

Jessica slouched into the couch. "It's complicated, Mom."

"It sounds to me like he doesn't want to make a commitment."

Jessica shuddered. Commitment? Was her mother already marrying her off? "I think you're jumping the gun, Mom. I've only been seeing him for two weeks."

"Is he seeing anyone else or are you exclusive?"

"I don't know. I don't think he's seeing anyone else. With his work schedule, I doubt he has time." Jessica thought over the last two weeks. She'd seen him about every day he had off, and Bobbie said he didn't date anyway. Maybe they were exclusive, if only exclusively screwed up.

"So you've been spending a lot of time together." Her mother sounded smug. She was marrying them off in her mind.

"Yes, but mostly we're working out."

"Working out?"

"Lifting weights, running, stuff like that."

"That doesn't sound very romantic. Does he ever do things with you that you want to do?"

Oh good, now she's up to our marital problems. "That is what I want to do, Mom." Calling her mother for someone to talk to had been a terrible mistake. Her mother would never be the objective observer Jessica needed.

"You want to lift weights?"

"Yes, Mom. I want to lift weights."

Her mother rephrased the question. "Do you want to lift weights because he wants to or because you want to?"

Divorce. Her mother had already managed to get as far as divorce because of irreconcilable differences. Kevin didn't want to get involved until after the exam, and her mother had their entire relationship plotted out to a bad end. "Because I want to. Mom, I am capable of separating my wants from his."

"I can't understand why you would want to lift weights. You did that for a while in college, didn't you? When you wanted to be an ambulance driver?"

"Paramedic, Mom." Jessica picked up a pillow and started combing her fingers through the fringe. In college, between dropping out of pre-med and before committing to a miscellaneous biology major, she started training for fire service. She'd sorted out a class load with the help of her advisor and started weight training. Her mother's handwringing had ended that, too.

"I still don't understand what the difference is," her mother said and giggled.

"You would if Dad were having a heart attack," Jessica snapped. "The difference between an ambulance driver and a paramedic could be life or death."

"Jessica!" her mother scolded. "You don't wish ill on your father."

"I'm not wishing ill on Dad."

"Your father is in very good heath for a man his age," her mother continued as if she hadn't heard. "He has many, many good years left to him. You should be ashamed of yourself for thinking such a thing."

"I'm not thinking anything bad. It was an example. You weren't listening to me again." Jessica threw the pillow across the room. "I said you would know the difference *if* Dad had a heart attack. I didn't say I wish Dad would have a heart attack."

"I should think not," her mother huffed.

"Good Lord, Mother, why do you think I'm training to be a paramedic? If I wanted to tote people back and forth to the hospital I'd just get a job with the ambulance company instead of working my butt off to get into the fire department."

There was a long silence on the other end of the phone. Her mother cleared her throat. "Training to be a paramedic? Is that what you're doing with your fireman?"

Jessica had said it deliberately, but not deliberately, and hated herself for it. When her father told her to pick her battles, he'd been referring to her mother. Jessica's mother was the only person who could drive her to the point of yelling. Once, when she was about fifteen, her father had come to her room after one of their pitched battles. He'd sat on her bed and told her, "Your mother only fights with you because she wants what's best for you. That doesn't mean what she thinks is best will always be the best, but it does mean she loves you. You're old enough now to start recognizing when she's right and when she's wrong and when it's worth fighting about. You have to learn to pick your battles, Jessica."

He'd been right. She'd learned to pick battles at school and at work. She could deal with Julie and irate customers. She could handle her boss and total strangers on the street. But fifteen years later, she could still not handle her mother, and she was still fighting back at every challenge. And fighting dirtier as she got older.

"Honey, I can't believe you're thinking about doing something so dangerous," her mother started fussing.

Jessica stopped listening. Her mother would fume for a while, say goodbye and start leaving little bombs on Jessica's answering machine. Statistics, grisly stories. She had done wonders after Jessica decided to go pre-med. How many pre-med students never made it through the program. How difficult internship was. How long it would take. The works. Jessica really shouldn't have called her mother.

But her mother had been her last hope. She had no one else to talk to.

* * * *

Kevin wiped his damp palms on his uniform pants again and stared down the road. She'd said four o'clock. It was two minutes till and she was punctual, if not early. That should please him. He'd always hated people who couldn't be counted on to show up on time, but he'd been dreading this meeting since she brought it up. Since Bobbie brought it up three weeks ago. Jessica would walk through the door and all the guys in the place would start sniffing around her like wild dogs around fresh meat.

Since they weren't an item, he couldn't do anything about it. If he could just claim her as his, the others would behave themselves.

He couldn't do that because…

The list of reasons was as long as a fire hose. He just couldn't think of any of them right now. All he could think about was whether or not she would show up in a tank top. The weather felt right for it. Hot and miserable. If she followed form, she would run or walk over since she only lived six blocks away, and if she ran, it would make sense for her to wear bike shorts and a tank top. Which would, in turn, drive the other guys into a greater frenzy.

Dan strolled out eating an apple. "What are you looking for?"

"Jessica."

Dan's signature leer spread across his face. "Jessica?"

Kevin didn't growl, no out loud anyway. "She's stopping in to take a look at the tools."

Dan grinned, and Kevin's entire body tightened up. He had that prowling look to him now and in a few minutes so would the other five guys on duty. Maybe not Lew. Lew didn't seem to prowl the way the other singles did. Kevin wished Jack was on duty. Jack, at least, wouldn't be on the prowl anymore.

"Hello, beautiful."

Kevin jumped at Dan's voice and spun around. She'd come from the other direction and she wasn't wearing bike shorts or a tank top. Kevin quelled a pang of regret and smiled. "Right on time. I expected you to come from the other direction."

"I decided to walk down Market." She shrugged. "Same distance."

He checked her over. Tan shorts and a white cotton short-sleeved blouse. He could still see a generous amount of leg. Her face was lightly coated with sweat from the heat, not exertion, and her dark eyes settled on him. At the gym on Friday, she'd seemed quiet, but now she'd become tense. With his audience, he couldn't ask why.

"Kevin says you want to look at our toys," Dan announced. He tried to hook his arm through hers, but she shifted just enough to discourage him.

"I need to know the tools for the exam. It's one of my weakest points," she said.

"I have better toys than he does," Dan said.

"But the tools on the engine are bigger." Doug walked out the door. "You must be Jessica. I've heard a lot about you."

Kevin cursed under his breath. Another good reason to wish Jack weren't still out. If Jack were here, bald, tactless Doug wouldn't be. He'd known this was going to happen. All night he'd been half awake worrying about it.

"Oh, have you?" Jessica raised one eyebrow. "What's my sign?"

Doug stared at her. "What?"

Kevin's heart swelled with pride. Seeing Doug get stopped was a rare thing, and that it was his Jessica who did it made it more wonderful.

Not his Jessica. Yet.

"You said you'd heard all about me, I thought you'd know my sign." Jessica folded her arms. "But maybe you weren't paying attention."

"Hello, Jessica." Lew stopped behind Doug, who was still trying to decide what she'd done to him.

"Hello, Lew. It's good to see you again," Jessica said.

"Come on. Let's get started." Kevin put his hand around her arm to tow her inside, away from Dan and Doug. "We could get a call at any time. I want to cover as much ground as possible as quickly as possible."

Lew beat him to the side of the engine and opened the bins. Jessica joined him and he started showing her the tools. Kevin breathed a sigh of relief. Doug went back to the day room, and Dan didn't seem to be interested in pursuing her any further. He hung back watching with Kevin as Lew took things out and discussed them with her. Lew, he could trust.

"Who's the chick?" Mark Davis asked. "Dave said we had a visitor."

"Kevin's wannabe," Dan answered. "But she's no fuzzy yellow thing, that's for sure."

"What do you mean?"

"She just shut down Doug like nobody's business. It was a beautiful thing to see."

"That isn't the only thing." Mark sighed. "I love a woman who can handle tools."

Jessica, at that moment, had a crowbar in her hands, testing its weight. Kevin felt his breath getting short. He knew the conversation wasn't going to get any better, and he couldn't think of a way to derail it.

"She's got a body on her, too."

"I know. Check out those legs."

"I was looking at something else."

Kevin ground his teeth together. He'd lost track of who was saying what because he was too angry to think straight. The memory of what it had felt like to have her body pressed under his in her kitchen smothered him. He could still taste the frosting on her lips and smell her skin.

"Gentlemen," the captain said. "Our guest isn't here for you to ogle. Mark, will you sweep out the dorm and then help Dan scrub the bathroom."

Mark opened his mouth to protest and then got a good look at the captain's face. He had on a scowl that brooked no argument. The two men scurried away to complete their tasks. The captain stood next to Kevin, watching Lew close one bin and open another.

"I'm sorry I couldn't make it to your birthday party last week." Cap spoke quietly so as not to bother Jessica and Lew.

Kevin swallowed hard. It might be better that he hadn't shown up. "That's okay, Cap. I think it was kind of last minute."

"I would have liked to be there. I was told by Captain Malloy up at Twelve it was very nice. Not the usual." He gave Kevin an odd look.

A little puzzled, a little curious, maybe a little doubtful. "Before she leaves, stop in my office. I'd like to meet her. She is very attractive."

"Thanks," Kevin murmured. Great, now he had the captain to worry about. Leaning on the wall, he watched Lew go through all the tools on the engine systematically. He should have asked Lew to help him train her instead of Bobbie. Lew seemed to be very good at answering her questions, leaving Kevin free to wonder what had upset her.

Her shoulders looked tense but that was all the emotion she'd displayed so far. She studied the tools Lew handed her with a coolness about her. Kevin wished he could ask her what was wrong. But he couldn't.

Lew closed the last bin and Kevin pushed away from the wall to join them. "Do you feel more confident now?" he asked.

"Yes. It's much easier to understand how things work when you can hold them in your hands." She folded her hands together. "Thank you for your time, Lew."

"Sure. Any time." Lew nodded and went in the direction of the day room.

"The captain wants to see you before you go." Kevin watched her face. A ripple of nervousness passed through her eyes before disappearing.

"All right. Where's his office?"

Kevin gestured. He wanted to take her arm again, just to touch her, but he thought she might shy away like she had with Dan. His chest ached from wanting to touch her. Her demeanor reminded him of the day at the bookstore when she'd been fighting with her friend, the day he'd been so impressed with her handling of the old woman. Had she had another fight with her little friend? Had she told her parents, and been fighting with them? He knocked on the captain's open door.

The captain looked up, smiling. "Jessica Decker, please come in. I'm Captain Stoker. Kevin, you can sit in if you like."

"Pleased to meet you." Jessica stepped forward and shook his hand. She sat down in one of the chairs in front of the desk. Kevin sat down next to her, admiring the way she held her head high.

"I've heard some very complimentary things about you." Cap grinned. "Captain Malloy from station Twelve says you are an excellent cook. I'm sorry I missed that party."

"I'll remember to invite you next time." She smiled, but it looked strained to Kevin.

"I've also heard you attack your workouts with enthusiasm from Captain Bartlett. He has a membership at your gym, and he noticed you working with Bobbie Kelly one day. I hope you don't feel spied on."

"Of course not. Not very many women try out for the department, do they?"

"They do, but not many of them are as qualified as you are." Cap lifted a paper off his desk. Kevin could see it was an application. Her application. Why did the captain have a copy of her application? Did they want her that badly? "You maintained a perfect grade point average through college, and you weren't taking simple classes. That's very impressive."

Kevin tried to read the application, but couldn't make it out upside down and across the desk. He could believe she'd had good grades in college, though he'd never met anyone who kept a perfect grade point average before. How did someone with a 4.0 end up in a bookstore? He glanced at her. Her cheeks were flushed. "I enjoyed my classes."

"Obviously. Why aren't you working in a research lab somewhere? Why a bookstore?"

"Research didn't appeal to me. I didn't feel like I was accomplishing anything putting stuff in Petri dishes and watching it grow. I ended up at the bookstore by default while I was trying to figure out what to do and unintentionally worked my way into management."

"What made you decide you wanted to join the fire department?" Cap folded his hands on the desk.

Jessica glanced at Kevin, but kept her composure. "I've always wanted to be a paramedic. I started out pre-med in college because I wasn't sure how to become a paramedic."

Cap laughed. "That usually goes the other way. From your transcript it looks like you had figured out what you needed. Why didn't you join the department out of college?"

"My mother."

Kevin saw the brief sour twitch of her lips. That must be why she seemed so tense today. She must have told her mother.

Cap laughed again. "Mothers. They always think they can protect us."

"Yes, they do. I think I'm beyond the need for protection though." She turned and fixed Kevin with an indecipherable look. He shifted in his seat, wondering if the look meant something or if she had just wanted to include him in the conversation.

"Very good." Cap stood up. "It has been a pleasure talking to you. I hope to have you sitting across my desk in a few months as a probationary firefighter, but I think I might be fighting a couple of other captains for you. If you have any questions don't hesitate to stop in."

"Thank you." Jessica shook his hand again and left the office. She went through the apparatus bay and down the drive like she was going to set off along the sidewalk without another word.

"Hey, Jessica. Wait a minute." Kevin hurried after her. She stopped in front of the Victorian next door. It had been for sale for months, but Kevin suspected that no matter how beautiful it was inside, no one wanted to live next to a fire station.

"Do they always take that much interest in hopefuls?" she asked before Kevin could ask her why she seemed so tense.

"No, not that I've ever noticed, but the captain told me a couple of weeks ago the department expects a shortage of paramedics in about a year. You could get lucky."

"I don't want to get lucky. I don't want anything handed to me," she insisted.

"I believe you. You won't get anything handed to you. I guess you just have a very good-looking application. Relax. You're not up to the oral exam, yet." Kevin almost reached out and put his hands on her arms, but managed to stop himself.

She nodded.

"What's wrong?"

"Nothing," she snapped.

"I thought we had this conversation."

"What conversation?" She folded her arms.

"When something bad happens you have to get used to talking about it." He felt a minor twinge of guilt for using this guise of helpfulness to get her to talk to him, but it wasn't enough to stop him. "You've been tense since you got here. What's wrong? Did you have another fight with Mindi?"

"No."

"Did you talk to you mother?" Kevin guessed again. He glanced back at the bay door to see if they were being watched. So far the coast was clear.

"Yes, I talked to my mother. Why does it matter?" Jessica demanded. "Look, I've got to be someplace tonight, and I need to go home and get ready." She started to turn away, but he grabbed her arm.

"It matters. You've been tense since you got here. What's wrong?" Kevin wanted to know what had upset her, but now he wanted to know where she was going tonight too. Was it a date? Some young guy she met at the gym? Was that why she was so tense? "Come on. We're friends, you can tell me."

"Oh, we're friends. Funny, I've never had a friend shove me against a wall and kiss me like that." She pulled her arm out of his grasp and started away again.

"Is that what you're mad about? Wait." Kevin chased her to the Victorian's property line. He hated the fact that she kept getting away. Why was she bringing their kiss up now where the guys might hear her?

"If you want to fight with me, will you please try to look at me while you're doing it? Don't worry, your buddies won't catch you with me," she hissed.

"What does that mean?"

"You keep looking back at the station. I saw your face when your captain said one of the other captains had been watching me at the gym. You are ashamed to be seen with me."

"What?" Kevin tried to remember what expression he might have been wearing when Cap mentioned Bartlett had watched her work out. Jealousy, most likely. After all, if Bartlett had seen her at the gym, he'd seen her in her bike shorts and tank top. Kevin couldn't remember right now if Bartlett was married, but he knew he had to be older. "What makes you think that? I'm not."

Jessica pinched the bridge of her nose. "I don't have time for this," she groaned.

"I'll prove I'm not. What are you doing August twenty-second?"

"I don't know. What day is it?"

"It's a Saturday." Kevin itched to hug her. Ashamed? Where had she gotten that idea? How did she manage to make him feel like such a heel all the time?

"I'm opening the store and going to the gym after work."

"Can you get the afternoon off?"

She sighed and checked her watch. "Yes, I can get the afternoon off."

"Good, then you can come with me to Jack and Kate's wedding." He wished he knew how to read minds because he couldn't make anything out from her face.

"Jack and Kate's wedding?" she asked, staring at him.

"My friend who's getting married. I told you I needed a date. I want you to be my date." Kevin would have preferred it to come out as less of an order and more a request, but somehow he'd turned it inside out in the asking. Behind his back he crossed his fingers. He wanted to believe he was solving two problems, gaining a date and convincing Jessica he wasn't ashamed of her. If he tried hard enough to convince himself, he might.

"You want me to go to a wedding with you that will be attended by all your firefighter pals?" she said.

"Yes."

Her eyes narrowed. "Why?"

"Because I still need a date." He shrugged, hoping she would believe his story.

"All right," she said. Her eyes still had a suspicious gleam. "I'll see if I can get the day off. The twenty-second?"

"The twenty-second of August." He remembered how easily she'd remembered the dates of the exams. Why did she need to confirm the date of the wedding? "It's informal. They're having the ceremony in the park and having a picnic reception right after."

"Okay. I'm meeting Bobbie at the gym tomorrow at ten, do you want to join us?"

"Sure." Kevin grinned at her. Jack would forgive him if he canceled out again. Jack owed him a couple anyway.

"I'll see you tomorrow. Bye." She walked away.

Kevin watched her sashay down the road and realized she didn't mean to, she just had those kind of hips. Generous, curvy, womanly hips. He remembered how it had felt to slide his hands around them. To feel them crushed against his.

And now he was taking her to Jack's wedding to convince her he wasn't ashamed to be seen with her while trying to convince everyone around him he wasn't interested in dating her.

* * * *

Jessica closed the door of her apartment feeling wired and drained at the same time. Somehow she had to make it through the opening at the art gallery tonight. Kevin had seemed pleased to see her when she first arrived, but then he'd left her to Lew. Lew was nice, but she'd planned on working with Kevin. She'd wanted to work with Kevin. All morning she'd been preparing to be professional with Kevin, not Lew.

She didn't think she'd done a bad job. Even though a gaggle of admirers had formed behind her, she'd managed to pay attention. When Kevin told her the captain wanted to see her, she'd kept calm and she'd pulled off the interview without screwing up. The fact that some man she didn't know was watching her at the gym did make her feel a little paranoid. Did they treat all hopefuls this way? The captain had a copy of her application. Kevin must have told him she was coming to the station. Was he short a crew member? If she got into the department, would she end up on Kevin's crew?

After her shower, she pulled on the halter top navy blue dress and sandals she'd set out this morning. At least at the opening, she'd have a chance to pick apart the entire encounter for hidden meanings and missteps among friends.

Julie and her husband stood near the door. Julie looked like she'd been sucking lemons all day. As soon as Jessica got close enough, Julie said, "Would you look at the garbage this woman does? How did your field trip go?"

Jessica looked at the art on the wall inside the door. It was a three-person show and only one of those three people was one from the store. Her friend Bess's art at least looked like art. Portraits, landscapes, etc. Not especially good, but not weird. The stuff on this wall fell into the weird category. The nearest one looked like smashed dinner plates cemented onto a two-by-six. Check that, it was smashed dinner plates cemented onto a two-by-six.

"My favorite is that one." Julie pointed at an empty white shelf with a card on it that read *think*.

"What is it?" Jessica asked. She looked around the room for Bess.

"A Think Space." Julie sneered, ducking her mouth behind the rim of her cup, which was probably spiked Kool-Aid knowing the group in this co-op. "The artiste is over there."

Jessica looked in the direction Julie had gestured. The weird artist girl who hung out at Meechan's stood across the room beneath one of the larger and stranger pieces, flailing her arms around.

"So how did the field trip go?" Julie asked again. Sonya had arrived at Julie's elbow and stood waiting for a report.

"I'm not sure. Kevin didn't go through the tools on the truck with me. This other guy, Lew, did."

"Is Lew cute?" Sonya asked.

"He's very deliberate. Reddish hair, green eyes. I guess he was cute. He was a good teacher, though. He showed me everything and explained how to use it. Then the captain wanted to talk to me. I guess

I'm being watched."

"Watched?" Julie wrinkled her nose. "That sounds creepy."

"One of the captains has a membership at my gym, and he's been spying on me when I work out, and one of the others was at the party."

"That's got to be good," Diana announced. Jessica hadn't noticed her join the group.

"I hope so. Captain Stoker said I was very qualified."

"Okay, so the captain likes you, blah blah blah. Let's get to the good part. What happened with Kevin?" Julie encouraged.

"We talked before I left the station, and he asked me to his friend's wedding."

The three women gasped. Julie's husband looked puzzled.

"I think it's just a friendly thing." Jessica was glad she hadn't told them about the kiss or they'd have lynched her for that comment.

"No," Sonya said. "Not to a wedding. Not in the ambivalent state you two are in. He likes you."

"He's been worried about finding a date since I met him. He might just be getting desperate." Jessica ground her teeth together. She didn't want him to be desperate; she wanted him to have chosen to take her. "And I sort of forced his hand."

"How?" Julie folded her arms.

"I told him he was ashamed to be seen with me. He kept looking back at the station like he didn't want to get caught talking to me," she added.

"Did you actually say that to him?" Diana asked.

"Yes." When she did it, it hadn't seemed that outrageous.

"Subtlety'R'Us." Julie smiled, rolling her eyes.

"Like you can talk. You are one of the least subtle people I have ever met. Besides, it makes me mad. He gets all freaked out any time he thinks his fellow firefighters are going to see him talking to me. Do I have an eye growing out of the middle of my forehead or something?" Jessica huffed. "He said it's because his one friend is a Lothario. Granted, Dan did hit on me as soon as I showed up, but I can handle myself. I'm a big girl." Jessica bit her lip. That was part of the problem. She was a *big* girl.

"He must not be ashamed of you if he's taking you to his best friend's wedding." Sonya patted her arm. "Is he in the wedding? If he's in the wedding party, you're going to spend most of the time sitting by yourself. Or rather, sitting with his buddies."

"He said it was informal, and he didn't say anything about being in the wedding." Jessica frowned. They seemed to think it was significant that he asked her, so why did she still feel like there was something wrong about the whole thing?

"I don't understand why it's important that he asked her to a wedding." Julie's husband Aron said. Jessica thanked him silently.

"Because it is." Julie said. "It's an important relationship-type occasion with family and friends and so forth. You just don't ask any handy girl to a wedding. You ask someone you have intentions with."

"But she said he needed a date. Maybe he didn't want to go alone." Aron shrugged.

"Doofus." Julie swatted Aron. "It's his best friend's wedding. He'd be better off going alone than taking the first bimbo that crossed his path. I've seen this guy. He's not lacking for company."

Jessica watched their silly exchange. For years she'd been watching them have basically the same conversation. She couldn't imagine ever having that kind of chummy chatter with Kevin. They always seemed to be on the verge of snapping at one another, but that might be her own frustration. This time, she could only hope Julie was right, and someday she and Kevin could settle into a relationship where they could banter like Julie and Aron did.

"What are you going to wear?" Diana asked.

Jessica stared at her. That question hadn't even occurred to her. "I don't know."

"Wear that. It looks great," Sonya said.

"It does. You have the shoulders of a Greek god, doesn't she honey?" Julie elbowed her husband.

"Goddess," Aron corrected.

Jessica glanced down at the dress. She always thought of it as her Marilyn Monroe dress because of the halter top. Kevin might like it. Maybe it would prove to him that she wasn't a big awkward Amazon. "Do you think so?"

"Come on. You are the only woman in this building who could pull that dress off right now." Julie nodded, agreeing with herself. "It would make me look like a sack of potatoes." Her husband rolled his eyes heavenward.

Jessica smoothed the dress over her hips. She had always liked it.

"Take a shawl with you," Diana suggested. "In case it gets cold."

"I don't have a shawl."

"I do." Sonya grinned. "I'll bring it in to work."

CHAPTER 10

Kevin sat on his bunk, pretending to read until Jack got out of the shower. It had been non-stop all day. They had been at the last scene for four hours in the pouring rain and hadn't been able to eat dinner until eight.

"What is it, and why haven't you been able to help me with my house?" Jack dropped onto the bunk next to Kevin's, rubbing his hair with a towel.

"I've been busy." Kevin closed the book without marking his place and tossed it on his pillow.

"With your girlfriend?"

"She isn't my girlfriend."

"Oh." Jack grinned. "So you're just very good friends?"

"Cut it out. This is serious." Kevin started picking a string out of the blanket draped across the foot of his bed. "I don't know what to do about Jessica."

"Didn't your father have this talk with you?"

Kevin collapsed backward and thumped his head on the wall. He stared across the room, wondering why he ever thought Jack would be any help at all.

"So this is serious," Jack said. He dropped the towel into his lap and finger-combed his hair into place. "What's wrong?"

"I think I'm in love with her," Kevin groaned. He hoped no one was listening. The other guys should have headed to the day room, which was why he'd asked Jack to meet him in the dorm. With his luck, one or all of them was standing outside the door eavesdropping just to harass him later.

"This is bad because..."

Kevin started listing off his reasons on his fingers, hoping he wouldn't forget any. "First of all, she's too young. She's seven years younger than I am. Second, the department is gun-shy about couples, and she's wanted to be a paramedic since she was a kid so it wouldn't be fair for me to screw up her ranking because I think she's cute. Third, the department needs her. Cap said they think there'll be a shortage of paramedics in about a year. Fourth, she's not my type."

"Any more?"

"Give me a minute." Kevin pouted. None of his reasons sounded as good out loud as they had inside his head.

"That's a nice list of excuses you have, anyway."

"They aren't excuses." Kevin closed his eyes. Jack was supposed to be agreeing with him, not pointing out flaws in his argument.

Jack leaned forward with his elbows on his knees. "She's too young. Seven years isn't exactly cradle robbery. Now if it was twenty-seven years, I'd be telling you to get off the playground. If the department is nervous about couples for whatever reason, they'll put her on a different shift, so unless we have an earthquake and they issue a total recall, you won't be working together. If the department needs her so bad, they'll find a way around the whole couple problem, if it is a problem."

"She's still not my type," Kevin offered.

"What do you think your type is?"

"I don't know." Kevin swallowed. "Someone smaller. More petite. More feminine."

"Someone more like Kate."

"I wasn't going to say that."

"And my sister."

Kevin glared at Jack. "That was just a cheap shot."

"Revenge is a dish best served cold. You got to harass me about my exes. The only two of yours I ever met were cold-hearted, manipulative lizard wenches with pretty faces and nice bodies. I never did understand why you didn't go gaga for Leia. She's your type."

"I swore off cold-hearted lizard wenches." Unfortunately, Jack was right. Kevin reviewed his last few girlfriends. The last one had been looking for a wedding ring and a steady paycheck so she could stay home eating bonbons and watching soap operas without giving anything in return. She'd just about made him celibate for life. The ones before her hadn't been too much better. Jessica was the first woman he'd been more than vaguely interested in since then.

Jack slicked his hair back again. "What about Jessica's personality? You had to like something about her to agree to work with her."

"She's got a great personality. She's nice, and she's smart. She's enthusiastic and competent in a crisis. She's been to Ireland."

"Really?"

"She went to Ireland by herself." That still impressed Kevin. The idea that she had the courage to go overseas alone.

Jack whistled. "That took guts. Most people won't eat in a restaurant alone. She seemed nice enough when I talked to her. What does she think of you?"

"I don't know. Most of the time she seems irritated by me. Bobbie's mad at me too." Kevin sat up and went back to work on the blanket.

"Why is Bobbie mad at you?"

"I don't know. I met her and Jessica at the gym Monday, and Bobbie huffed off early." The knot in his stomach reformed. When Bobbie stormed out, he and Jessica had both been puzzled, but Jessica seemed to know something. Bobbie hadn't shown up at all on Thursday, and Jessica said she hadn't heard from her.

"You have a way with women."

"I do not," Kevin snapped. He worked the string loose and pulled it, puckering the fabric.

"Okay, you don't. Let me ask you one question."

"Do I have to answer it?"

Jack shrugged. "I guess not, but you asked me for help."

"What's the question?"

"Why did you kiss her at your birthday party?"

Kevin glared at his friend. "I didn't kiss her," he lied. Lying was getting easier.

"Oh yeah? You had her fingerprints on your back, and she came downstairs looking like she'd just been hit by a train and walked away without a scratch. You're lucky she was carrying a cake or every other guy at the party would have noticed too."

Kevin cradled his head in his hands. Why had he kissed her at the party? He'd gone inside to tell her they were not and never would be a couple and then attacked her. Since the party, he hadn't been able to stop thinking about that ten-second span when he'd held her. "So what do I do now?"

"Just a wild, off the cuff suggestion. Have you tried talking to her?"

"Yes. She gets defensive."

"Unlike you."

Kevin frowned at Jack. "I don't like you anymore."

Dan stumbled into the dorm, his shoes squishing, and dropped onto the end of Mark's bunk across the aisle. "I just had the weirdest experience of my entire life. This chick walked in out of the rain, demanded I kiss her, and then walked away."

"That must have been terrible for you." Kevin sighed. How easy life must be for Dan. Bouncing from relationship to relationship. Always a new woman on the horizon. Kevin looked at his friend again. He was soaked like he'd been standing in the rain for a long time. Maybe this time, instead of being able to sail away, Dan had gotten himself stuck. Kevin understood the feeling. About now he felt mired to his chest and there was no elephant wandering by to get him out. Even if there was, he hadn't decided if he wanted out.

Dan tried to fix his gaze on Kevin, but couldn't seem to focus. "I've got to find her. Jack, Kate's lived in this area for a while. Do you think she'd know her?"

"No, Kate doesn't socialize in the neighborhood much." Jack rested his chin on his fist. "One of the cops she knows might have an idea. I'll ask, but don't count on me."

"What about your girlfriend, Kevin? She lives around here."

"She's not my girlfriend," Kevin growled. "Quit calling her my girlfriend."

"Whatever she is, do you think she would know? Jessica? That's her name, isn't it?" Dan leaned forward.

"I don't know. Ask her next time you see her." Kevin sneered. "In between hitting on her."

"Yeah." Dan stood up, still looking dazed. "I can ask her the next time I see her." He wandered out of the dorm.

"I leave for a couple of weeks, and you guys all get weird." Jack turned away from staring out the door. "So what are you going to do about Jessica?"

"I already asked her to your wedding." He hadn't decided yet if that had been a mistake and he didn't think he'd know until the wedding ended.

"That's a start. Now you have to start thinking about your next date. Something that doesn't involve weightlifting."

"I can't date her. She's going to be a probie."

Jack rolled his eyes. "You have excuses for all seasons, Marshall. Look, you like her. You might even love her."

"Whoa. Don't start with that. I'm not in love with her." Lying wasn't very difficult with practice. Kevin hoped someday to be able to convince himself.

"Whatever you say." Jack smirked while the thought settled in. "So you like her. You have a lot in common with her. What are you afraid of?"

"I'm not afraid."

"And I'm a Hispanic woman with a doctorate in nuclear physics. I dye my hair to get it this color."

"I didn't know you had a doctorate," Kevin answered. He'd asked Jack for help because he couldn't sort this out on his own and now when Jack was trying to help him, he started getting evasive. What he needed to do was stop sabotaging himself. "If I start dating her, everybody is going to think that's why I trained her. I'll never hear the end of it."

"Okay, then I have another question you won't be able to answer. Why *did* you offer to help her?"

Kevin sat up straighter. "I felt sorry for her. She said she'd always wanted to be a paramedic and when I told her the cut-off age was thirty-one, she panicked. She'd turned thirty that day."

Jack frowned mockingly. "Kevin Marshall taking pity on the poor girl. Sorry, I can't see it. I think it had more to do with her smile or her hair or her trip to Ireland."

Kevin grunted. It had less and less all the time to do with her trip to Ireland.

"Search your feelings. You know it to be true."

"I still don't want to screw up her chances in the ranking."

"How gallant of you."

"The department needs her."

"No, the department wants her. Doubtless, only slightly less than you do." Jack ignored Kevin's dirty look. "Do you know why the department wants her so much?"

"She's smart. She was pre-med. She took good classes in college and got good grades."

"And *you're* training her."

"That has nothing to do with it."

"That has everything to do with it." Jack tossed his towel to the foot of the bed. "You met up with her on what, the twenty-third, twenty-fourth of June? I started getting phone calls on the twenty-sixth. Everybody thought if you agreed to work with her, she must be something special, and since you're not Dan, we figured she wasn't special in the thirty-six/twenty-four/thirty-six way. I hate to break this to you, but you have a good reputation around here. If you choose, out of left field, to work with somebody nobody's heard of, there must be a reason."

"So everybody already thinks I'm a lovesick moron."

"No, everybody wonders what kind of treasure you found up there at the bookstore. The fact that she's got a great body, a great personality, and can cook is gravy. When I heard about her, I assumed she was some mongrel who could bench press a cow." Jack stood up and picked up his towel. "Accept the fact that somewhere along the line you're going to look like an idiot for her. I'm pretty sure it's a requirement. Start acting less like a jackass. Maybe she'll stop acting as if she's angry at you all the time. Then, maybe you have a chance to only look sort of silly instead of like the village idiot."

* * * *

Kevin walked into the gym the next morning prepared to follow Jack's advice. Bobbie should be there to act as a buffer, which would help. It didn't matter if the guys thought he had ulterior motives. She was very qualified. If she also happened to be attractive then it was, as Jack said, gravy.

Rounding the corner out of the hallway, he spotted her talking to a man. Talking and smiling. Talking, smiling and laughing.

Kevin picked up his pace. He needed to be between her and whoever this guy was. From this perspective he could only see the man's back, but he could see Jessica's expression. He wanted her to look at him that way. Like she admired him. Like she thought he was interesting and funny.

"Oh Kevin, you're here," Jessica said when she caught sight of him. She looked almost relieved. "I suppose you know Captain Bartlett."

Kevin forced himself to smile and tried not to swallow his tongue. Captain Bartlett from Four. The one who'd been watching her work out.

"Marshall." Bartlett held out his hand.

Kevin shook it, trying to figure out what had just happened. What had they been talking about?

"The captain finally decided to come out of the shadows and introduce himself. He's been giving me tips for the exam." Jessica laughed.

Kevin didn't recognize her laugh. Given, she didn't laugh much around him, but this laugh had a coy, anxious ring to it. Was she interested in the captain? He had to be over forty.

"I promise you. You walk into the room and slip the proctor a fifty, you'll ace the test." He patted Jessica on the shoulder. "But I don't want to interrupt your workout. Remember, if you need anything, don't hesitate to give me a call. You have my number, right?"

"You watched me put it in my phone."

"Good. I look forward to seeing you at the fire academy." He nodded to Kevin and walked away.

"Have you seen Bobbie?" Jessica asked. She looked over Kevin's shoulder toward the door. "I've left her a couple of messages, but she hasn't called me."

"What was that all about?"

"What? Bobbie?" Jessica frowned, bewildered.

"No. You and Bartlett. You two looked awfully cozy." Kevin glanced back at the doorway Bartlett had gone through. At least he wasn't still hanging around. He had expected the other guys to start sniffing around Jessica the moment she showed up, but the captains too?

Jessica blinked and shook her head. "What are you talking about? Neil has been watching—"

"Neil?" She knew his first name? How chummy had they gotten in the few minutes before he'd arrived? Was she just attracted to power? A captain had more power than a lieutenant. What would she do the first time she encountered a chief?

"Neil. That's how he introduced himself. What is wrong with you?" Jessica put her fists on her hips.

"Nothing. It just seems a little strange. Every time I walk in here you're surrounded by admirers, and today it happened to be a captain."

"This isn't a jealousy thing, is it?" Jessica narrowed her eyes at him.

"No, I just wondered how you got to be so tight with a captain you met this morning." Tight? Kevin's entire body felt tight. He wanted to grab her and kiss her. When she was angry she really did get more beautiful. Her eyes sparkled and her face tensed into hard, clean lines.

"I don't know how I got to be so *tight* with a captain I just met, and I didn't realize I was surrounded by admirers every time you arrived. Gee, maybe I'm arranging it that way." She smirked. "I'm using my considerable feminine wiles to bind you into my web."

Kevin heard a tang of harshness in her voice and regretted his reaction. Bartlett could be pretty charming when he wanted to be, and Jessica wasn't known to be a shameless flirt. She wasn't using him and she wasn't going to jump ship for Bartlett. If she were attracted to power, she wouldn't be looking in the fire department. Even cops got to carry guns. Once again, he felt like a complete heel, but this time it was his own fault. "I'm sorry. I wasn't thinking. What did you say about Bobbie?"

Jessica studied him. "I haven't heard from her since Monday when we worked out. Have you talked to her?"

"No. I'll call her and see what's going on." If he could just touch her, pat her shoulder like Bartlett had or brush his fingers through the stands of hair that had already worked loose from her ponytail. This morning he'd been ready to start over with her, but he'd blown it as soon as he walked through the door. He needed to go back in time a couple of weeks and start this whole relationship over again as a relationship. "Did you get the day off for the wedding?"

"Part of it. Your message said the wedding starts at one, can you pick me up at work at noon? There isn't anybody to open the store." She stood less than an arm's reach away watching him.

"That's fine." Kevin considered reaching out and taking her hand. How would she react? She might like it. She also might deck him.

"Are we going to get to work at some point or just stand here contemplating the floor?" Jessica asked.

* * * *

Jessica felt the brick grab her foot and knew the exact moment when she had no chance of recovering her balance. She fell face first into the street, attempting to catch herself with her hands and succeeding in tearing up her arms as well as her cheek and her knees. Lying in the street, she clenched her teeth against tears of anger and frustration. She could feel the scrapes on her cheek, her arms, her hip and thigh.

"Are you okay?"

She rolled onto her back and looked up at Kevin. "Fabulous." She groaned.

"Did you hit your head?"

She rolled her head back and forth on the street. "Just scraped my cheek."

"Here, let's get inside and get you cleaned up." He reached for her.

She pulled away. "I'm fine."

He flinched. "Okay, but you need to get bandaged up. You're bleeding."

Jessica touched her cheek. It felt sticky. A wedding to go to in less than three weeks and she'd torn up her face. "Great." She sat up. "I just need to get cleaned up, and we can get back to work."

"No. You haven't tried that knee yet. You could have damaged it. Let me help you up." He held out his hands again.

"I can stand." She didn't trust herself to rest her hands in his right now. This day of training had been a comedy of errors. After Kevin's bizarre behavior in the gym yesterday, she hadn't been able to sleep so she felt like a limp rag. The day had dawned brutally hot. All her normal workout clothes were dirty. One of her shoelaces broke when she put on her shoes, requiring her to stop on the way here and making her late. If she took his outstretched hands now, she might break and fall into his arms. That wasn't going to improve the day in the long run. Sure, the short run would be fun, but she didn't want to start out at the fire department as *the easy one.*

She rolled onto her hands and knees. When she fell, she'd twisted so she didn't take the brunt of the impact in her knees, but on the side of her leg. From the way it felt, she'd torn her sweat pants to the hip. Good thing all her running pants were dirty or she'd have taken off a nice layer of skin instead of ruining a pair of pants. As she worked her way to her feet, she sensed Kevin standing right beside her, ready to catch her if she slumped. The fact that he didn't trust her to know how badly she'd hurt herself irritated her, but that was cancelled out by the warm fuzzy feeling of having someone watching out for her. By the time she'd stood up completely, Kevin had stepped back as if he hadn't been a foot away the entire time she'd been working her way upright. He lifted the duffel bag over his shoulder and followed her to the house.

"Are you hurt bad?" he asked.

"I don't know yet." She watched her feet as she walked up the porch steps. "I don't think I damaged the joint. It just looks cool." She tried to smile, but he frowned at her.

"The bathroom is at the top of the stairs to the right. Bandages and stuff are under the sink." He dropped the duffel on the living room floor with a thump.

Jessica worked her way up the stairs. Her leg stung, but mostly just felt exposed. She had torn the material from knee to hip. In the mirror over the sink she checked the scrape on her face. It wasn't as bad as it felt. The peroxide, cotton balls and bandages were under the sink where he'd said they would be.

"You need any help?" Kevin asked from the door.

Jessica looked at his reflection in the mirror. She could see how much he wanted to help, and it almost matched how much she wanted him to help her. "I guess." She swallowed. Outside she hadn't wanted him to lay a hand on her, and now she was inviting him to bandage her upstairs in his house? Where had her common sense wandered off to?

Kevin dampened a washcloth and cradled her cheek with his other hand as he tried to brush the dirt and brick shards out of the scrape. She hissed and pressed her face against his palm. "I'm sorry." He lifted the cloth away from her face.

"Not your fault. I'm the one who can't keep my feet." Jessica tried to laugh, but it came out tight and weird because she couldn't think beyond his hand on her cheek.

Kevin brushed the cloth across her scrape again. The cool water accented the heat welling inside her. Dropping the cloth in the sink, he doused a cotton ball in peroxide. A delicate movement for such powerful hands. Jessica tried to take a deep breath, but her chest was strapped in iron. His big, warm hand cradled her cheek, making her entire body shiver with the contact. She wanted to feel that hand everywhere. He dabbed the peroxide on her cheek. The sharp clear pain made her squeeze her eyes closed and cringe away.

"Jessica," he whispered.

"Go ahead. I'm not that big a baby." His hand trembled against her face. Licking her lips, she tried to breathe again with as much success as last time. The desire to lean forward and press her uninjured cheek against his shoulder so he could put his arm around her waist and finish cleaning the wound. When she opened her eyes, she found him watching her. For a long moment they stared at one another. All the reasons she shouldn't do this still held true. Nothing had changed. No matter how much she wanted it to.

She reached up and put her hand on his wrist. "Maybe I better do this myself," she said.

"Jessica…" he said again.

"No. Let's not just now." She stepped away from him, slipping his hand off her cheek as she did. "Perhaps next time if you ask nice, but not now."

His face clouded for an instant. Then he set down the cotton ball.

"I'll be downstairs," he said, backing out of the bathroom.

Jessica stared at herself in the bathroom mirror trying to decide if she'd lost her mind or if she'd just found it. She took her time cleaning herself up, hoping her heart rate would settle back to normal. By the time she went downstairs, Kevin had stretched out on the couch.

"Ready to get back to work?" she asked.

"You're done for today."

"Why?"

"Because I said so."

Jessica put her hands on her hips. She felt a little more at home with this conversation since they had it so frequently. "Since when has that been a good enough answer for me?"

She thought she saw a smile flicker across his face. "You've been off your stride all day and now you're dressed in rags. You need a half day of rest. There's lemonade in the fridge."

In the kitchen, she poured herself a glass before going back to the living room and dropping onto the mismatched easy chair. "So how am I doing?" The notebook he used to keep track of all her records was on the table, but she didn't have anything to measure against so the numbers meant nothing.

"You're doing fine. You're making good progress. Slow and steady wins the race." He took a long swallow from his glass. Jessica watched his throat work, fascinated.

"By the way, you're out of peroxide," she said before anything else could come out. "I can bring some more over, next time I come."

"I think I can spring for first aid supplies."

"It's poker night, isn't it?" she asked, trying to get as far away as possible from the incident in the bathroom.

Kevin nodded.

"If we're done, I'll head home before the guys get here." She started to sit up.

"I'll drive you. Relax. I just want to wait until somebody shows up so everybody isn't locked out of the house."

He wasn't rushing her out before the guys arrived. Her crack about him being ashamed to be seen with her must have sunk in. Leaning back in the chair, she clutching the cold glass. Maybe she'd been wrong in the bathroom. Maybe something had changed. What if Diana, Julie and Sonya were right, and the invitation to the wedding did mean something?

"I bet it never gets this hot in Ireland," Kevin groaned.

"No, from what I understand it's lukewarm or chilly and damp. It ranged between those two when I was there. When you go, pack layers."

"If I go."

"What happened to *sometime before this day next year*?" Jessica grinned. She could remember every instant of that first conversation. For the past five weeks, she'd been reviewing it in her mind daily.

He shrugged, still focused on his lemonade. "Just doesn't sound like fun going alone."

"There are drawbacks, but on the plus side, you don't have to do anything you don't want to. If you don't want to go to the National Gallery, you don't."

"Did you?" He set down his glass to focus on her.

"No. I had to pick between the National Gallery and the National Museum. I picked the National Museum. I didn't have enough time to do both. Especially after the unfortunate trip to the Guinness brewery." She smiled. Until now they had managed one conversation that hadn't been fraught with sexual tension or anger. This made two. Both about Ireland.

He smiled. "I can't see you getting that drunk."

"It only happens when I'm being plied with the heavy European stuff. It isn't so bad going alone, you know. Tours pick what you're going to do for you, and friends or family can get under foot."

"But weren't you ever standing on a train platform in the middle of the night wondering where you were going to sleep?"

"Almost. I got off a bus at about eleven at night in a little town that had already rolled up its sidewalks not knowing where I would sleep, but I found a place."

"Didn't you wish you had someone to share it all with?"

Jessica thought for a minute. She had photo albums full of pictures and a journal she'd kept while she was there, but he was right, there were things that needed another person to really enjoy. "I guess. The whole falling down the side of a mountain in Carrowkeel would have been funnier with an audience."

Kevin laughed. "You fell down a mountain?"

"It wasn't a mountain, just a tall hill. There are a series of passage tombs on the ridge. You know, those heaps of rock with the cross-shaped chambers inside. Like Newgrange."

He nodded, his eyes focused on her as if nothing else mattered. It was a nice place to be.

"I was trying to take a picture of the landscape below, and I took one step too far forward trying to focus." She shrugged. "I only tumbled about twenty feet."

Kevin chuckled. "Maybe I can't spring for first aid supplies, if you're that clumsy."

"I am not that clumsy when I'm not trying to focus a camera on a landscape."

He threw a pillow at her. "I don't know, that was a pretty beautiful slide you took a bit ago in the street."

"You two look comfortable." Jack opened the screen door. "Nice leg. Nice scrape too."

"She fell."

"So I gathered from the bricks pulled up in the middle of the street."

Jessica cringed. "I pulled up bricks in the street?" She limped to the window and looked out. Three or four bricks were piled haphazardly where she'd fallen. "I better go fix that."

"Jack can take care of it." Kevin stood up.

"Jack can?" Jack asked.

"While you're holding down the fort," Kevin said. He sat up, setting aside his glass without taking his eyes from Jack's. "I'm going to drive Jessica home so she doesn't have to walk on that leg."

Kevin and Jack stared at each other like they were communicating silently. The telepathy stretched out between them until Jessica wondered if there had been a breakdown. Jack sighed. "I guess Jack will take care of it."

"Thanks, buddy." Kevin grinned. "I'll be back in a few minutes. I just have to get my car keys and we can go."

Jack stared up the stairs. "And he thought I was a pain," he grumbled. Jessica only had a second to consider what that might mean before he'd turned to her. "So you're coming to the wedding with Kevin."

"I guess so." Jessica flexed her hand. It had started to feel stiff, and she needed something to focus on.

"It's going to be a pretty low-key deal. Kate wanted to get the paperwork in order before the school year started, and she knew what she wanted. She was supposed to get married a couple of years ago, but he died."

"I know. From the paper." She gestured over her shoulder as if the newspaper in question were behind her on the couch.

"It was pretty sensational when it happened." Jack looked at the floor. "So…" he began, but Kevin came down the stairs.

"Ready?" he asked.

Jessica wished Kevin had spent a few more minutes looking for his keys so she'd know what Jack had been about to say. He probably wanted to ask why she wanted to be a firefighter or why she hadn't joined before now. Something mundane. Or he might have been about to tell her something important. Jack smiled and turned toward the front door. She followed Kevin to his car and let him open the door for her. Jack was kneeling in the street fixing the bricks when they pulled out.

CHAPTER 11

Kevin parked in the garage. He wished she hadn't stopped him in the bathroom, but he couldn't fault her for it. He'd told her they had to wait. Lew and Dan's cars sat in the street, so the gang was accounted for. As he walked through the front door, he saw Bobbie park down the block.

"Hey," Lew said as soon as he walked in. "I hear Jessica took a spill."

"She just tripped. No big deal." Kevin put his keys on the table.

"Seemed fine when I got here." Jack walked out of the kitchen. He was carrying a bowl of pretzels which he must have broken out himself. Kate was turning him into a regular hausfrau.

"She was telling me about Ireland."

"I know, I stood on the porch and listened for a minute before I came in." Jack smirked and headed through the archway to the dining room table. "I got everything set up here, and I fixed the road too. Is there anything else you'd like me to do?"

The screen door closed behind Kevin. He turned around. Bobbie looked at him and then at the floor. "Hey, guys."

"Bobbie!" Dan jumped out of the chair. "Come to lose your shirt again?"

"Ha ha," she said. "I've been busy."

"You haven't shown up at the gym either," Kevin pointed out.

"I said I was busy," she snapped.

Kevin tried not to flinch away from her. He glanced at the other guys to see if he was imagining her hostility. They were also exchanging baffled looks.

"Are we going to play cards or are we going to stand around all night?" She started toward the dining room table.

Dan sucked a breath through his teeth as she passed him.

She spun around. "What?"

"Nothing. Let's play." Dan stood up, trying to stay out of her range as much as possible without alerting her.

They gathered around, dumping their change on the table with Dan at one end, Kevin at the other, Jack in front of the door to the kitchen and Bobbie and Lew under the window. Jack dealt first and no one spoke, even to joke about the deal.

"How's Jessica doing?" Bobbie asked, arranging her hand and not looking at any of the guys.

"Fine," Kevin said. He looked at the cards in his hand. Mismatched garbage.

"She fell today," Lew added.

Kevin glared at him. Bobbie turned to Lew. "What happened?"

"Jack said Kevin said she tripped over the bricks on the street. She pulled up a couple." Lew set his cards face down on the table. "You have any beer, Kevin?"

"Fridge."

"So she's okay?" Bobbie turned to Kevin. "You should be more careful."

"I should?"

"Yes, you should. She might get hurt." Bobbie focused on her cards again. "Jack, you deal nothing but crap."

"Of course it is, it's my good marked deck," Jack said. He used the joke once every poker night. Normally they laughed to be nice, but not tonight.

"Do you think she'll pass the test?" Bobbie asked, not looking up from her cards.

"Sure. At the rate she's going, she should rank pretty high."

"Of course," Bobbie mumbled. "Everybody going to the wedding? Who gets Leia this time?"

"Not me." Dan rocked back on his chair. "I found a date. I'm clear."

Lew walked in. "I'm bringing *my* sister. Is Leia really that bad?"

"Much, much worse," Jack said to his cards.

"What about you?" Bobbie turned to Kevin.

"I'm taking Jessica. It's a good chance for her to meet everybody." He swallowed. "Anybody else want a beer?"

The others shook their heads.

"Whose turn is it? What's the bet?" Bobbie demanded.

"We haven't anted yet, motor mouth," Dan quipped.

Bobbie fixed him with a glare that made him shift in his seat. "Then ante," she snarled. Dan tossed a nickel toward the middle of the table. It rolled across and fell on the floor.

Kevin returned to the table.

"So she's doing great, then," Bobbie said.

Kevin looked around the table. The kitchen wasn't far enough way for him to have missed any of the conversation. Jack looked at him and shook his head. "She's, ah, she's doing fine."

Bobbie nodded. "What about you two?"

"Us two who?" Kevin put his cards on the table face down before his shaking hands dropped them.

"You and Jessica. That's why I haven't been around lately. Watching the sparks fly between the two of you is kind of nauseating after a while."

Kevin picked up his beer can and drank about half of it, trying to sort out a response. Nothing good came to mind. "Bobbie, what are you talking about?"

Dan leaned on his elbows with his cards face down in front of him. "Yes, Bobbie, what are you talking about?"

Kevin braced himself not to cringe. He couldn't be sure what Bobbie knew, but whatever it was, Dan would love to hear it. Then he would love to tell everyone he could get his hands on. Dan and discretion were only passing acquaintances.

"Oh come on, Dan. There's nothing to know. Bobbie's just jerking Kevin around." Jack stared at her across the table, flicking a nickel toward her. "Aren't you, Bobbie?"

Bobbie stood up. "I left something in the oven. I gotta go. Tell Kate I can't make it to the wedding." She walked out without picking up her money.

"My, wasn't that interesting?" Dan said. "Kevin, would you like to elucidate?"

"Elucidate?" Jack repeated.

"I told you. I've got a word-a-day calendar this year."

Lew flipped over Bobbie's cards. "She had a natural flush," he pointed out.

"Lucky at cards, unlucky at love." Dan studied Kevin across the table. "Isn't that the saying?"

"I thought it was cold hands, warm heart," Lew said. He held up his cards. "Get it? Cold hand—warm heart?"

Kevin sighed. Overall, the day had been good. He'd enjoyed some peaceful time with Jessica. She'd made a rational decision when he hadn't been able to. Jack had averted both Dan and Bobbie for him. Other than Bobbie acting like a nut case, he'd done well. He stood up. "I'll call her house. See if I can find out what's wrong."

"I'll give you three guesses," Jack grumbled, gathering up the cards.

* * * *

Jessica struggled to balance two large boxes of empty plastic security keepers as she walked away from the registers. Kevin was due to pick her up any minute, and Mindi hadn't shown up to replace her yet.

Kevin had been acting strange for the last three weeks. Ever since he asked her to the wedding, in fact. Like he was on his best behavior. He was trying so hard, it made her nervous.

Why was he bothering? What did he hope to gain? At his party he'd made it clear that he was attracted to her, but they couldn't do anything about it until after the exam. In his bathroom the day she fell, she'd made it pretty clear she could wait until after the exam. She still felt certain he wouldn't be interested any more after the exam, but she'd made her decision. There had to be other men she would be just as attracted to out there somewhere, even though she hadn't found any in years of determined searching.

Unless she'd read that wrong, too. Maybe he would sustain an interest after she didn't need him anymore.

She couldn't hang her heart on that idea. It would be all too easy to find herself attached to him only to have him dump her. Starting off on a new career, surrounded by men she was just meeting while living with them one day out of every three, single, and carrying a reputation she didn't want.

Then there was Bobbie. She'd thought she had an ally, but she'd always sensed something odd about Bobbie's relationship to Kevin. Bobbie had always acted high-strung around Kevin. Jessica thought she might be enamored of him, but she never said anything, and he didn't seem to pay her any more attention than he paid to any of his male friends. Two weeks ago, Jessica had gotten tired of waiting for Bobbie to not return her phone calls and had gone to Bobbie's station. She'd been greeted enthusiastically by the men and evasively by Bobbie. The whole trip had solved nothing, but it gave her another shot at the tools and a chance to talk to their captain. He didn't have a copy of her application like Kevin's captain had.

Jessica stopped at the office door and looked at the keypad at the door. If she put down the boxes to punch in the numbers, she would have to pick them up again. Picking them up required a very unladylike maneuver in a dress. Of course, attempting to type in the code while balancing the boxes increased her likelihood of dumping one or both boxes, scattering the contents and requiring a similar unladylike maneuver to gather them up and get them into the office. Unless she put the boxes on the floor, opened the door and kicked the boxes into the office, around the corner and to her desk. That idea had a little merit even though it wasn't very professional. She wondered why she never thought twice about kicking and dragging things in jeans, but she felt obligated to attempt to be graceful in a dress.

"Need a hand?"

Jessica's heart throbbed. Twisting her head she peeked around the corner of the box even though she didn't need to see to know. She knew who it was. No one else had that voice. He looked very nice in a tan sport coat, white shirt and navy blue slacks. "Actually, yes. Almost. Can you grab one of these?"

Kevin lifted the top box out of her arms.

Jessica punched in the code to unlock the door. "Bring that back here, could you?" She walked through the office feeling as though the box in her arms was balanced more precariously than it had been before. Her throat tightened thinking about him following behind her. At the moment she didn't look great. She'd opted to wear tennis shoes to work in and had left her sandals at her desk, and the dress code forbade sleeveless tops so she had worn a baggy yellow sweater all morning. Her hair was pulled into its traditional ponytail. The coffee bar girls had dubbed it the *frumpy librarian* look and begged her not to go to the wedding dressed this way. If Mindi had managed to be on time this once, she'd have been waiting near the front door, dressed to go with her hair down and combed, although she should have known better than to expect Mindi to be on time. She dropped her box on the floor beside her desk. "Just dump it there."

Kevin set the box he'd carried on top of the one she'd just dropped. He looked at the wall over her desk. "Quite a gallery."

"Yes, well, Julie saves everything for me." Jessica sloughed off her sweater and sat down at the desk to switch shoes. Kevin hadn't stopped looking at her pictures. Most people had pictures of actors over their desks. Jessica had fires and firefighters. The few pictures she had had of actors had been taken down in favor of more fires over the last few weeks.

"Why do you have a picture of Jack and Kate on the wall?"

Jessica glanced up at him as she slid the strap of her sandal over her heel, then she followed his gaze to the wall. He was staring at the "Cop Hero's Widow Finds New Love" picture. Julie had given it to her the day Kevin offered to train her. The same day Mindi started hating her. She wanted Mindi to understand, but she suspected she never would. It didn't help that she'd also lost Bobbie to a lousy quirk of fate. At least Julie would be entertained by the fact that *this* wedding was *that* wedding. "Julie gave it to me."

"Why is it on the wall?" Kevin asked.

Jessica bit her lip. Everybody here found it amusing, but Kevin didn't seem to see the humor. "It sort of goes with the theme. Julie, the magazine clerk, cuts all this stuff out of the papers for me. I hang up the interesting ones." Jessica hesitated. Something about that picture bothered him. Just about every female in the building had announced it was romantic, and she agreed. If it was his friend, why would it bother him? She pulled her hair out of its semi-permanent ponytail, hoping it would fall attractively. If Mindi had been on time she would have had time to brush it out in front of a mirror.

The office door banged open. "Sorry I'm late," Mindi called.

Jessica stood up and picked the pale blue shawl Sonya had loaned her off the back of her chair. "Are you ready to go?"

Kevin turned, and his eyes went round. "You look great."

"Thanks." Jessica ducked her head. She felt kind of glamorous having him look at her that way.

Mindi stepped around the corner. "Isn't that Sonya's shawl?"

"Yes, it is. She loaned it to me." Jessica folded the shawl over her arm, keeping the beaded fringe from tangling.

"That purse is Diana's."

Jessica picked up the purse Diana had loaned her. It matched Sonya's shawl and Diana insisted she use it. The glamour had faded when Mindi started picking apart her wardrobe. Always a confidence builder, that Mindi. "Tony left for lunch ten minutes late, so he's going to be ten minutes late getting back. I already warned Druanne she's stuck at register for a few extra minutes." She couldn't meet Kevin's eyes. So she didn't have a fashion model's wardrobe, why did it matter?

"Happy hunting."

Jessica glared at her. "What?"

"Happy hunting. Isn't that what we usually do at weddings?" Mindi smiled. It had all the warmth and camaraderie of the Donner Party. "It's nice to see you again, Kevin. You should come around more often."

Jessica heard Mindi's tone drop seductively. All Mindi needed to do was start batting her eyelashes and complementing him on his muscles and it would be college all over again. Kevin looked a little stunned by her display already. "I'm ready to leave, Kevin. Mindi's here to hold down the fort."

"Let's go then." Kevin took her arm and walked her out of the office. "What was that about?"

Jessica had been keeping her head down, taking deep even breaths so Kevin wouldn't get a look at her scarlet face which clashed with the blues in the rest of her outfit. How had she ever considered that woman a friend? "Mindi has always hated this idea. She didn't want me to train from the start. She's almost as bad as my mother, but she's got geography on her side."

Kevin pushed open the front door. "What about the happy hunting crack?"

"Your guess is as good as mine. I don't think I ever really knew her." Jessica waited while Kevin unlocked and opened her door. She should be enjoying his gallantry, not thinking about Mindi. But Mindi seemed intent on pushing her past the point of reason.

Kevin climbed in the driver's side and turned to look at her. "It happens sometimes. Family and friends are either proud of you or they fight you. Sometimes both at the same time." He put his hand over hers. "You look beautiful in that dress. I'm glad you agreed to come with me."

Jessica looked down at his large hand covering hers on her thigh. If only she could be a little more sure about him. She felt like she was walking across ice, and she could hear it crackling under her weight. Nothing was as she thought it was, not Mindi, not Bobbie, nobody except her mother had reacted the way she'd thought they would.

Did that mean she had misread Kevin and he would still be interested when she no longer needed him?

Or did it mean that she wanted him to love her so much she had read him right and didn't want to accept it?

* * * *

The exchange of vows took place on the lawn of one of the lodges that overlooked a ravine in the park. All of the guests gathered in a semicircle around the couple for the short ceremony. They couldn't have ordered better weather. The heat of the past few weeks had toned down to warm instead of sweltering. Jack wore a dark suit. Kate wore a tea-length, ivory lace gown and didn't seem at all bothered when Jack's dog Archer put a large muddy smear on her knee while trying to catch her attention during the vows. Archer wore a bowtie which he had off within the first half hour and had torn to shreds before the reception started.

Jack had to endure the heckling of his coworkers during the photos following the vows while the caterers set up inside the lodge where the reception was to take place.

Jessica stood near the fieldstone fireplace watching the ebb and flow of the crowd as the caterers put out the food. She already knew many of the groom's guests, and a couple of the bride's guests were regulars at the store. Kevin had stayed by her side for the ceremony, but had been hauled away for a picture he didn't look happy about. Archer and one of the other dogs in attendance were playing tug-of-war with the remains of his bowtie.

It wasn't the wedding Jessica would choose for herself, but it suited the bride and groom. Jessica had always envisioned a big fairy tale wedding for herself. She supposed Kevin would prefer a nice quiet trip to a justice of the peace.

Not that she would be marrying Kevin anyway. She sighed and looked around the room. It was a well put together reception. The room was dotted with round tables covered with ivory table cloths. Each table had a vase in the middle with a single red rose in it. Ivory and red bunting garnished the door sills and draped across the front of the head table in front of the fieldstone fireplace on the other side of the room. Kevin was trapped between Jack and Dan with all the other guys from his shift against that fireplace for a photo. He caught her eye across the room and grimaced. She raised her glass to him.

"Did you come with Kevin?"

Jessica turned. A bubbly little blonde stood beside her.

"I'm Arianna." Arianna stuck out her hand. "I'm here with Dan. Isn't he adorable?"

Jessica shook Arianna's hand. She had a light, helpless grip that felt more like shaking hands with a damp dish towel than a person. "It's nice to meet you."

"I met Dan at the grocery store, of all places. I was buying apples, but most of them were bruised, and I don't like bruised apples."

Jessica nodded, trying to decide if this story had a point.

"Well, I pulled one apple out and all the others just tumbled onto the floor." Arianna's voice rose to an annoying squeak.

"I'll bet several of them got bruised then." Jessica looked across the room. She needed Kevin to come rescue her from this. If he didn't, she was going to have to fake an injury. No, that was no good, Dan was a paramedic, Arianna would hang over his shoulder chattering about apples while Dan diagnosed her as a faker.

"Oh, it was terrible. I felt so bad. But Dan helped me pick them up. He's so sweet. We're not *dating* dating, but…you know. I always eat an apple a day. My hairdresser says apple skins are good for your hair."

"Really?" The group photo started breaking up.

"There are just so many things that damage your hair. The ozone and chemicals in the air." Arianna's hands fluttered around her head as if she could chase away the ozone like a moth.

"Think of what it does to your lungs." Jessica smiled to cover her clenched teeth. The guys had fallen into a conversation on the other side of the room.

"It's just terrible, isn't it? And your skin. All those things in the air give you premature wrinkles. It's just awful. It must have been much easier to keep your skin in good condition before all that awful stuff went into the air." Arianna patted her cheeks like she might be able to feel them wrinkling under her hands.

"I don't know if women worried about it as much before the industrial revolution," Jessica murmured.

"They didn't have to, did they? It just wouldn't have been an issue."

"They were probably more worried about death in childbirth, or the plague, or something like that." Jessica cringed. A touch more sarcasm and she was going to offend Dan's girlfriend, who he wasn't *dating* dating.

Arianna blinked. Her face went blank for an instant, then lit up again. "I work at the mall in the card shop."

"I work at the bookstore."

"Really? That must be really boring. I like cards. They're pretty." She sighed. "God, I need a cigarette."

Jessica had been trying to recover from the fact of Arianna thinking the bookstore would be boring and she blurted out the first thing that came to mind. "They give you wrinkles."

"They do?" Arianna's crystal blue eyes were shocked.

Jessica studied her, trying to decide if she was stupid or just a good actress. It was looking like stupid. Dan and Kevin strolled over.

"You two seem to be engrossed in conversation." Dan grinned and draped his arm around Arianna's shoulders.

Jessica forced a smile. She hoped he would take Arianna away before she started talking again. "Are all of the pictures finished?"

"I hope so," Kevin grumbled. He hadn't made any move to put his arm over her shoulders, but she couldn't be sure if that meant anything.

"Ari, why don't you go find our table?" Dan suggested.

"Okay." Arianna smiled and wandered away.

"Ari, why don't you go look at a shiny thing?" Kevin mocked. "Where do you find them? I'm surprised this one's smart enough to remember to breathe."

"I needed a date and she looks great." Dan peered over his shoulder after Arianna, who was engrossed in the task of finding their place cards. He turned back to Jessica with an odd intensity in his eyes. "You live in the neighborhood. Do you know a woman with black hair and, I think, blue eyes? I know she lives somewhere near the station."

"Oh man. Will you give this a rest?" Kevin folded his arms. "You lost her."

"Black hair and blue eyes?" Jessica asked.

"Yes. She's about this tall." Dan held his hand at about his eye level. "Kind of thin and willowy."

Jessica shook her head. "It sounds like the weird artist girl who hangs out at Meechan's, but I could be wrong."

"Weird sounds about right." Kevin snorted.

Dan didn't even give Kevin a glance. "Meechan's? Is that the restaurant up on Market? You think she hangs out there?"

"There's an artist who I see up there pretty often who matches your description." Jessica wondered if she should define *artist* for him. Probably not, better he should find out for himself. Kevin could harass him about his choice of girlfriends, but Jessica didn't think she rated that comfort level yet.

"Meechan's, thanks. I'll give it a try." Dan followed Arianna to the table she'd found.

"What was that about?" Jessica asked Kevin.

"This strange chick kissed him a couple of weeks ago, and now he's obsessed with finding her. I guess she just walked out of the rain and demanded he kiss her." Kevin shrugged.

Jessica looked around the room. There was a smallish blonde reaming out one of the caterers. Jessica looked closer. That caterer worked with her at the store. She started over to rescue him. In years of working with him, she'd never seen him do anything to deserve the public upbraiding he was receiving.

"Hello, Mike," Jessica said.

Mike jerked, wild-eyed. He didn't seem to be at all relieved to see her.

"I'm telling you, this table is a mess," the blonde continued. She gestured at a table that didn't yet have a tablecloth on it. The cloth lay on top of a cardboard box. Two other caterers were darting back and forth between their van and the food tables.

"We're working on it. It'll be completely fixed in a few minutes." Mike kept sidling to one side as if he wanted to escape, but the woman kept following him.

"I want it fixed now."

"It'll be fixed soon," Jessica said. She planted herself in the woman's way so Mike could gain some ground.

"Who are you?" the woman demanded.

"Hello, Leia," Kevin said. "Enjoying the festivities?" He slipped between Leia and Mike so Mike could complete his escape.

"Kevin." Leia sneered. "It's nice, for a little wedding. Just what I expected from my brother." She sighed. Jessica's impression of Jack and Kate's simple wedding rose a notch.

"Yeah. It is nice, isn't it? Very low key. Jack has good taste." He nodded and looked around the room as if he were admiring it. "How have you been?"

Jessica heard a falseness to his voice she'd never heard before. This woman must be Jack's sister, but she had a hard time imagining them coming from the same family. To think, a few minutes ago she'd been bored and watching Jack's dog. In such a short span of time, she'd discovered Dan's obsessive side and Jack's evil sister. What other surprises did the day hold?

"I got a partnership. I'm sure you don't know what that means." Leia folded her arms and leaned back.

"It means your firm had to print new stationary, doesn't it?" Kevin's tone had a cruel edge to it. Jessica felt pretty sure she wouldn't have liked Jack's sister anyway, but Kevin's disdain sealed it for her.

Leia snorted. "Something like that. Excuse me."

Kevin watched her walk across the room. "Every bride's worst nightmare."

"A bad wedding guest?"

"A bad in-law. That woman is poison." He gave a short laugh. "Come to think of it, I guess my sisters wouldn't be much better."

Jessica giggled. "Should we stand guard and make sure she doesn't attack the caterers again?"

Kevin frowned conspiratorially. "I think the caterers are safe for the moment, but I'd love to get Leia and Dan's dingy date into a conversation."

"Dan's dingy date?" Jessica repeated. "Why Kevin, you're alliterating."

"Ah, love a good alliteration," Kevin drawled.

Jessica laughed, but part of her already mourned losing him. She would miss these rare moments of comfortable conversation. All too soon her training would be over, and they wouldn't see each other much. Never long enough to share a light joke like this.

Kevin seemed to notice the moment too. He looked at her soberly as if he wanted to capture the feeling before it escaped them, but by then it was already gone. "Come on, we should go sit down. Unfortunately, I think we're near Dan and Arianna."

Jessica followed him to the table. They had been seated next to Lew and his sister. Dan sat next to Lew's sister. Jessica still felt too close to Arianna for safety.

"Your sister?" Dan scoffed at Lew.

"You had me convinced that I was doomed to spend the day with Leia if I didn't have a date." Lew draped his arm across the back of his sister's chair. "Besides, I like my sister."

Lew's sister, who looked barely out of high school, blushed and said nothing.

"Jessica, how's your training going?" Lew asked.

"She's right on schedule," Kevin answered. "She'll be ready for the test in two weeks."

"The written is in ten days," Jessica corrected.

"You've been ready for the written for two weeks now."

"But I don't think I'm ready for the physical, which is twelve days away."

"You'll be ready."

"My times aren't good enough."

"Your times are fine."

"Fine isn't good enough."

Dan leaned forward to look around Lew's sister. "Aren't they cute when they bicker?"

Jessica looked at the table. Kevin's discomfort radiated off him. They had argued about that aspect of her training off and on all summer, but always without an audience. Kevin seemed determined to ignore the dummy drag. She'd gone so far as to convince a couple of people at work to let her drag them around the store before it opened, but she was running out of candidates. Every time she cut a corner too close, her current dummy ended up with bruises and wouldn't do it anymore. She couldn't convince Kevin that dragging him around his padded living room was a much better solution. Unfortunately, a nice public argument destroyed any chance of a nice private moment between them for some time.

"Hey, did you see the new truck Harville got?" Lew asked.

"No, how's it look?" Dan asked.

Jessica pulled inside herself when she heard them launch into a technical discussion of the new fire engine in the neighboring suburb. She looked down the table and spotted an empty chair. She'd be willing to bet the name card at that chair read Bobbie Kelly. What was she doing here? Why had she started this in the first place? Her mother was right. It was too hard, but not for the reasons she'd been leaving on Jessica's answering machine for a month now.

She'd disrupted Kevin's life immeasurably.

She'd forced Bobbie away from her friends.

She'd wrecked her own friendship with Mindi.

She'd freaked out her mother. Again.

And she had to wait ten more days before she could even start to find out if any of it had been worth it.

CHAPTER 12

Kevin had felt Jessica draw away. She was doing it again, making him feel like a heel on a moment's notice, but she was more than prepared for the test. If she didn't rank near the top he'd be shocked. If she didn't make it in this time, there would be another test. She'd only been training for a few weeks now.

After dinner, a string quartet had started to play on the lawn outside. Jessica had physically kept near him, but seemed distant. Cool and rigid. He wasn't sure if she'd been interested by the conversation going on around her or if she'd endured it, waiting for the day to end. When someone else came over to talk she acted more animated, but otherwise spent her time looking around and saying nothing.

Over the past couple of weeks, she hadn't responded to his efforts to be nice. Instead, she'd acted suspicious. He'd imagined her reacting in a more accepting way. More like Arianna, who was at this moment fawning over Dan on the dance floor. Watching her display, he decided there were things more embarrassing than bickering with Jessica.

He stole a glance at his date. Jessica had picked out a point on the wall and was studying it as though it might be on the test. He'd been almost floored when he got a look at her in the bookstore. When he'd caught up with her at the office door, she'd been dressed about as he'd expected, except for the tennis shoes. Navy blue skirt, cardigan. Perfectly acceptable. While she didn't look like a fashion plate, he wouldn't be embarrassed to be seen with her.

Somehow she'd transformed while he looked at the pictures over her desk. He felt like he'd been punched in the gut when he saw her bare shoulders and the plunge of the neckline. Distracted, he hadn't noticed he'd stopped breathing until lack of oxygen made him dizzy and by that time he'd missed a large section of the conversation she'd been having with Mindi. All he caught was *happy hunting.*

That still bothered him. Happy hunting? What was that supposed to mean? Jessica said she didn't know, but was she telling the truth?

Kevin looked around the lawn. Dan was still dancing with his date, whose high heels sank into the grass with every step. Lew stood talking to a bunch of guys with his arm draped around his sister. Every other couple in the room was touching. Even Jack's sister was dancing with his grandmother.

He hadn't been able to bring himself to put his arm around her yet. Too dangerous, but it might be what she was waiting for.

"You want to dance?" Kevin asked.

Jessica blinked at him. "Dance?"

"Yes, dance. You and me."

Her eyes narrowed and she fussed with her shawl. "All right." She held out her hand so he could lead her into the swirling couples.

When he got her into the middle of the crowd he realized he had no idea what to do. Checking the nearest couple for hand position, he rested one hand on her waist as he clasped the other around her hand.

She seemed to have some idea what they should be doing, so he let her set the pattern.

"Are you having a good time?" He guessed she wasn't, but thought she'd be too polite to say so. It made for conversation anyway.

"It's a very pretty wedding. I'd have never thought to hold it here." She looked around at the trees lining the clearing.

She'd side-stepped lying, and she wasn't having a good time.

"You know, maybe next week we can work on the dummy drag," he said. No one had moved close enough to hear their conversation, but he knew they were watching. Kevin the celibate had not only shown up with a date, he was dancing with her. He tried to convince himself this was all part of the *looking a little silly* Jack had told him would be necessary. It felt closer to being the village idiot.

She looked at him suspiciously. "Why the sudden change of heart?"

"I just think it's a good idea. I didn't realize the test was coming up so soon." That, he conceded, was a flat-out lie. When she joined the department there wouldn't be any reason for her to hang around with him anymore. His hand tightened against her waist. Very likely, in ten days, he wouldn't hear her voice on his answering machine, and he wouldn't see her standing outside his front door.

She paused, licking her lips. "Do you want me to come to your house tomorrow morning?"

"That'd be good." The thought of her having her arms wrapped around his chest made his heart pound and he now had less than eighteen hours to get it under control. The dress wasn't helping. "I think you're ready."

"I hope so. I'm running out of time." She looked away, and her hand tensed in his.

Running out of time? Time for what? Did she think it would take her until next June to rank high enough? Or did she realize they only had a little time left too? In a couple of weeks, she was going to be done with him. She'd be off at the academy for a while and then settling in at her new station. It could be months before she had a spare minute. Who knows what could happen before then. "You have plenty of time. You know you can always call me if you need anything," he said. He should have kept his mouth shut. *Call me if you need anything?* Like what? How desperate did he need to sound?

She nodded, but didn't say anything.

"We can head home anytime. If you're tired." Kevin could have spent the rest of the night swaying with her in his arms, but she seemed melancholy now. He wanted to be alone with her so he could draw her out. To convince her he wasn't desperate. "We are going to start early tomorrow."

"That might be best then," she said. "If we went home."

"Do you need me to take you back to the store to get your car?" Now that he'd convinced her to leave, he wanted an excuse to hold her for another minute. He couldn't decide if she sounded eager to get home or not.

"No. I got a ride to work this morning. I thought it might be closer for you to take me home." She took a deep breath and stepped back. "Are you ready to say good night to the bride and groom?"

"If we can find them."

"I saw them headed over there." She gestured toward the lodge and started walking in that direction.

Kevin followed her. It didn't seem late, but the party had started breaking up. Jessica wove through the gathering knots of people. Inside the lodge, she went to their table for her purse before she went to where Jack and Kate were standing in front of one of the fireplaces. "I guess we're going to hit the road," he said.

"Okay, thanks for coming out." Jack shook his hand.

"Jessica, I wish I'd had your help planning this." Kate took Jessica's hands in hers. "But I'm so glad you could come. Your exam is coming up soon, isn't it?"

"Ten days," Kevin answered.

"Ten days, is that all?" Kate sighed. "Good luck, although I'm sure you don't need it."

"You're going to need the luck stuck with him," Kevin commented to Kate.

"It's your fault if I do." Kate smiled at Jack.

Kevin watched the two of them together. They matched. He was glad he'd bumped into Kate in time to talk to her before Jack quit the department for her. Their problem had been easy to fix. If only someone would come along with the easy fix to his problem with Jessica. A way to fix time so he was younger. Some magic spell to keep her interested after she didn't need him anymore.

"It was a lovely wedding. You did a fine job planning it, and your ring is just beautiful." Jessica smiled. Kevin wondered for a minute what she would look like in Kate's dress.

"Thanks." Kate held out her hand so her ring caught the light.

"We had the stone from my other ring mounted into a new setting. It's supposed to be symbolic."

"It's very nice."

"I have my grandmother's ring," Kevin announced. As soon as the comment left his lips he wondered why he'd said it. All three of them turned to look at him.

"Why do you have your grandmother's wedding ring? Why didn't she give it to one of your sisters?" Jack asked.

"Because it's family tradition that the oldest child gets the ring and because none of my sisters are much into tradition." Kevin shrugged and tried to think of a way to change the conversation.

"So is it a family heirloom?" Kate asked.

"Sort of. It's not like that. It's a plain Welsh gold band and it's really beat up. It belonged to her mother." Kevin hoped no one would ask why it had come up now, because he wouldn't have been able to tell them. He'd remembered it the moment he told them about it. It was in a small velvet box his mother had given him in the bottom of his underwear drawer. "Too bad you have to come right back on duty Monday," he told Jack.

Jack blinked. "Duty?"

"Not much of a honeymoon." Kevin glanced at Jessica and knew she hadn't been fooled by his sudden change of topic. Kate didn't look convinced either.

"Oh, that. We had that before the wedding." Jack put his arm around Kate's shoulders and kissed the top of her head.

"While you were gimpy," Kate protested. "You owe me."

"I'll see if I can make it up to you."

Kevin wondered if he could get the conversation back to his grandmother's wedding ring. He hadn't thought there was a worse topic of conversation, but here they were soaking in it. "We're going to go now. Congratulations. See you Monday, Jack." He put his hand in the middle of Jessica's back to guide her away, forgetting for a moment that her dress was backless. As soon as his hand touched her flesh he wanted to jerk it away. Or pull her against him.

She turned away from his hand, waving a cheery goodbye over her shoulder, and beat him to the driveway. Walking beside her to the parking area, he wondered if he could get away with touching her again. The way she'd leaped away, probably not. At the car, he opened the door for her and walked around to the other side. He couldn't tell where he stood with her. If he asked Jack, he knew the answer he'd get. *Ask her.* Somehow, Kevin couldn't picture himself asking Jessica if she liked him. It sounded juvenile.

"So, how many sisters do you have?" Jessica asked before the silence in the car got so oppressive he had to say something.

"Four. And two brothers."

"Big family." She looked out the passenger window as if she were going through the motions of the conversation.

"And scattered to the four winds. I think only two of us live in the same city right now. Every one of them works in business and transfers where the job takes them, or where their spouse's job takes them."

"Do your parents live here?"

"Used to. My dad transferred to San Diego about five years ago and retired out there."

"Oh." Jessica sighed and folded her hands over her purse. "So are your brothers and sisters married?"

"All of them but the baby. Irene is picky." Kevin adjusted his grip on the wheel. He didn't want to think about Irene's issues. "What about you? Any brothers or sisters?"

"No. I'm an only child. This way my mother gets to focus all her energy on making my life miserable." Jessica leaned her head on the head rest. "That's not fair. My mother has just always had my father around to take care of the hard stuff, i.e., everything. She isn't very independent, and she doesn't understand how I could be. She always thought I would settle down right out of high school and spend the rest of my life polishing my nails or something." Jessica looked at her hands. Kevin glanced at them too. Her nails were short and ragged. She'd worn polish, but it had chipped. "What about you? I bet your mother didn't have time to be over-involved."

"With seven kids eleven years apart? She was too tired. I ended up taking care of them most of the time. I remember once in high school, while I was packing the little kids' lunches for school the next day, announcing that I was never having kids because I never wanted to have to take care of anyone again."

Jessica laughed. "How did that go over?"

"Oh, my mother started to cry and my father grounded me. Every year it gets funnier." Kevin grinned. Every family gathering someone told that story, and it did get funnier as his brothers and sisters had their kids.

"So do you still not want to have kids?"

"Need a wife for that." Kevin turned onto her street. He had to drop her off soon. Would she invite him in or would she want to be away from him as soon as possible? Only ten days until the written test.

"Hypothetically speaking then. If your friend Jack's Kate had a twin sister who was available."

"Irish babies tend to weigh in around eight or nine pounds." Where in God's name was she going with this conversation and why? Was it idle curiosity? Time filler? Pointed?

"We women are tougher than we look. Come on, quit dodging the question. Hypothetically, if the stars lined up just right, would you?"

"I guess so. I like spending time with my nieces and nephews. I see a lot of the other guys' kids and they're fun." Over the years he'd had conversations like this with different guys and different guys' wives. He liked kids, and they seemed to like him. Plus, he'd had plenty of experience changing diapers. But kids required a wife. He pulled up her driveway.

"Home already?" Jessica sat up. "You want to come in for a minute? I think I've got some coffee."

"Sure. That would be nice." Kevin followed Jessica up to her door. He wondered how he was going to screw this up. Waiting on the top step for her to unlock the front door, he watched her. Her dark hair brushed against her tanned shoulders. She walked through the apartment with a confident gait.

"I should have coffee, but I doubt I have much else." She dropped her shawl on the chair and set her purse on top of it.

"Coffee's fine." On the bookshelf in the dining room she had a few framed pictures on the top of the shelf under the high window. One looked like a family portrait. Jessica looked like her mother in coloring, but she stood half a foot taller. Jessica's mother also looked like she could be snapped in half by a strong wind. Another one of the pictures showed what must have been a Cast-Off Thanksgiving Dinner, judging by the sweaters, the turkey and the missing couch.

"There's a photo album on the lower shelf if you're interested."

Kevin turned around. She'd stopped inside the room and leaned against the wall with her hands behind her back. Her lips curled into a faint, mocking smile. He wanted to run his fingers through her hair. "That's okay. This looks like one of your Thanksgiving dinners." He pointed to the picture he'd been looking at.

"It is. Those two are the next door neighbors." Stepping closer, she pointed to a couple near the head of the table. "Most of the others work at the bookstore. Except that guy. He's just a customer, but he's in all the time, and everybody likes him pretty well. He usually carves." She tapped the glass near a tall balding man.

Kevin tried to follow her description, but he found himself watching the line of her lips. He remembered kissing her in the kitchen at his birthday party. He'd been trying to forget it. Get a little perspective. Focus on approaching her gently. That rash act could have cost him her company. He was lucky she hadn't decked him for it. He had already decided she wouldn't slap, she would punch. Somehow he didn't mind.

"What?" she asked. Her eyebrows pulled into a suspicious frown.

"Can I kiss you?" he asked before he could think better of it.

Her mouth opened, but nothing came out, and she closed it. Her dark eyes lingered on his for a long moment, until he wondered if he hadn't made another terrible tactical error. She had said she might if he asked nice. Maybe he should have said please.

"If you like," she whispered.

He leaned down and brushed his lips across hers at first. When she didn't leap away, he put his arm around her waist and pulled her against him. Her hands rested on his shoulders. He brushed his hand through her hair. "I've been wanting to do this all day," he murmured.

"I admire your restraint." Her voice sounded weak and uncertain.

He pressed his lips against hers again. She shivered, molding against him as he teased open her lips. Her mouth felt warm and soft and tasted strangely sweet. Psychological, he decided. The icing on the wedding cake had been hours ago, and he had been imagining and dreaming about how she tasted for weeks based on the kiss at his party. He dragged his mouth along her jaw and she arched her neck to give him greater access. A roar filled his mind, but he didn't know if it was his pulse, his breathing, or his thoughts crumbling to dust.

When he hooked his arm under her knees and lifted her off the floor, she gasped, clinging to him, but didn't protest. He wanted to carry her to her bedroom. To that passionate cocoon she'd created from her bed. The one he hadn't been able to stop thinking about every time he saw her, but didn't want to rush her.

He carried her to the couch so he could feel the length of her next to him.

She lay against the arm of the couch breathing through her open lips, watching him through wide, limpid eyes.

Wanting to draw out the moment, he sat on the edge and brushed her hair off her cheek, contemplating the smooth porcelain texture of her skin before he leaned down to kiss her again.

Spark Of Desire | Charlotte McClain

The phone rang.

"Ignore it. Let the machine get it," Jessica whispered. She pulled him closer.

"Are you sure?" Kevin asked. The phone unnerved him. It reminded him too much of the world outside the apartment.

The phone rang again.

"I'm sure. It's probably somebody from work wanting something stupid." Her voice had a rattled, almost panicked edge to it. Was she reminded of the world outside too? "I should have turned the stupid thing down."

He stretched out next to her, enjoying the way her body fit against his. Her hips curved against his and her shoulder slid under his, leaving her hand free to stroke along his spine. He caressed down her neck and along her shoulder, trailing down the edge of her dress to feel the swell of her breast.

The machine clicked on and her familiar message started. "Hello, it's Jessica. I can't get to the phone so please leave a message."

Kevin hovered over her mouth as she arched toward him.

"Hello, baby girl, it's Dad."

"It's your father," Kevin growled.

"He won't leave a long message." She squeezed her eyes closed.

Kevin shifted away from her. With her father's voice in the room he couldn't continue to touch her. It was almost as bad as having the man standing there.

"You mother told me what you're doing and I wanted to tell you we're both very proud of you. She'll stop leaving her encouraging

Page | 218

messages."

Jessica sighed. "That's good."

Kevin sat up. Seven years younger and somebody's baby girl. Jessica reached for him. She frowned, confused that he was moving away. Didn't it bother her that she'd just been necking on the couch and her father was on the phone? He didn't want to think about what that might imply.

"She also told me about your new boyfriend."

They hadn't been involved until about five minutes ago. Where did her father get the idea they were dating? He stood up, needing to get some distance between them so he could think. Why did she tell her father they were dating?

"You do whatever you need to be happy. Call us if you need anything. Love you, pumpkin. Bye."

You do whatever you need? What did that mean? *Happy hunting?* What had *that* meant? And why all the talk about Kate's ring? All the talk about families and kids? *My mother has just always had my father around to take care of everything.* The pieces were starting to fit together. He paced to the opposite side of the apartment.

"What's the matter?"

He turned around. She had sat up. Her hair hung in disarray, and she was blinking against the light in the room. His first impulse was to take her into his arms and take care of her, but that had been the plan, hadn't it? For her to find someone to take care of her. "What's going on?"

"It sounded to me like my father is going to stop letting my mother leave evil messages on my answering machine. What did it sound like to you?" She brushed her hair back.

"Don't misunderstand the question."

She stood up. "I'm not. The question didn't make sense in the context."

"What's going on here?"

"Where?"

"Between us."

"Starting when you offered to train me two months ago or when you asked to kiss me five minutes ago?"

Kevin's mind creaked into gear. The training. The party. The day he saw her talking to Bartlett. "Was that part of it too?"

"Was what part of what too?"

"The training. Did you plan to use me to get into the department and then decide it wasn't enough? You wanted to trick me into marrying you, too?" The guys were never going to let him hear the end of this. They would all get a huge kick out of how he'd been fooled.

"Marry you? I don't remember that being part of the bargain. Why would I want to marry a man who wants to turn loony on me all the time?" Jessica clenched her fists.

"You're not going to get the chance."

"The chance to what?" she shouted.

"I'm not going to be lured into that trap. Happy hunting, your friend said. Husband hunting, that's what she meant."

"You aren't seriously taking Mindi's word as gospel, are you?" Jessica looked aghast.

"You told your father I was your boyfriend."

She faltered. "I told my mother that," she said. "But I was trying to avoid another conversation at the time and—"

"So you admit you lied once."

"Yes, I lied once. I've lied more than once to my mother. You've never lied? You've never let anyone assume something for the sake of peace and quiet?" Her lower jaw jutted out. "Listen, old boy, I don't need this. I've got a lot going on right now, and more stress I don't have time for."

"Fine. I was just leaving." He started for the door.

"Wait. This is crazy." She tried to step between him and the door, but he'd already brushed past her. "Let's talk about it. We have to calm down."

Kevin jerked the door open. "What's the problem? Your little plan falling apart?"

"I don't have a plan," she wailed.

He slammed the door behind him.

* * * *

Jessica blinked at the closed door. She could still hear Kevin's footsteps pounding down the stairs. If she wanted to, she could catch him.

But he thought she was trying to manipulate him. That she was trying to trap him.

He thought the same thing Mindi had thought.

Scratch that, he thought several degrees worse. Mindi assumed she was working out with him to spent time with him. Kevin thought she was using him to get into the department and trying to trick him into marrying her, too.

Then she'd done that thing to him she always did to her mother. Called him *old boy* just to set him off. She hadn't even known she was doing it until he stormed out.

Outside, his car roar to life. He had stomped on the gas, revving the engine. He must really want to get out of here.

Fine. Go. Jessica swallowed hard. She didn't need any more help. She was going to pass the exam without him and then he'd have to deal with her professionally. Professional didn't require nice.

CHAPTER 13

Kevin walked into the station and took off his sunglasses. He hated wearing sunglasses, but being up most of the night for the past two days had made him sensitive to light. Fortunately, at no time during the last two days had he given in to the temptation to bang his head against a wall or he'd have a raging headache as well.

He would have married her, manipulated or not.

At the moment he wasn't sure he'd been manipulated at all, but since he'd shouted at her, the likelihood she would accept him back was slim to none.

Lew was the only one in the locker room when he went to put away his stuff. He grunted hello and hoped Lew would be too engrossed in whatever he was doing to ask questions.

"Rough night?" Lew asked.

No dice. "You could say that."

Lew studied him while he hung up his spare uniform and started changing into the other one. "Did you have a fight with Jessica?"

Kevin frowned at him. "No," he lied. He winced as he remembered accusing Jessica of lying to him. One guess what she would say to that.

"Really? The last time you were acting like this you were having problems with Jessica." Lew sat down. "So what is the problem?"

As slow as Lew could be, he had the patience of a saint even when everyone around him was losing their cool. Especially when everyone around him was losing their cool. "I guess it is Jessica. It's nothing."

"You look like you haven't slept," Lew pointed out.

Jack walked in, already in uniform. "Ouch, what happened to you?" he asked Kevin.

"Nothing." Kevin buttoned up his shirt. Normally, twenty-four hours with these guys wasn't so bad. Today, he didn't know if he could make it to the other end without killing himself or one of them.

"Oh good, are we picking on Kevin today?" Dan asked. He had his uniform on too. "What did he do?"

"Nothing," Kevin, Jack and Lew answered in unison.

"Oh, it's one of those." Dan hung up his spare uniform. "He looks like he's been run over by a truck, so it's not a minor problem. We'd have heard if a tree fell on his house, so it's not the house. His car is parked out back, so it's not the car. That leaves a hard night partying or a woman. It's Kevin and yesterday was a Sunday."

Kevin threw his clothes in the bottom of his locker, slammed the door, and walked out of the room.

"It's a woman," Dan announced.

"It's Jessica," Lew added.

"Jessica?" Jack followed Kevin out with Dan and Lew right

behind him. They tracked Kevin to the dayroom where they found him attempting to make coffee. Or throw coffee grounds all over the counter, one or the other. "What happened with Jessica?" Jack asked.

The previous shift, which had been discussing plans for their days off until Kevin walked in, turned as a group to watch.

"Nothing." Kevin swung around with the carafe in his hand to fill it, and Lew scooped it away before he smashed it against the faucet.

"Nothing?" Dan asked. "I don't know. It looks like something. Something about this tall woman with dark hair, dark eyes, and a burning desire to be a paramedic. Get it? Burning desire."

"Will you leave me alone? You guys are all like a bunch of vultures with a fresh kill." Kevin walked through them and out of the dayroom.

They trailed him out to the exercise yard behind the station. "Come on, man," Lew said. "Let us help you. You and Jessica looked happy at the wedding."

"If I tell you, will you leave me alone?" Kevin asked.

The three men looked at each other and shrugged. "Maybe," Dan said. "Spill."

Kevin sighed. "I found out a few things about her I don't like."

"Such as?" Dan asked.

"She was trying to manipulate me into marrying her."

Dan burst out laughing, Jack struggled not to, and Lew scratched his head. "Why do you think that?" Jack asked after a labored pause.

"Something her father said when he called. He said she should do whatever she needed to be happy."

"He wasn't perchance talking about the department, was he?" Jack folded his hands together. Dan leaned against the fence wiping tears from his eyes, still giggling.

"Quit laughing. I'm not exactly dog meat," Kevin shouted.

"Okay, okay. I can't imagine someone like her being that manipulative or someone that manipulative going after a firefighter. You aren't bringing down six figures." Dan snorted. "Jack's right. Her father was probably talking about the fire department. Even if he was talking about you, he might just be being overprotective. Daddies are like that about their little girls. Even when their little girls are five foot ten and thirty years old. Trust me, I've had personal experience here."

"When we left her store a friend of hers said 'happy hunting'. You know, husband hunting."

Lew frowned. "If she's got you, why would she be hunting?"

Unfortunately, he'd already had that thought and decided it made sense. "Okay, what about that whole conversation about my grandmother's ring then?"

"*You* started it." Jack folded his arms. "Where did all these conspiracy theories come from, anyway? You know, you haven't been the same since you bought *The X-Files* DVDs."

"There're other things. Things that never made sense to me before." Kevin looked at his feet. One of the things that didn't make sense was why he was standing here trying to convince them of something he didn't believe himself. He had started the conversation about his grandmother's wedding ring, and he'd aided and abetted the conversation about kids. "Okay, maybe I'm an idiot. It doesn't matter. It's too late."

"What did you do?" Jack asked.

"Nothing."

"Nothing?" Dan smiled. "Do we have to go through this again?"

"We had a fight, and I said some pretty bad stuff."

"What did you say?" Jack asked.

"I called her a liar, and I said she was manipulative." Kevin looked around at each of them. They didn't look very sympathetic so far. In their shoes, he doubted he would be sympathetic either. He never had been in the past. "She said I was old."

"Damn, I wish my girlfriends would stop at old when they're cursing me out." Dan smirked. "They usually get a little more, um…colorful."

"Or they hurl things," Jack added.

"True, sometimes objects are thrown," Dan agreed.

"She also said I was a loony," Kevin muttered. That still didn't sting as much as old had, but he felt the need to slander Jessica a little more to keep himself from looking like as much of a fool as he felt.

"If you had started in on me with that stuff you just said, I'd have called you loony too," Lew announced.

"Thank you," Kevin muttered.

Dan draped his arm over Kevin's shoulder. "Listen, I have a lot of experience with this kind of problem. This is what you do. When you get off duty, go to the florist and pick out a big bouquet, preferably with roses. Red ones. The more the better. Take them to her job and apologize in front of all her girlfriends so they know how contrite you are."

"I don't know if I'd go to her job," Jack shook his head. "Try her at home. You have no scene control at her job. People walking in and out all the time. It's too risky."

"Okay, if you're not sure how she'll react, then do it at her house. You know when she'll be home. Get there before she's due home and wait at the door. It works like a charm." Dan nodded.

"I'm not doing it," Kevin growled and tried to walk away, but his friends crowded around him again, blocking his way.

"Why not?" Jack asked. "It's just an apology. You know you were stupid."

"She wouldn't accept my apology. She hates me, and there's no hope." Kevin shook them off and headed inside the station, leaving the other three men standing confused behind him.

* * * *

Jessica walked into Eric's office. "I need next Sunday and Monday off," she announced. She was about to turn around and walk out again, but Eric's nervous squeak stopped her. The last couple of days, employees and customers alike had fled her path. Anyone unlucky enough to talk to her had been happy to escape her snarling presence. For Eric to even whimper at her now boded ill. "What?" she demanded, turning on him.

"It's just— Well, that week's bad." Eric started leafing through his day planner. "See, Mindi has the second through the eighth off, and Sonya asked for Sunday the sixth, too. I have a family reunion on that same day, and I had planned on being gone until the eighth so I had time to drive home, and then Tonya is off the seventh through the twelfth and she can't come in until after six on the sixth. So if you take the sixth and the seventh," Eric coughed. "We won't be covered."

Jessica put her hands on her hips. "I can't open on the day of my oral exam. You scheduled me to work on all my exam days." *Provided I get that far.* She pushed the thought out of her mind. She would get that far, rank high enough to be hired, survive training, and become a paramedic just to spite Kevin Marshall, or die trying.

Eric coughed again. He shrank into his chair. "I guess I could open the seventh. I'll just drive straight home after the reunion instead of staying at my grandmother's house."

"So I still have to work that Sunday."

Eric swallowed and stiffened. "Yes. It's just a swing," he added.

Jessica groaned. She had wanted that day to relax and prepare herself, but when the schedule changed last Monday, she had to work Sunday, Monday, Tuesday, Friday, Saturday, and the written and the oral fell on consecutive Mondays. She'd managed to trade off the thirtieth and thirty-first, but not the sixth and seventh. "All right. I guess I can do the ten to seven." Making it sound like she was doing him a favor. Kevin was right. She was manipulative. Walking out of the office, she caught a glimpse of herself in the window. The new haircut didn't look like her for a second.

Things about her had changed in the last couple of days. Her tension and anger was reflected in the faces of her friends. All her time was spent either studying or working out. When she went in for the usual trim yesterday, she'd gotten her hair cut very short instead. She told herself she'd gotten it cut so it would be out of the way. The boyish cut was because it had looked best with her face.

She couldn't quite convince herself it had nothing to do with the memory of Kevin running his fingers through it. Or that the purpose of the boyish cut was to make her look as masculine as possible. She didn't want to think that she was trying to look and behave as little like a woman as possible.

Even though she knew she was.

* * * *

Jessica picked eggshell out of the mixing bowl. She shouldn't be baking cookies. Right now she should be soaking the aches out of every muscle in her body or sleeping to recover from the physical exam. But if she stopped to do anything, she ended up getting mad at Kevin and mad at herself for wasting energy getting mad at Kevin. Stupid Kevin. She tried to crack the second egg on the side of the bowl without smashing eggshells in the batter again.

The phone rang. Jessica's hand slipped and half the eggshell slithered into the batter. Probably Kevin calling with excellent timing to get her all wound up again. She snatched the phone off the cradle. "Hello?"

"Um, Jessica? What are you doing home?"

Kevin's voice would never get that high. "Who is this?"

"Bobbie."

Jessica grinned. "Bobbie? Really?"

"Yes. What are you doing home?"

"Resting my sore, tired body." Baking cookies and hating Kevin Marshall to distraction. She carried the phone into the kitchen.

"I hear you ranked third so far. That's, well, that's really great. How come you're not out celebrating with Kevin?"

Jessica snorted. "Kevin. We had an argument. He stormed out. I haven't seen him since." She started picked eggshells again, flicking them into the trash.

"When?"

"After the wedding. I don't know, two weeks ago." Something new started to ache in the vicinity of her chest. She'd been so stupid to look forward to that event. Such a big deal to be invited. Going to a wedding always meant something. Ha. What about that nitwit Dan brought? And Lew had brought his sister.

"You're kidding. I thought you two were a couple." If Bobbie followed the pattern of Jessica's other friends, she'd move on to flabbergasted pretty fast. Unless she was like Julie, who'd leaped right past that in favor of outrage. Julie had been all for making a voodoo doll and burning it in the alley behind the store. She'd even hunted down the kit on the sales floor.

"No. According to him, I was trying to manipulate him into marrying me. I was using him to get into the department, and I was willing to lie to do it." She picked up the mixer and surveyed the bowl for any remaining eggshell pieces. Hell, they were calcium. Leave the damn things in there as a nutritional supplement.

"That doesn't sound like Kevin," Bobbie said.

"It sounded just like him when he was snarling at me in my living room." Jessica cringed at the sound of her own voice. No wonder people were avoiding her. She was sweating fury like she was in Hell's best sauna.

"What a jerk," Bobbie howled. Straight for outrage. Jessica thought she should introduce Bobbie to Julie. "He said you were using him to get into the department? What's the point? You didn't need that much help, and there isn't a casting couch anyplace in City Hall. Did he think you were stupid?"

"I don't know." Jessica sighed. She felt comforted by Bobbie's reaction. Having her friends pronounce him a jerk was almost a requirement. Having his friend do it was confirmation. "But I haven't heard from him."

"Have you tried to call him?"

"No," Jessica snapped. "My best friend assumed I was chasing Kevin, too. You're the only one who didn't assume I was doing all this to catch a man." Her voice tightened and she switched on the mixer to cream the dough.

"Nobody else knows how hard it is. And Kevin is cute, too. He never looked at me the way he looks at you."

"Fat lot of good it does." Jessica turned off the mixer to scrape down the sides of the bowl. Bobbie was right. All this training was hard. Really hard. How pathetic did Mindi think she was to go through all this to catch a man? This went way beyond running to catch the bus. "At least I proved I didn't need him." Jessica turned on the mixer again to give the dough a final whirl before adding the dry ingredients.

"Yeah, you did," Bobbie said. "You always seemed like you'd be good together. He'd never have been happy with me."

Jessica pinned the phone between her shoulder and her ear so she use both hands for the cookies. "I don't think he'll be happy with anyone."

"He would have been happy with you if he'd given you half a chance. He's just too stupid to see it."

"The worst part about it is I did everything I could to play it cool. I didn't attack him, I didn't lure him. I didn't do anything. He kissed me in the kitchen on his birthday, and he asked to kiss me when he was here after the wedding. He was the one who wanted to keep it quiet." Jessica sneered despite that fact that no one would see her. He'd stood in her dining room and asked if he could kiss her. Very gentlemanly and sweet.

Just a few minutes before he went insane.

"Why did he want to keep it quiet?"

"At his birthday party he said something about the department not wanting couples and that it might mess up my ranking. I guess it doesn't matter now." Jessica ground her teeth, scraping off the beaters with her fingers. They hadn't paid any attention to each other until they couldn't have one another. He'd been shopping there for years. How many times had they talked without him ever noticing her? What if she stayed at the bookstore? Would he like her better then? Would they have a chance? Would she be miserable without him or without the job? Not that she seemed to have any say in the matter.

"You have your oral on Monday, right?"

"I find out tomorrow what time."

"Good. Let me know. I'll take you out for a congratulatory dinner if Kevin's too much of a pig to do it."

"You don't have to." Jessica tore open the bag of chocolate chips and dumped them in the dough. Would anybody congratulate her when she passed? Would anybody be that excited? Bobbie sounded more determined than enthusiastic.

"Of course I don't have to. I want to. I'll talk to you later, okay?"

"Okay. Bye," Jessica muttered. Kevin had dumped her on Bobbie, and now Bobbie felt required to see this through. At least Bobbie would have a little class about this if Kevin couldn't.

"Bye."

Jessica took the phone back to the dining room. When she went back to the kitchen, she looked at the bowl of cookie dough, deciding whether or not to just eat it. With the way her luck had been running she'd end up in the hospital with salmonella poisoning from the raw eggs and miss the oral exam. Then she'd never be able to glare at Kevin from inside the department. Stupid Kevin.

* * * *

Everyone in the living room jumped when the pounding started at the door. Jack, Dan and Lew had been brave enough to show up for poker, but they had decided to call the game due to Kevin's inability to be civil. To be honest, all three of them had only come out of loyalty and not to spend time with Kevin. For four shifts in a row he'd been impossible to work with and impossible to avoid, and he knew it. He didn't deserve any of them. Somebody should be kicking his ass from here to the second Monday of next month.

Kevin opened the door and as he did, Bobbie pushed into the living room.

"You fool," she bellowed at Kevin. She looked even worse for wear than Kevin did. If they hadn't known her as well as they all did, they would have thought she was drunk. Her hair sprang out at odd angles and her eyes were red-rimmed and puffy.

"Hello to you too, Bobbie," Kevin quipped, backing up a couple of paces.

"Don't get smart with me." She poked him in the chest. "You know, Marshall, I used to think you were the greatest. You were smart, and you were good-looking, and you were fun to be with. I wanted you in the worst way. You're a..." Her voice deteriorated into sputtering.

"Bobbie, what is wrong with you?" Kevin tried to keep his voice calm, but if Bobbie couldn't manage to vent in English, he worried she might start throwing things. He might be getting that ass-kicking after all. Dan and Jack were sitting up, ready to jump if he needed them. Lew had already stood and come around the coffee table. At least only those three were here to witness this.

"Wrong with me?" She sobbed. Tears flooded out of her blue eyes. "You jerk."

He reached onto the coffee table and picked up a box of Kleenex. "Here." He held it out.

She swatted the box out of his hands. It sailed across the room into the dining room, bounced off the table and into the wall.

Dan muttered an awed curse. Jack stood up.

"What *is* wrong with me, huh? I was here first. I tried to be what you wanted. But you never even looked at me. Then you found her." Bobbie wiped her nose on her sleeve. "You found her, and you couldn't keep your hands off her."

"Her?" Kevin stammered.

"Jessica," Bobbie shouted. "I saw you kissing her at your party. You were practically having sex against the wall in the kitchen."

Kevin bit his lip. He had thought that was just between him and Jessica, but there was a clear line of sight between her front door and kitchen.

And Bobbie had disappeared before the party ended.

Dan whistled.

Bobbie turned on him. "You just shut up." She whirled back around and shoved Kevin back a step. "You ignored me for three years, and you can't keep your hands off her for three weeks?"

"Bobbie, it's not that there's something wrong with you." Kevin searched for an acceptable answer. It wasn't anything wrong with her, it was something right with Jessica.

"You know what the worst part about this is? I really like her. She's nice and fun. She's the only friend I have who's a girl and I couldn't even be friends with her because of you." Bobbie pounded on his chest with her fists. Not little girly flailing, either, but serious body blows that would leave bruises.

"Ow, hey!" Kevin put his arms up in front of him to block her blows. "Bobbie, stop it."

Jack grabbed one arm and Lew got the other. They managed to drag her back a step, but she struggled out of their grip, barely acknowledging them. "Do you know how she's ranking? She's third. She tied for first on the written and dropped to third after the physical." Bobbie wiped the tears off her face with her hands. "She's really good. And you dumped her."

"I didn't dump her."

"You liar. I talked to her."

Kevin paled. He could imagine the conversation. Two women who hated him. Both of whom he would be working with soon. Dead things in his locker were going to be the least of his problems. "I'm sure it didn't happen quite the way she said it did."

"She said you called her a liar and accused her of trying to trick you into marrying her."

Kevin sucked his teeth. "Okay, it did happen like that. Listen, I screwed up. It happens. She's better off without me."

"You idiot. She's perfect for you." Bobbie sobbed and rubbed her eye with the heel of her hand. "She's perfect, and it's not fair." She stormed out the door, slamming it behind her and cracking one of the panes.

"We can't let her drive home like that," Dan said. He looked at Kevin.

"I don't think she wants to see me." Kevin shook his head.

Jack shifted. "She hits. I don't want to go out there. Crying, I'm trained on, hitting is different."

"I'll go." Lew walked out the front door.

"You certainly have a way with women. I didn't know you were that hot and heavy with Jessica," Dan said, retrieving the Kleenex box from the dining room. It was more egg-shaped than rectangular now.

"I wasn't that hot and heavy with Jessica. Bobbie is blowing it out of proportion."

"I don't know." Jack sat down on the edge of the couch. "Bobbie's pretty reliable about that stuff even when she's hysterical, and you did have icing on your back."

Kevin sneered at Jack. "Thank you for the detail."

"Icing on your back?" Dan laughed. "Will you please just apologize to her? I mean Jessica. Bobbie might kill you if you get too close to her right now."

"She wouldn't accept it either. You heard Bobbie. She hates me now." Kevin hunched onto the easy chair and clasped his hands around the back of his neck. He missed Jessica with a gnawing ache that never left. At night he lay awake thinking about going over to her house, hoping her defenses would be down at three in the morning. Last week he'd called the bookstore with bogus questions hoping she would answer the phone so he could hear her voice. The only bright spots in the week had been when her ranking came back for the written and the physical. He'd entertained the idea of sending her flowers as congratulations and signing them from the station, but he thought she would see through it and torch them in his driveway.

"Man, she is upset. I'm soaked." Lew stopped inside the door, brushing a damp spot on his shirt. "He still won't apologize, will he?"

"Look, you're gonna have to move on if you won't talk to her." Jack sat on the couch. "There's an Irish singer at the bookstore on Sunday. Kate and I were going to go. Why don't you come with us? She doesn't work Sundays, does she?"

Kevin groaned. Jessica didn't work Sundays, but the rest of the staff knew him and probably knew what he'd done. He hadn't been greeted warmly last time he stopped in. Without Jessica, he now had to find a new favorite hangout too. "I don't think that's a good idea."

"I think it's a great idea," Dan said. "You stay in this house much more and you're going to mold. Who knows, maybe the guitar player will whack you upside the head with his guitar and knock some sense into you. I hope he has one of those solid body electrics."

"You are all so helpful." He closed his eyes. Tears burned behind them. He didn't want to cry in front of these guys, not over a woman. He stood up. "I'll think about it. Maybe I'll just meet you there." He retreated upstairs and locked himself in the bathroom until the sensation passed.

CHAPTER 14

Kevin drove past the front doors of the store hoping the truck he'd seen hadn't been Jack's, but it was. Jack and Kate loitered near the front doors waiting, and both looked up when he passed the doors. If he didn't go in now, he'd never hear the end of it. Jack had managed to enlist the help of everyone on his shift to harass him into this night out. They were all tired of his moodiness. Of course, the parking lot was packed. Quite normal for a hot, humid Sunday night. Kevin found a spot in front of the computer store, not far from where he'd jump started Kate's car back in June.

Jessica. Kate had been talking to Jessica inside when he offered to jump the battery for her. He remembered looking at Jessica and thinking she seemed very together. Very confident. There had been something marvelously attractive about it. A momentary insight he hadn't remembered until now.

God, he missed her.

He missed the sound of her voice and the ring of her laugh. The way she smelled and the way she moved. The way her hair felt on his fingers and the way her lips tasted.

He really missed the way her lips tasted.

But she hated him and she had every right to. No apology would ever be enough. He'd seen something in her eyes. A flash of betrayal. Whatever he'd said, it had been exactly wrong. He couldn't remember what he'd said now anyway. How could he apologize when he didn't know what to apologize for?

He locked up his car and went inside.

"You made it." Jack grinned. "Congratulations. It's the first step to becoming a bearable member of society again."

Kate elbowed Jack without looking up from the book she held open in her hands. "Be nice."

"This is nice." Jack put his arm around her shoulders. "Come on, honey. You can bring the book with you."

"I don't want to mess up the display. I just want to look." She turned a page and kept reading.

Kevin glanced around. All the employees were staring daggers at him. He was getting paranoid now.

"Bring it with you. I'll buy it for you," Jack was saying.

"I know you will, but I don't want to mess up their nice table."

"Oh, look who's here."

Kevin tried not to cringe when he turned around.

Jessica stood behind him with her arms folded and her lips pursed. She'd cut her hair short. Really, really short. Kevin remembered his mother cutting his hair that way when he was about six. Bangs straight across his eyebrows, short over the ears, shaved up the neck.

"Congratulations on your ranking." Jack stepped between them and held out his hand.

"Thank you," she said. She shook Jack's hand and then folded her arms again before Kevin had a chance to move. "Are you here for the performer in the coffee bar?"

"Yes. Do you know if he's any good?" Kate asked. She put her book down.

"He's the husband of the magazine clerk. He's no professional, but he won't play *Danny Boy*. I know that will please Kevin." Her lips curled into a cruel smirk. Instead of chilling him, the expression reminded him what great lips she had.

Kevin wondered how she would react if he grabbed her and kissed her. With that look on her face, she might bite him. But he wanted to kiss her. He wanted to touch her. Maybe she would accept an apology. Maybe if he begged for forgiveness here in full sight of all her friends, she would accept him back at least as a friend. Maybe given time she would—

"Here. I didn't bring a gift to your wedding, so why don't you each have a drink on the house?" Jessica held out two business cards to Jack. Turning to Kevin, her face darkened. "I suppose I can't leave you out. Even though you seem to think I'm the world's stupidest gold digger." She slapped a card into the middle of his chest.

The imprint of her hand sank through his skin and bone, clenching around his heart and stopping it. He reached up to try to catch her hand, but ended up with only the card.

"Here I am, surrounded daily by doctors, lawyers, and CEOs, and who do I decide to make my gravy train? A city employee. Yeah, you must think I'm pretty stupid." She grimaced at Jack and Kate. "I hope you enjoy the show. Although, you might be seeing more of me. Good night." She spun on her heel and walked out the door.

"Oh my." Kate gasped. "That was ugly."

"If I didn't know better I'd think that *you might be seeing more of me* was a threat." Jack looked at Kevin. "She hates you. If I were you, when she makes paramedic, I'd try really hard not to get hurt."

Kevin felt too numb for any of it to sink in. "She cut her hair," he said.

"What?" Jack asked.

"She cut her hair," Kevin repeated.

Kate looked out the doors. Jessica had already reached the opposite side of the parking lot. "She did, didn't she? That's not a requirement?"

"No, women can have shoulder-length hair. She butched her hair off, though. You don't think it's because of you, do you?" Jack asked.

Kevin didn't answer. Couldn't answer. He watched Jessica start up her car and drive away.

"Come on. Let's go sit down." Jack reached for Kevin's arm. Kate hooked hers through the other side and between them they towed him to the coffee bar. They got into line, and Jack and Kate started discussing the menu. Kevin looked at the card in his hand. He'd thought having Bobbie attack him in his living room had been traumatic, but it barely registered next to this. The card was pretty standard. Business-card size. Free-drink-of-your-choice wording. Jessica had written her initials in the upper left-hand corner. He didn't want to give it up. Her initials on this card were all he had.

"The usual?" the annoyed voice on the other side of the counter asked.

Kevin looked up. The woman glaring at him from behind the counter only worked in the espresso bar. He'd seen her at the party and around the neighborhood too. "Usual?"

"Large hot cocoa, shot of caramel." She didn't smile. She'd always smiled at him before Jessica had turned the entire staff against him.

"Sure. That's fine."

She reached across the counter and snatched the card out of his hand. Then she turned away and started making his drink.

"Hot chocolate? Are you nuts? It's ninety degrees outside," Jack said.

Kate wrapped her arms around herself. "It feels like it's sixty-five in here."

"That's what I usually get." Kevin looked at the menu board. For some reason he couldn't read it. In the corner of the café, the musician was setting up. He had two guitars with him. Behind him stood the magazine clerk with a third guitar in her hands. For a moment when she caught sight of him, she seemed confused, then she glared.

"Here." The counter woman set the drink in the center of the counter. "I didn't spit in it, if you're wondering, but I didn't do you any favors either. Like Jessica says, professional doesn't require nice." She turned to Jack and Kate, smiling. "Now what can I get for you?"

Kevin found a table large enough for the three of them. Jessica had gotten to the whole staff. If he couldn't make his friends understand he'd done something unforgivable, how could he explain to hers that he was sorry?

"Hey, your magazine is in."

Kevin looked up. The magazine clerk had fixed him with a glare from two tables away. Her husband looked up, confused.

"What?" Kevin asked.

"Your magazine. It came in Monday. You can find it yourself." She turned back to her husband and snapped something at him before she walked toward the coffee bar counter. Her husband caught Kevin's eye and shrugged before he went back to work getting himself set up.

"They all hate me," Kevin whispered when Kate sat down.

"They don't all hate you." She patted his hand. "They're being loyal. Nobody understands why you won't try to talk to her."

"Because it's a waste of time. She wouldn't listen to me. She has no reason to." Kevin stared at the whipped cream dissolving on his hot cocoa. Hot cocoa. It was ninety degrees outside and he had a cold spot in the middle of his chest that hot cocoa was not going to fix.

Kate's small fingers closed around his wrist. He met her eyes. "It's okay to be afraid. I don't have any statistics for you, but I'm pretty sure everyone is afraid at one point or another that the person they love doesn't love them back. All we usually need to fix it is confirmation."

Jack set a mug in front of Kate. "Hot chocolate. I can't believe you two. It's broiling outside." He slipped into his chair. "Am I interrupting something?"

"No." Kate drew her hand back across the table. "Just talking. So he's the magazine clerk's husband? Wasn't he at your birthday party, Kevin?"

Kevin studied the table top. Confirmation. Jack had given Kate confirmation that he loved her. He'd wanted to quit the department for her. Kate had given Jack confirmation by talking him out of it. Did Jessica want that? Would she accept an apology if he swore he loved her?

The guitar player fiddled with his microphone. "Hello, I'm Aron McGraw. The first song I'm going to play tonight is *Down by the Sallee Gardens.*"

He's no professional, but he won't play Danny Boy. That should please Kevin. Her words echoed in his mind. They had never talked much about music. Once he'd mentioned not liking the canned Irish-American music everyone assumed he should. She hadn't played any of it at his party, and she'd bought Guinness for him. Why had she paid so much attention to his preferences?

Why hadn't he paid attention to hers?

He wasn't even sure what he'd said that had hurt her so much.

Except for that gold digger comment. He'd accused her of trying to trick him into marrying her. For a few moments, two weeks ago, he'd believed she was capable of using him as a means to an end and told her so. What had he been thinking?

What had she thought?

He had fallen in love with her. He wanted to see her succeed, and he wanted to be with her when she did. But he'd accused her of not being in love with him. Of worse than that. Of using the love she'd cultivated against him. How was he supposed to fix that?

The singer launched into another song.

Kevin picked up his drink. The whipped cream had melted, leaving a milky film on the surface. He could still feel where she touched his chest. How could he let someone who affected him like that go? He looked at Jack and Kate.

They seemed engrossed in the song, but they were disappointed in him. Jack had his hand lying over Kate's, and she leaned toward him. When he first met Jessica, he'd tried to convince himself he wasn't in love with her. That he had only wanted what Jack had, that he'd wanted stability and any handy woman would do.

Jessica just happened to come with added drive and ability. He convinced himself that he liked her the same way he liked Bobbie or Dan. Liked her as a potential crew member.

Then he tasted frosting on her lips.

"Okay, this next song is actually by Andy M. Stewart. It has a sing-along chorus if you'd like to join in. You'll pick it up pretty fast. The song is called *Take Her in Your Arms*."

Kevin sipped his drink. It was getting cold. Any other day he'd have asked the staff to heat it up for him again, but not today.

Jack laughed. "That sounds like you."

Kevin looked up. He'd been too busy thinking to hear a word, but he knew the song well enough. Jessica had played it at his party. The man in the song was too lovesick to even shave, and although Jessica had never appeared painted and scented as the woman in the song did, it had still been enough to drive this man demented. Yes, he knew if someone polled the guys at the station, *demented* would be the description of choice.

Kevin remembered the chorus as the singer reached it. It was all about how hold a woman and telling her you loved her could fix everything.

He'd never told her he loved her. Maybe, as Kate said, she just needed confirmation.

It seemed too easy. But if he held her tight enough she wouldn't be able to hit him until he'd explained himself.

He jumped out of his seat. "I gotta go."

By the time he got to his car, he'd decided she wouldn't believe a heartfelt apology. He had to do something to prove what he said. This had gone on too long and he'd been too cruel. She needed physical confirmation.

He went home.

The house sounded empty. It sounded like this every time he walked in, but today his footsteps echoed as he ran up the stairs two at a time. He kept the ring in his underwear drawer. Yanking open the drawer, he reached in the front left corner.

And it wasn't there.

The whole plan thus far depended on that ring.

Groping along the side of the drawer, he found nothing, so he started across the front. Still nothing. He hadn't had it out for years. When he'd moved into the house last year, he hadn't even emptied the drawers, they'd pulled them out and reassembled the dresser once they got it inside.

He pulled the drawer out and dumped it on the floor.

The ring box tumbled off the top of the heap. He scooped it up and opened it. The ring itself wasn't much to look at. It needed polishing and had a couple of scratches. His great-grandmother had worn it until his grandparents married before they emigrated, and his grandmother had worn it until her death when she willed it to him. Now, maybe, it would gain him the forgiveness he needed and the woman who would give him a fifth generation to hand it down to.

He stuffed it in his pocket and ran out the door, barely remembering to lock the house behind him.

* * * *

Jessica opened the front door and left it open, locking the screen door to help cool off the apartment. She'd been considering staying to watch Julie's husband until she noticed Jack and Kate lingering near the front doors. That would only mean one thing. If she had a little more class, she'd have been able to hide out in the office until they were ensconced in the coffee bar.

Changing into shorts, Jessica dropped onto the couch with her chenille afghan wrapped around her shoulders. Without the afghan she'd be twice as cool, but she needed to be hugged by something, even if it was her own afghan.

She didn't have that much class. She'd gone out hoping for the confrontation. Hoping he'd say something.

He hadn't. The entire time she'd been standing right in front of him by the new hardcover table, he'd stood stunned and saying nothing. It hadn't exactly been a triumph all around. Jessica stared at the movie she'd popped in when she came home. She didn't even remember what she'd put on. Her ranking should make her happy. Her parents had sent flowers to prove how proud they were. Her father was, anyway. Her mother hadn't written out the card. The flowers sat on the table. At work they'd gotten her a cake. Vanilla. Sonya hadn't saved her the frosting roses.

What were Sonya and Julie doing? She almost felt sorry for Kevin trapped in a room with them, even a room as big as the store. Both of them had been furious and neither had much subtlety.

She'd thought she'd steeled herself to have him drop her as soon as she didn't need him anymore.

But she hadn't. No one could have been prepared for his sudden wild accusations. Not after the way he'd touched her and kissed her. Acted like he wanted her. Some harpy in his past must have saddled him with a fear of women that she now had to pay for. Closing her eyes, she tried to clear her mind. No time to worry about this now. Tomorrow was the oral exam. She had to focus on the oral exam.

A car pulled into the parking area. It didn't alarm her until she heard footsteps on her stairs. She cringed into the corner of the couch. At best, it was a friend coming to make sure she hadn't hung herself from grief. At worst, it was Kevin.

"Jessica? Can I talk to you?"

Worst it was. Kevin couldn't see her from the door. If she didn't move off the couch, he might think she'd stepped out and left the door open. Pigs might fly, too.

"Jessica, I know you're in there. I really need to talk to you."

She heard a small clang from the door. Either he'd leaned his hand or his head on it. Tears formed on her eyelashes. Would it be so bad to open the door? Even if he thought she was only with him because of money or connections or something? She had no idea what he thought he had that was so valuable, and it wouldn't matter when he realized he didn't love her and dumped her.

Why did she always look ahead to see the end of the relationship?

"Jessica, will you please listen to me?" He sighed. "I'm sorry. You can't imagine how sorry I am. I'm a fool, and I got cold feet."

Cold feet from what? He might not know it, but she hadn't planned to go all the way that day. She had been prepared to pull him up short. Why would he have cold feet from the thought of having sex, anyway? He was a guy. Weren't they always up for sex?

"I can stay out here all night. You have to come out sometime. You have to be downtown at ten-thirty, so you're going to have to leave the house by ten and, knowing you, you'll leave at nine-thirty to allow for Los Angeles-style traffic in Arden."

Jessica bit her lip. He'd been paying attention. Her theory had always been, why be on time when you can be annoyingly early. Did it mean that he'd noticed something about her?

"Jessica, I wish I could tell you why I stormed out on you two weeks ago."

His voice was now coming through the window. That meant he'd moved down the stairs to the third step and was leaning toward it. Did he realize what a spectacle he was making of himself, talking to a window? What if she'd been taking a bath? She might have no idea he was out there. She pressed her hand against the wall, wallowing in the idea that he was on the other side of it.

"Jessica, I love you. If you'd let me in, I'd hold you and try to tell you how much, but I don't think I know the words." His voice had dropped to that low rumble that made her ache all over. "I brought something I want to give you that might prove how much I love you. I figured after the way I acted you wouldn't believe me if I told you the moon was made of rock."

No, I wouldn't. But I would want to.

"I brought you my grandmother's wedding ring. I thought maybe when the time came we could give it to our oldest. Or we could give it to my sister's oldest boy. He's my oldest nephew. You never said if you wanted to have kids. I think I was monopolizing the conversation then. I'm sorry for that, too."

Jessica sat up. She hesitated to believe he might be asking what she thought he was asking. Although, it would explain the cold feet comment. She hopped off the couch and hurried to the door. The screen door latch stuck for a moment and by the time she got it open, he'd turned and come up one step. Jessica stopped and stared at him, trying to get some order out of her thoughts. "Did you just propose to me?"

"I—yes." He looked doubtful. "I guess you have to backward-engineer a little to get there, but that's what I meant."

"No." Jessica's throat closed, but after the word was out. Her heart would have leaped into his arms shouting *yes*, but her mind still remembered the sting of being called a liar and a gold digger.

"No?" Kevin repeated. He looked down at his hand and she realized he had the ring in his palm. "Is there anything I can do to change your mind?"

CHAPTER 15

Jessica pulled the afghan tighter around her shoulders. "I can't live with someone who thinks what you think about me."

Kevin reached across the stairs to grip the banister as if he needed the support. "I don't believe that. You aren't a gold digger and if you were, you're digging in a copper mine. I just got scared. I panicked. And I'm sorry."

Jessica lifted her chin. "What about being a liar?"

"I have been lying since I met you. Lying to myself, to my friends, to everyone, because I was afraid you couldn't love an old man like me."

Jessica rolled her eyes. "You aren't that old. My father is twelve years older than my mother."

"Does that mean you could be in love with me?"

Jessica swallowed. He looked desperate. If she told him the truth, how far out of hand could it get? He had proposed, but would he still love her when she didn't need him? Would she end up in a sham marriage he wouldn't end because of some point of pride, and she wouldn't end because she was weak and craved any little bit of him he would allow? "Don't get any ideas."

"I'm looking for small victories right now. I'll take anything I can get." He put one foot on the step above him, and she moved back a step. "Are you cold?"

"No."

"Then why are you wrapped up in a blanket?"

Jessica dug her fingers into the afghan. She wouldn't have given it up now for any reason. It was a shield. "After tomorrow I'll be a full-fledged member of the department. I won't need your help anymore."

"So?"

"So, you might be less interested in me when I don't need you. I'm not exactly clingy." She almost added *despite the fact that I am clinging to an afghan on a hot night.*

Kevin laughed. "Believe me, that's the last thing I want in a wife."

Jessica reached behind her for the door. When he said *wife*, some of the strength went out of her knees. "How can I believe you now? When you kicked me to the curb and ignored me for two weeks?" she wailed.

"Isn't this enough? It's the most valuable thing I have to offer." He held out the ring.

She looked at it balanced between his fingers. The porch light glinted off it. It wasn't round anymore. Heavy wear left it oblong and thin along the sides. No one would call it beautiful, but it was his great-grandmother's wedding ring. He hadn't meant what he'd said before. What if he did still want her when she didn't need him? What if he wanted her more?

"Jessica," he said, "will you please marry me?"

"Yes," she answered.

Leaping up the last two steps, he pulled her into his arms. He pressed his face against her neck. "I wanted to talk to you, but I thought you hated me. You had every right to hate me. Bobbie was right. I am an idiot."

"Bobbie?"

Kevin brushed his fingers through the little hair she had. "Bobbie came over to my house last week to ream me out for breaking up with you." He kissed her forehead. "I missed you."

Jessica leaned against him. Her whole body still trembled with the tension she'd been carrying around for two weeks. "Why don't we go in the house? We're letting all the bugs in."

Kevin scooped her off the ground and carried her through the door.

"What did you do that for?" Jessica asked when he put her down inside.

"Practice. I have to be ready for after we get married. Here, let me have your hand." He sounded almost giddy.

Jessica held out her hand and he slid the ring onto it. "It's way too big," she pointed out. "Do you really want me to wear it?"

"Maybe not to work." Cupping her face in his hands he leaned down and kissed her.

Jessica sagged into his embrace. The afghan slipped off her shoulders and dropped to the floor behind her. She wrapped her arms around his neck so she wouldn't slide to the floor with it. It felt so good to be in his embrace again. One hand around her waist, he stroked across her shoulders and back with the other. She moaned when he pulled away from her lips to kiss her neck. A surge of emotion welled up from her belly, a heady cocktail of nerves and desire. His hand reached under her shirt, and she shivered.

"Jessica," he whispered. He started to step back.

"No," she whimpered. She tightened her grip on him, needing to be touching him right now, needing contact.

"I'm not going anywhere." He reached back and untangled her from his neck. Closing his eyes he held her hands against his face, breathing deeply. "I won't go anywhere, I promise."

She watched him, still shivering. For a long moment he kept her hands against his cheeks before he opened his eyes again, searching her eyes until her breath became short. He kissed her hands. She wanted to say something, but she couldn't think of what. What would he think if she asked him to stay the night? Would she even be able to form the sentence? *Have sex* sounded juvenile and *make love* flowery. In books and movies, the hero and heroine fell into bed, and it seemed perfectly acceptable. At least all the ones she could remember right now. Memory seemed to have deserted her along with her voice. But in a powerful and inarticulate way, she wanted to feel him against her and within her.

Kevin brushed his fingers through her hair. His hands trembled, she noticed. She had worked him over when she didn't answer the door. Telling him no the first time he proposed hadn't helped either. "I'm sorry," she said.

"For what?"

Jessica licked her lips. Now that she thought about it for a moment there were a couple of things. For not answering the door. For telling him no the first time he asked her to marry him. For being so nasty at the store. She shook her head because her voice abandoned her again. The ring hung around her finger, reminding her of its presence. "Can you stay?"

"Stay?"

"The night?"

He looked baffled, as if he hadn't planned that far ahead.

Or maybe he hadn't planned to get this far, she thought. He might have assumed she would turn him down. Bitting her lip, she said, "I mean, if you're comfortable with that."

He glanced at the living room, grinning. "Almost too comfortable. We should close the front door."

"Go ahead. I'll meet you in the bedroom." Turning away from him, she walked away, listening to him close the door and lock it. She turned on one lamp on the dresser, but otherwise left the room in darkness. The fan in the bedroom window drew the cool night into the room, creating a quiet hum. The coverlet hung over the foot of the bed where she had draped it a few weeks ago when the heat became too much at night. Kevin walked around in the other room, turning off the television. Should she change into lingerie or not? She considered the idea nervously. That was the fantasy and she had a few pieces, but he was already standing in the doorway. She smiled. "Here we are."

"Here we are," he repeated. He drew a ragged breath. "I didn't bring any protection."

"I take birth control," Jessica said. A slow, amazed smile crept across his face. Delicious tension built across her skin. He would be touching her soon.

He moved across the room faster than she expected. This time she didn't have time to pull back like she had in the kitchen that day long ago. His hands slid around her waist and up under her shirt in one fluid motion, dragging his callused fingers across her skin. Lifting the shirt over her head, he pressed his hot mouth against her shoulder. The electric contact skimmed across her skin until the connection closed at the apex of her thighs. Her knees gave, and she toppled over backward, pulling him down on top of her. His mouth covered hers, pillaging her until she couldn't think anymore. He pressed her into the mattress with his heavy and hard body, his manhood urging against her. For an instant she feared she might be too small to accommodate him. Strange thought. That anything of hers might ever be too small. But her body seemed to strain for him, opening, blooming. The back of her bra opened.

Wanting to feel his skin pressed against hers, she tugged at his shirt. He had to roll off her to get out of the shirt, and she pulled off her bra. For a moment he lay next to her, admiring her. The cool air from the fan whispered across her skin, teasing her already deliciously tense nipples. She stared at him, wanting to ask him to touch her or kiss her or something. Something more than just lie there looking at her, but she couldn't find the words. She couldn't find any words. When she reached toward him, he caught her wrist and pushed it back onto the bed beside her so she lay helplessly, watching him look at her.

Kevin traced his coarse fingers down her neck, across her collarbone and down her side to the underside of her left breast.

Jessica's breath caught in her throat. Her whole body ached with a need she couldn't describe. She closed her eyes and focused on the sensation of his hand cupping her breast.

"You're going to be my wife," he murmured, his mouth brushing her temple.

She shuddered. That little word had gained power over her in the last fifteen minutes, leaving her defenseless. He leaned against her so she could feel the length of his body pressed along hers.

"My beautiful wife." He shifted up to his hands and knees.

He loomed over her until her eyes focused on his before he moved again. Then he pounced, covering her bare skin with kisses, nuzzling under her breasts and teasing his tongue around her belly button. Her body throbbed under the assault. She writhed under his touch, arching toward him, moaning for more while her body ached with near pain. Squeezing her eyes closed, she reveled in the feel of his mouth and his hands on her bare skin.

When he reached the waistband of her shorts he sat back, breathing hard. His fingers played around the edge, but didn't attempt to move under the fabric. Jessica opened her eyes to look at him. If she'd had words she would have begged him to stop or continue, but not to stall here. Her belly coiled and twisted under the light, teasing touch of his fingers.

Moonlight fell across him, showing her the focused expression on his face. He studied her every helpless motion as if he were waiting for some signal. She could see his broad chest clearly defined and wanted to touch it, but didn't think she had the strength to reach for him. Clenching the sheet with her sweaty hands, she heard it pop up from the corners of the bed. As she met his eyes, she felt his hand slide under the waistband of her shorts. Her body crested in a paroxysm of desire. She felt wrung out and worn, but a knife edge of desire still cut through her.

Kevin stood up to slide his jeans over his hips. "You smell wonderful, Jessica," he moaned. "You taste wonderful." He teased his tongue along her throat. "I love you."

Jessica moaned in response and felt him enter her. She wanted to tell him she loved him, too, but her body was more concerned with the feeling of him inside her to interest itself with language. Her hips shifted, rising to meet him.

"You've never done this before," he said, drawing himself out.

Shaking her head, she reached for him before he slipped away. He eased in again, and a sharp pain startled a cry from her. He covered her mouth with his, wrapping his arms around her shoulders. The pain disappeared under the sensation of him moving deep inside her and the glimmer of breeze across their sweaty bodies. Another crest took her, blotting out everything and taking another cry from her. An instant or an hour later she felt him roll off her. She felt more spent now than she had after the physical exam.

But the physical exam hadn't left her with this sense of shuddering relaxation and deep completion. She didn't even have the strength to keep him from moving away from her.

"I'm sorry," she said when she had the strength to form thought again.

Kevin had propped himself up on his elbow next to her. "Sorry about what?"

"I should have told you I was a virgin." She decided the darkness was a good thing. He couldn't see her blush this way.

"Don't be sorry. I would have done things differently if I had known, but it doesn't matter now."

The low thrum of his voice hummed along her overworked nerves. She moaned.

He shifted, chuckling. "You're going to make it easy to seduce you."

"As long as I can keep you interested, we'll be fine." She reached over, running her fingers through the coarse black hair on his chest.

He caught her hand. "I don't think you'll have a problem."

* * * *

Kevin woke up in the watery pre-dawn light. For a moment he couldn't place where he was. Not home, not the station. Then he remembered last night when Jessica had given him three shocks in the space of an hour, each of which should have killed him. First, she'd said no when he asked her to marry him. He'd tried to convince himself she might say no on the drive over, but he didn't seem to have heard himself. No man expects a woman to say no when he asks her to marry him. Then she'd asked him to stay the night. Despite his apparent conviction that she would agree to marry him, he hadn't expected to get through her door, let alone into her bed.

Where, third, he'd realized she was a virgin.

If he'd known that before, he wouldn't have teased her so long, would have moved more carefully. But how could he have guessed? Most women at her age weren't, but then most women didn't want to be firefighters. He smiled, deciding he'd managed to find himself his own personal enigma so he could spend the rest of his life trying to figure her out.

Stretched out on her stomach, she had **one arm** crooked under her pillow and the other hanging off the side of the bed. He hoped she didn't sleep that way all the time because if she did, the guys she ended up working with were going to use it against her. Last night they hadn't left the bedroom. They hadn't left the bed. The light on the dresser still burned. They had lain curled together in her bed, talking a little and floating in their own euphoria. When she moved into his house, they would sleep in her bed, and she should move in soon. Within days, if possible.

Lightly he touched her shoulder. Turning toward the touch, she sighed in her sleep. He caressed along her hip, feeling her warm satin skin with his palm.

She twisted around, her eyes drowsing open. "Good morning." Her hands teased down his sides, shifting him on top of her. "I love you," she whispered.

Immersed in a warm salty sea, he moved inside her, half aware of what was happening. She arched, exposing her throat and pressing her heavy breasts against him. Her tension twisted through him until her body tightened and her mouth formed a taut, silent O. He squeezed his eyes closed and buried his face against her neck as his own climax took him.

She stroked her fingers through his hair as he brought his breathing back under control. "You learn fast," he murmured.

"I thought you would have noticed that by now." Her voice was low and sultry. "You know, you didn't have to propose to get me into bed. You could have managed that with a sincere and garbled apology."

"I had to propose if I wanted to be doing this when we're a hundred and two." Kevin realized that that's what he'd wanted all along. He'd wanted the right to wake up next to her every morning for the rest of his life. Two mornings in three until retirement. Well, one morning in three once she got her assignment. That would be enough.

She laughed. "I'll be a hundred and two, you'll be a hundred and nine."

He caressed her cheek. "At that point, I don't think it'll matter."

"I don't think it matters now."

He kissed her shoulder. "We should get up."

"Why? I don't have to be downtown for hours." She stretched and her body moved against his.

Why hadn't he liked full-sized women? There had been some reason. He seemed to remember thinking her inappropriate because she was too big. Whatever it was, it had been, as Jack so delicately put it, an excuse.

"Well, if you're going to lie there awestruck and not entertaining me, I'm going to take a shower." She swung her legs off the side of the bed and sat up. "I don't think I need the run this morning. I've had enough exercise."

"I have one question. Why were you on birth control?"

Jessica shrugged. "I wanted to be prepared in case I had the chance to pick up a firefighter in the Reference section."

He watched a blush spread across her face. "Are you embarrassed about this?"

"How could I get to thirty as a single virgin on birth control and not be?"

Kevin rolled over and put his hands behind his head. "I didn't think anything embarrassed you."

"That was it." She wrinkled her nose. "Too bad you can't use it on me anymore." She kissed his cheek and stood up.

"Maybe not, but I want you to do me one favor."

She stopped in the bathroom door. "What?"

"Will you grow your hair out?" He wanted it to be a joke, but knew there was too much truth to the request.

She looked at him for a long moment. "You hate it." She touched her hair. It was too short to get very messed up.

He remembered the day of the wedding, the day they had been kissing on the couch when her father called. When she was trying to make sense of his raving, her hair had been tousled around her head. The sight had nearly made him stop and take her in his arms, promising to take care of her if that's what she wanted. Strange how it wasn't what she wanted at all. "I liked it better before."

"Okay. I only did it to irritate you anyway." She walked into the bathroom and turned on the water.

"Hey, does this mean every time you're mad at me you're going to cut your hair?"

She shrugged. "Maybe." She stepped into the shower.

Kevin rolled onto his back. There were worse things she could do. He could live with the occasional haircut, and it would make for a pretty clear indication of how badly he'd screwed up. He could hear the guys now. 'Hey Marshall, your woman chopped off her hair again. What the hell did you do this time?'

* * * *

Kevin leaned on the rear bumper of his car, waiting for Jessica to come out. He'd read the entire paper, including the comic strips he usually skipped. Any time now she would be out and, short of threatening the mayor with death, she'd be a member of the fire department. He sighed. Now things would get interesting.

A car pulled into the lot and parked nearby. Jack jumped out, slamming the door. "So, it went okay?" He strolled over to join Kevin leaning on the bumper.

"Great. We're getting married in about a year and a half, once she's through her probational year and before she's eligible for the paramedic exam."

Jack nodded as if he'd expected this outcome.

"Kate's car?"

Jack picked up the front page. "Yeah. Needs an oil change, so she took my truck to school today."

"Domestic bliss already?"

Jack shrugged. "You'll see. It's got its perks." He dropped the paper on the trunk.

Another car pulled in and parked in the next aisle. Lew and Dan got out and came over.

"So does this mean there's good news?" Dan asked.

"Marriage," Jack said.

"Oh, that's terrible. I'm so sorry." Dan grinned. "Does this mean we can't play poker at your house anymore?"

Kevin snorted. "What are you two doing here, anyway?"

"We thought she might need some post-exam company." Lew folded his arms. "But it looks like there's plenty. Including Bobbie."

The other three men watched Bobbie's car pull in. She parked beside Dan and sat there for a minute before she got out to join them. Her face seemed a little paler than normal and her eyes glittered with tension.

"Hi, Bobbie." Lew grinned at her.

"What are you guys all doing here?" Her voice was faint and uncertain.

"Waiting for Jessica to get out of her interview," Jack said. He stood away from the car so he was between Kevin and Bobbie. "What about you?"

"Same." Her eyes narrowed as they settled on Kevin. "You?"

"I—I drove her here," Kevin stammered and swallowed. He didn't want them knowing all the details. Jack raised an eyebrow at him and Bobbie's eyes narrowed a little further, but Dan and Lew didn't seem to pick up on the significance.

"Is that so?" Bobbie said. "I guess you don't need me here then, do you?" Her ears started to turn pink.

"Bobbie, you don't have to leave," Kevin murmured. How many years had she had a crush on him and he hadn't noticed? Had he talked about other women in front of her like she was one of the guys? How could he make up for that track record of insensitivity?

"That's okay." She took a step backward. "I can go."

"Bobbie!" Jessica cut through the middle of the group and hugged the other woman. "I passed. It's not official yet or anything, but they told me I passed. I start training in a month. I want to play with your chainsaw some more before then, is that okay with you? Hey, are we still on for dinner?"

"Dinner?" Bobbie asked. Her cheeks were beginning to match her ears.

"You said you wanted to go out to dinner to celebrate."

"But... I thought... What about Kevin?"

Jessica glanced over her shoulder at Kevin, but turned back to Bobbie before she had a chance to move. "What about Kevin?"

"I just thought you'd have dinner with him." Bobbie shifted her feet, managing to gain another half step away from the group.

"Why would I do that when I already had plans with you?" Jessica asked.

Kevin registered the false innocence in Jessica's voice. She was babbling at Bobbie to keep her from bolting. Bobbie had to be humiliated after her spectacular display at his house a couple of days ago, and she didn't even know they were getting married yet. The other guys were watching, covering their fascination as best they could. Jessica might just be able to work out this little problem he had with Bobbie.

"I thought that might have changed," Bobbie whispered.

"No. Why would it?"

Bobbie looked at the ground. "I don't know."

"So I'll meet you at your place about six. Is that okay or do you want to go earlier?"

"Six is fine," Bobbie answered. Her voice rasped like she'd eaten too much smoke.

"Okay then, I'll see you at six."

Bobbie nodded and turned away.

"Hey, Bobbie," Kevin called before she got too far away. He needed to take a lead from Jessica. If Jessica was going to keep plans she'd made with Bobbie before, then he should too. Bobbie turned back. "You coming to play poker next week?"

"Sure. I guess so." The smile Bobbie directed at Dan and Lew before retreating to her car and driving away had a serious twitch.

Dan whistled as Bobbie pulled out of the parking lot. "You don't play poker, do you?" he asked Jessica.

"No, why?"

"Because if you decided to use that talent for evil, you could be a rich woman."

Epilogue

Jessica limped through the door and looked around the dining room. "They aren't here yet."

"Of course they aren't here. We're fifteen minutes early." Kevin crowded through the door behind her. "You go find a table while I order."

"But why Wendy's?" Jessica shifted her crutches for better balance.

"I don't know. Jack said something about reliving a first date and getting to needle his sister at the same time. Go find a table before you fall off those things."

Jessica worked her way through the maze of tables. Kate had been right, not many people chose to eat at Wendy's on Valentine's Day. They had considered going to Meechan's, but decided since they all ate there pretty regularly it wouldn't be much of an occasion. Jessica eased into a chair. At a fire this morning, she'd twisted her ankle on a slippery sidewalk. It would be healed up in time for her to go back on duty the day after tomorrow. Unfortunately, it limited her mobility on her one day in three with Kevin.

She watched Kevin at the counter. The department had solved its problem of having a couple working together by scheduling them on different shifts at different stations. He came home from work about half an hour after she'd left. Her parents had been amused by the exchange when they visited over Christmas. Her mother referred to it as the changing of the guard.

She had never been so glad to see them leave as she had been this year. Normally, they stayed in a hotel because she'd never had a guest room. Kevin had a guest room and had offered to let them use it. Ten days of her parents being within sight or hearing had driven both of them crazy. They'd left all the decorations up and pretended it was Christmas Eve the day her parents left. Kevin had learned to manage her mother much better than Jessica ever did. He'd gotten along with her father like an old chum. Now she had his family to conquer.

"What are you smiling about?" Kevin asked, setting the tray on the table beside her.

"I still don't know how my father talked you into the model train extravaganza in the basement."

"Oh." Kevin chewed his lips. "You know, we were talking, and one thing led to another and the next thing I know we're at the hobby shop on River Road talking about track." He moved a chair and pushed another table against the one she'd chosen.

"It's taking over down there," Jessica pointed out. "Funny how Dad hasn't put down a single length of track since after New Year's, yet it keeps getting bigger and more elaborate."

"Isn't it, though? I'm afraid it might build itself a scaffold so it can come up to the first floor. Now that a certain professional artist is finished painting the nursery at Jack's, I might talk her into helping me build some scenery."

Jessica raised an eyebrow. Scaffolding and scenery. The model trains were out of hand. "You are planning on paying that professional artist, aren't you?"

"Of course. Dan wouldn't let me get away with not paying her now that he's her fiancé slash manager." He kissed her cheek. "You need ketchup, don't you?"

Jessica looked at the tray. "Ketchup, napkins, straws. The works."

Nodding, he headed for the condiments. He acted like a little boy with those trains. Between him and her father, they would work model trains into the wedding someplace. Not that she would mind. It made him happy. She touched the chain around her neck, where his great-grandmother's wedding ring hung. In summer it had been loose, in winter it flew off if she gestured. The chain around her neck had been a good compromise. Not that everyone in the department didn't know that by this time next year they were going to be calling her Marshall instead of Decker. They did it now sometimes, claiming it was practice, but she knew it was part of a running joke.

She looked up and smiled when Kevin set napkins on the table. Bobbie had a date tonight. A third date. They had even reached a point where they could discuss Kevin without awkward pauses.

Jessica leaned her head on Kevin's shoulder. Everything would work out in the end. Kevin turned and kissed her.

"Will you two cut it out? That is just disgusting," Dan announced, dropping his coat over the back of a chair.

Dan's fiancée, Rebecca, leaned across the table. "He'd be doing it too if he thought he could get away with it." She winked.

Dan tugged her braid. "When are you going to learn to respect me?"

"When you deserve it."

Kevin sighed. "Go order already, or you'll be stuck in line when the festivities start."

"Oh, that's right." Dan grinned and hurried away from the table.

"What festivities?" Rebecca asked.

Kevin bit into his burger and smiled.

"They won't tell me either. Something to do with Leia and Lew, though." Jessica dipped one of her fries into her ketchup. "Want to start a betting pool, or do you think you know, too?"

About Charlotte McClain

http://www.lyricalpress.com/charlotte_mcclain

Charlotte McClain is a literary omnivore. Two years spent overseas honed her ability to enjoy all sorts of reading material from board books to history tomes. She writes as she reads and revels in putting her characters in difficult, painful and goofy situations, all at the same time. She believes that in any good relationship each partner should help the other be the best person they can be.

When not reading or writing she loves to travel, though it doesn't like her. Her strongest memory of the Philippines is hanging over the side of a boat saying, "Look! Little blue jellyfish!" She has been motion sick in nine countries on four continents. Rumor has it she also belly dances, but no one has ever seen it.

She is married to an artist and musician who also has a good sense of humor, but don't tell him she said so.

Charlotte's Website:

http://charlottemcclain.wordpress.com/

Reader eMail:

mcclaincharlotte@gmail.com

GO GREEN!

Save a tree read an Ebook.

LaVergne, TN USA
10 May 2010
182189LV00001B/23/P